She became aware of another sound—a grating, scraping noise. Then there was a strangled gasp, as though the air in the lungs that was its source had been suddenly cut off.

Amber felt fear then, black, abysmal terror. Whatever had lain asleep for eons in the heart of this fragment was now awake, that she knew beyond question. She tried to turn, to flee back to the relative safety beyond the wall, but it was as if her legs were no longer subject to her will. Heart pounding, unable to stop herself from looking, Amber stepped into the light.

And saw the glowing crystal sarcophagus of her nightmare, and, standing within it, a form that no nightmare, no matter how demonic, could have conjured—a Chthon like none she had seen before, standing easily ten feet in height. She had a brief impression of a long, segmented tail like that of a manticore's rising to curve over the head, which was an obscene crossing of human and arachnid features, and two arms that ended in lobster-like claws. One of them held Trisandela as if the Lady of Bats were a child's toy.

Then the head turned, and the eight burning eyes of the monster fixed their gaze upon her.

THE BURNING REALM

MICHAEL REAVES

THE BURNING REALM

Copyright © 1988 by Michael Reaves

A Baen Books Original

Baen Publishing Enterprises
260 Fifth Avenue
New York, N.Y. 10001

First printing, February 1988

ISBN: 0-671-65386-5

Cover art by David Mattingly

Printed in the United States of America

Distributed by
SIMON & SCHUSTER
1230 Avenue of the Americas
New York, N.Y. 10020

DEDICATION

For Brynne, as was the one before;

And for Diane Duane and Peter Morwood,
for knowing what it was like.

The Way of the Samurai is found in death. When it comes to either/or, there is only the quick choice of death. It is not particularly difficult. Be determined and advance. To say that dying without reaching one's aim is to die a dog's death is the frivolous way of sophisticates. When pressed with the choice of life or death, it is not necessary to gain one's aim.

—Yamamoto Tsunetomo, *Hagakure*

Prologue

There was once a world of green and gentle continents, separated by cerulean oceans, warmed by sunlight and favored with life. Shining cities were built by the hand of man, and empires rose and fell. In measureless caverns beneath the ground, an inhuman race known as the Chthons, together with their servants, the cacodemons, pursued their own ways, incomprehensible to those who dwelled in the light of day. By and large the two races had little to do with each other, save for occasional bloody skirmishes.

All of humanity was, to some small degree, born with the ability to control the force that would eventually come to be known as "magic." A small percentage, those whose mastery over that force was greater than others, purloined knowledge of how best to use it from the Chthons, and these few taught others who had the power within them. Deeds both good and bad were done with this knowledge and power, as is the way of mankind.

1

One who had risen to the highest rank of sorcerer dared to explore further. He learned the means of invoking a force that even the Chthons feared—the nearly limitless power that still smouldered in the dust of all who had lived through the previous ages. He created his own rank, beyond that of sorcerer, and named himself the Necromancer. Ensconced in a gigantic castle called Darkhaven, he ruled over the largest empire the world had ever seen. But legend had it that the Necromancer was still unsatisfied. It was said that, since he could not bend the entire globe to his rule, he decided to destroy it.

Whatever the cause, the world was shattered by a cataclysm that sent the fragments spinning into the void. A cabal of sorcerers, warned of some form of looming disaster by various signs and portents, managed to instigate thaumaturgic spells that prevented total destruction. They were unable to completely reverse the disaster, but they did what they could: their cantrips provided an envelope of air that encased the myriad whirling pieces of the world, and created runestones, repositories of ectenic force that provided weightfulness on the surfaces of the fragments and kept them orbiting each other in a complicated and orderly fashion. The shattering had also disturbed the world's path about its sun, causing it to pursue a new course that brought it, on occasion, terribly close to the fiery orb. The spells of the magicians protected against the extremes of periodic heat and cold that this caused as well.

The Chthons, their ancient underground warrens for the most part destroyed, congregated on the dark fragment of Xoth, which rotated perpetually in the shadow of a larger, nameless worldlet. They hated humanity for breaking apart the world and exposing them to sunlight, which was anathema to their kind, and sought revenge in devious ways.

Though millions of people had been annihilated in

the destruction, enough survived to repopulate the fragments over the following centuries. They built boats capable of sailing the abyss of air that separated the worldlets. And eventually, stories of the unbroken globe assumed the status of myth and legend . . .

But all magic, no matter how powerful, decays eventually. A thousand years after the world was destroyed, the ectenic force behind the runestones began to weaken. The new generation of magicians realized that another source of power had to be found that would revivify the runestones.

One sorcerer, Pandrogas, thought to find that source in the limitless libraries of the castle Darkhaven, part of which had survived the worldbreaking. Though the fact that it had served a home to the Necromancer had been lost in the chaos of history, it was still shunned as a place of evil. Pandrogas studied for years, seeking in vain to find a common, unifying theme behind all the disparate schools of magic that had developed since the Shattering. He pursued his studies alone, save for a few servants, until a storm brought two uninvited guests to Darkhaven. They were Tahrynyar, the exiled Marquis of Chuntai, and Amber, his wife. During the course of their stay at Darkhaven, Amber and Pandrogas fell in love. Tahrynyar was aware that he was being cuckolded, but was also afraid to confront the sorcerer with this knowledge. In an attempt to gain revenge, he unwittingly activated a spell that allowed entry to the castle the Demogorgon Sestihaculas, Lord of Snakes and ruler of the Chthons, who had an old grudge to settle with the sorcerer. Pandrogas was able to expel the Serpent Lord from Darkhaven only by agreeing to meet Sestihaculas in battle at a later time.

Pandrogas and Amber found their relationship new and exciting, but also difficult—Amber, though untrained in magic, possessed the raw power necessary to become a great sorceress. Her intrinsic capabilities far exceeded those of Pandrogas, and the sorcerer, to his private shame, found himself jealous of what his lover might in time become.

Pandrogas was unaware that others were instigating their own plots to save what was left of the world. A group calling itself the Circle, believing that the world had been shattered because mankind had turned away from worshiping the One God, decided to take the desperate measure of reviving the Necromancer's corpse to learn a way of somehow reuniting the fragments once more into a whole. To do so they needed a specific runestone, and the only way to find it was to investigate each fragment's stone in turn until they found the one they sought. One of those charged with gathering runestones was the enchantress Ardatha, also known as Demonhand. Ardatha hired a master thief, one Beorn of Osloviken, to steal the runestone of Darkhaven.

Beorn was a shapechanger as well as a thief; he had been cursed at an early age with the necessity of periodically assuming the form of a bear. The parameters of the curse insured that, should he remain too long in the form of his bestial counterpart, his human mind and identity would be subsumed and he would be a bear until the end of his days. Ardatha promised to lift the werecurse from him in payment for the runestone. Beorn, whose dream was to be free of the bear and retire from thievery to the idyllic fragment of Tamboriyon, readily agreed.

Beorn managed to steal the runestone, but had to become the bear to escape with it, gravely injuring Tahrynyar during the course of this. He fell out of a cavern in the lower reaches of Darkhaven and was blown into the Abyss by a storm.

Pandrogas performed a healing spell upon Tahrynyar; the unpredictable spell resulted in the Marquis's will, as well as his body, being strengthened.

After Pandrogas and Amber departed Darkhaven to find Beorn, Tahrynyar joined with Ardatha in their own pursuits—Ardatha in search of the runestone, and Tahrynyar in search of revenge on Pandrogas. They were accompanied by Balandrus, a cacodemon whom Ardatha had bound to her will, and who hated her for the indignities she heaped upon him.

During the course of his flight, Beorn met Kan Konar, a cloakfighter from the fragment of Typor's Fist. A warrior of superb skill and training, Kan Konar was seeking revenge against the Chthon Xhormallion, also known as the Lord of Spiders, for visiting a grisly death upon his leige, the Daimyo Ras Parolyn. The cloakfighter and the thief journeyed together to Dulfar, City of Lights, on the fragment of Rhynne.

Pandrogas and Amber, following them, became separated. Amber followed Beorn on board the *Elgrane*, a ship crossing the Ythan Ocean. Also on board were Mirren, a werewolf with whom Beorn attempted to have an affair, and Ia, a dryad.

During the course of her journey, Amber several times had to rely upon her untrained power to save her life. Her strength was formidable, but unreliable.

Ardatha and Tahrynyar also followed Beorn's trail to Dulfar, where they recruited Kan Konar to help them search. Instead of the thief, however, they found Pandrogas, whom they attempted to take prisoner. This attempt was thwarted by Sestihaculas, who took advantage of the situation to magically transport his enemy, along with the Enchantress, the cloakfighter, and Tahrynyar, to Xoth.

Beorn and Amber forged an uneasy truce on board the *Elgrane*, intending to part company when the boat reached shore. But a cataclysmic manifestation of the various decaying orbits prevented this: a small fragment struck the Ythan, causing a tsunami that swamped the *Elgrane*. Mirren and Ia were hurled into the raging sea, and the thief and Amber barely managed to escape on the back of a winged gryphon. In so doing, however, Beorn was faced with the choice of retaining the runestone or rescuing Amber, and elected to do the latter. The runestone fell into the maelstrom.

Meanwhile, a new character entered the drama: a masked sorcerer known only as Stonebrow. It was he who had employed Ardatha to bring him Darkhaven's runestone in the hope that it might be the one which would resurrect the Necromancer. He pursued his lonely task in a citadel carved from a spire of rock on Graystar Isle, in the middle of the Ythan. When the aerolith struck he barely escaped in time, but sensed the presence of the runestone on the ocean's floor and retrieved it. Convinced that this was the talisman he needed to revive the world-shatterer, Stonebrow began the long journey to the fragment of Nigromancien, which was assumed to be the tomb of the Necromancer.

Beorn and Amber were taken on board the *Dark Horizon,* a dragonship which sailed the Abyss, its sole purpose being to hunt and kill dragons. The captain refused to alter course to another fragment for them, and so they found themselves part of a dragonhunt that brought them closer and closer to the hell-fragment of Xoth. Eventually, during the ship's confrontation with the dragon, Beorn and Amber managed to escape in a small lifeboat. But the sails were destroyed by a swipe of the dragon's tail and they drifted into the shadow of Xoth, where they were captured by cacodemons.

On Xoth, Sestihaculas imprisoned Kan Konar, Ardatha and Tahrynyar and brought Pandrogas to the great hall of the Chthons, intending to destroy him publicly. As further torture, he reunited the sorcerer with Amber, intending to kill them both. But Pandrogas invoked the terms of his agreement with the

Serpent Lord, which stipulated that they do battle on neutral ground. Sestihaculas transported the three of them to the Cliffs of the Sun, a small area on one edge of Xoth unprotected from the sunlight by the shielding nameless fragment.

Beorn was incarcerated with Ardatha, Tahrynyar and Kan Konar. He explained to the enchantress that the runestone had been lost at the bottom of the sea. Ardatha managed to engineer their escape from the cell and called upon Balandrus to ferry her and Beorn back to Rhynne to search for the runestone. Tahrynyar and Kan Konar remained on Xoth for reasons of revenge—the cloakfighter intended to face the Spider Lord, and the Marquis hoped to find and kill Pandrogas.

Tahrynyar witnessed Kan Konar's battle with Xhormallion, which ended with the Spider Lord sinking its fangs into the cloakfighter and bearing him off into the depths of his web. Tahrynyar was expelled from the web, along with the cloak that Kan Konar had dropped during the battle. Driven nearly mad by what he had witnessed, Tahrynyar donned the cloak and began making his way through the mushroom forest of Xoth.

Xoth, and the nameless fragment that shielded it, were near the outer edge of the cloud of fragments that pursued its eccentric orbit about the Sun. The waning magic was no longer able to protect the fragments' surface from direct contact with the burning rays during part of the year; the Cliffs of the sun had been turned into a parched desert that teemed with snakes. These creatures Sestihaculas set against Pandrogas and Amber, but the latter managed to use her power to destroy the snakes. At this point, Tahrynyar emerged from the forest and hurled Kan Konar's heavy cloak at the Serpent Lord, causing him to fall into the deadly sunlight.

Ardatha and Beorn followed Stonebrow to Nigromancien, where the sorcerer and the enchantress prepared to raise the Necromancer from his tomb by using the runestone of Darkhaven.

Pandrogas saved Sestihaculas from immolation by the sun and in turn exacted the Serpent Lord's aid in their search for the runestone. Sestihaculas provided a cacodemon to instantaneously transport them to Nigromancien. They arrived in time to witness the rite intended to revive the Necromancer, but were unable to stop it. To the astonishment of all, the tomb was empty save for a complicated map. They realized that Nigromancien was a cenotaph, a false lead, and that the Necromancer was in fact buried in Darkhaven at the heart of a labyrinth of traps.

Stonebrow and Ardatha ordered Balandrus to take them back to Darkhaven. Pandrogas and Amber found Beorn within Nigromancien, and there they also found the runestone, the power of which had been totally depleted by the spell designed to open the tomb. There seemed to be no way to reach the Necromancer's tomb before Ardatha and Stonebrow did. But Beorn volunteered to use his knowledge of thievery to bypass the traps of the Labyrinth, and Amber's power might be sufficient to lead them to the catacombs beyond the Labyrinth.

The three of them made their way carefully through the gauntlet of traps designed long ago by the builders of Darkhaven. They barely avoided death a score of times. During the course of this trial, Beorn realized that he was falling in love with Amber. He did not speak of it to her or to Pandrogas, but resolved to do whatever he could to see to her safety.

Eventually they passed through the maze of death-traps and through the catacombs beyond, where they found the Necromancer's tomb guarded by a chimera. With time running out before Darkhaven crashed into Oljaer, Beorn once more became the bear and lead the chimera on a chase into the catacombs, while Pandrogas and Amber hurried to stop Stonebrow and Ardatha from ressurecting the Necromancer. They were too late, however—they found Stonebrow dead on the steps leading to the open sarcophagus. Pandrogas investigated the vault, and was enveloped in an ebon cloud that issued from it. Before Amber could attempt to rescue him, she found herself facing Ardatha. The enchantress tried to use her magic to destroy Amber, but the latter's intrinsic power protected her long enough for her to cut off Ardatha's demon hand with a sword. With Ardatha's demonic strength now severed from her, she was powerless to prevent Balandrus the cacodemon from appearing and carrying her off to a revenge of his own choosing.

Within the black mist, Pandrogas faced the essence of the Necromancer. He learned that the Necromancer had not, after all, been responsible for the shattering of the globe—that he had, in fact, tried to prevent another heavenly body from colliding with the world but had been unsuccessful. Pandrogas realized that the power of the dead was not necessarily a power of evil, and, trusting this knowledge, he opened himself to the force resting in the catacombs of Darkhaven, allowing himself to become a conduit for it, that it might recharge the runestone and restore Darkhaven to its former orbit. To do so exhausted him both mentally and physically, however, and when the Necromancer's essence retreated, Pandrogas collapsed in a coma.

Beorn, meanwhile, faced the chimera in battle and defeated it, but was wounded by the monster's venomous fangs. Feverish and delirious, his only thought was to return to Amber. Though he could feel his human personality slipping away from him, he remained a bear long enough to carry Pandrogas on his back from the tomb and back into the inhabited portion of Darkhaven, with Amber following.

By then it was too late for him to metamorphosize back into his human form, and the bear's personality became dominant. Beorn had, in effect, sacrificed his life to save that of Pandrogas. The bear was taken to Tamboriyon and set free in the forest by the sorcerer and Amber, who had come to love and respect the thief.

Pandrogas and Amber, realizing that the adventures that they had gone through had changed them both irrevocably, agreed to separate for a year in order to re-evaluate their relationship. Amber remained on Tamboriyon to study magic in the Taggyn Saer Temple and learn to channel her power. Pandrogas returned to Darkhaven, to study Necromancy in hopes that it would prove the salvation of the world.

Both mourned those who had died during the tribulations they had endured. But neither realized that, in two cases, the mourning was premature . . .

BOOK ONE

Resurrection

From one thing, learn ten thousand things.
—Musashi,
A Book of Five Rings

CHAPTER I

Escape From Xoth

He had not died. His fate had been far worse than that.

Kan Konar, cloakfighter from Typor's Fist, late a retainer of the Daimyo Ras Parolyn, had met the Spider Lord Zhormallion in battle. His objective had been simple and clear: to destroy the Chthon who had sent a plague of arachnids to poison his master, or to die in the attempt. To this end, he had joined forces first with Beorn, the thief and shapechanger who had stolen the runestone of Darkhaven, and later with Ardatha Demonhand, the enchantress who pursued him. After a long, circuitous route that had taken him to many of the world's remnants and imperiled his life a score of times, he had arrived by sorcerous means at his destination: Xoth, the legendary fragment of hell. And there, in the company of Tahrynyar, the former Marquis of Chuntai, the cloakfighter had faced Zhormallion in the latter's gigantic infundibular web.

The confrontation had been short, and even Kan Konar had known that it could have had but one ending. The certainty of its outcome, however, had left him no less determined to see it through. He had been bound by the code of his warrior class to give his own life in the defense of his Daimyo, and, failing that, to avenge him at the same cost if necessary.

He had not been afraid of death, not even of death from the poisonous fangs of the Spider Lord. He had been prepared for it. The most he had hoped for had been Zhormallion's death along with his own. Had he, by some absurd miracle, survived the battle and triumphed over the Chthon, there was no doubt that he would have died shortly thereafter by the will of Sestihaculas, Lord of Snakes and ruler of the Land of Night, or one of his countless demonic minions. That would not have mattered. Death was to be sought, rather than avoided, as long as it was death with honor.

But neither of those eventualities had come to pass. What had happened had been the one thing he had not foreseen—Zhormallion had defeated him and let him live.

The cloakfighter knew he would not survive for much longer, however. He recalled with merciless clarity the burning sensation of the venom as Zhormallion's fangs had pierced his flesh while the Spider Lord's eight unblinking orbs glared with utter inhumanity into his own. The pain had spread rapidly through him, leaving coldness and numbness in its wake, and his limbs had stiffened and locked in paralysis. He had been unable to move as much as an eyelid while sheets of disgustingly warm silk had been wrapped about him.

His eyes were still open; his inability to blink over the unknown length of time he had been encysted had left them agonizingly dry. There was nothing to see, however, save the filmy gray webbing over his face. The material was sufficiently porous to permit him to breathe, albeit with difficulty. The bitten area itched maddeningly, and he had felt initial waves of nausea and dizziness which gradually subsided. His heartbeat had remained unusually fast.

He knew what was in store for him; he had seen precedents in nature. Though he knew of no spider that paralyzed its prey, he had read of wasps that so treated other hapless insects, stinging them and then laying their eggs on the still-living corpse, that the larvae might have a vibrant first meal. And there was no reason why Zhormallion should be bound by the limitations of the vermin he chose to emulate.

So, then—the likely explanation was that the Spider Lord had preserved him against later hunger. Sometime in the future—when, he had no way of knowing—the Chthon would return, and Kan Konar would once again feel those fangs enter his flesh, this time to draw out his living blood . . .

He could not even shudder or scream. He could only wait.

The bitter irony of it did not escape him. He could not even die honorably, let alone be responsible for his enemy's death. All the exhaustive training and rituals he had subjected himself to since before puberty had been worthless against the Spider Lord.

He recalled the fugue-like statements and aphorisms of his mentor, the aged one known to him only as Shadowmaster—an honorific bestowed due to the old man's ability to manipulate the dark garment which served as weapon to those of the warrior class. "One must live as though one's body were already dead," the teacher had said. "A warrior's only thoughts must be of one's master, to the point of death and beyond." Kan Konar had accepted these precepts as gospel, and had lived his life accordingly. It was a point of pride to him that he had been willing to die for Ras Parolyn—and a point of shame that, at the final moment, he had screamed in fear.

Undoubtedly no one had heard that scream save the Chthon, and Tahrynyar, whom Zhormallion had no doubt dispatched within moments after Kan Konar's defeat. But that made no difference. He had shown fear at the last moment as the horror had rushed upon him. Had he command of his voice now, he would scream again, but in despair rather than fear. . . .

A dry rasping whisper issued from his throat.

The cloakfighter felt his heart pound even faster than before. There seemed to be the slightest play now in the muscles of his jaws and thorax, where a moment ago there was none. It was almost infinitesimal—before they had been carved of marble, and now they were carved of wood. And there was a tingling in his extremities, like the faintest twinges of recirculation.

The effects of the poison were dissipating.

And now began a new cycle of torment, as Kan Konar felt the immobility retreat with maddening slowness from his limbs. Before, he had had no way to measure the time—he might as well have been a disembodied spirit in a gray limbo. But now he could chart the glacial renewal of sensation in his body, and that was a thousand times worse. Before, he had had no hope. Now, though he tried with all the force of his iron will to ignore it, hope grew steadily with the flame of returning life.

Would he recover in time? It would be the final jest, he thought, if Zhormallion were to return just before he regained control. . . .

He could move his toes now, and his fingers,

which were bound tightly against his chest by the layers of spider silk. He stroked the rough fabric of his tunic. No woman's flesh had ever felt so exquisite. And he could blink as well, finally—that single fact gave him more joy than anything else, though his eyes felt as though they had been scoured with sand. Itching now consumed his entire body.

The process of revivification continued. Kan Konar felt a warm and wet sensation as his bladder abruptly relaxed, staining his breeches. He felt absurdly pleased at this. But the return of sensation was maddeningly slow; the thousand years that had elapsed since the Necromancer's final spell seemed short in comparison with the time it took for him to regain costive control of his limbs. Given that, he could do little more than flex his fingers and shift his arms slightly against the confining webbing. Kan Konar felt despair settle over him like the midnight folds of his cloak. The Spider Lord had taken no chances—even if the effects of the poison left his system entirely, he would still be bound like a mummified lich to the wall of the web.

Unless . . .

When manipulated properly, the edge of a cloak-fighter's garment became a slashing weapon as sharp as any sword. This was due to slivers of dragon ivory strategically mounted in the hems. Occasionally these would dull or break; against this eventuality, Kan Konar carried within his belt pouch replacement shards.

He could move his hand just enough to slip two fingers into the pouch. Carefully he brought out a thin length of ivory, wrapped in thin oiled leather, its edge as keen as the finest Bageran steel. He turned the sharp blade against the silk that ensheathed him—and felt the fibers separate.

Kan Konar was motionless for a long time after

that, his thoughts racing as fast as the blood within his veins. What gods there were had given him a second chance, it seemed. All that was left to him was to decide whether or not he wished to take it.

Did he deserve to live? Probably not. But equally as important a question was whether or not he deserved to die. He had failed in his quest to achieve an honorable death by avenging his master. He was no longer a warrior—no longer even a ronin, a rogue without class or purpose. He recalled the words of the sorcerer Pandrogas to him when the cacodemons found them in the fungaceous jungle above: *Your life will be over, and you will still be alive.*

The decision, then, was between dying a nightmarish death by the Spider Lord's fangs—or living without honor, without hope, without reason.

Perhaps, he thought, he had been granted this rebirth to continue his quest. He still possessed the skills and the body of a warrior—he did not doubt that it was his superb conditioning and strength that had allowed him to shed the effects of the venom before Zhormallion's return. But Kan Konar knew that he no longer possessed a warrior's heart. He could not bring himself to face Zhormallion in battle again. It was that simple, and that shameful.

There was only one way he could hope to expiate that shame. It was not by dying. It was by living.

He resumed his slow sawing of the web's filaments. As the opening grew larger, his hand was granted increased maneuverability. It was tedious and difficult work, for his fingers were still partially numb, and the after-effects of the toxin caused him to be wracked with spasmodic shivers. More than once he dropped the ivory blade and had to fish another from his pouch. Nevertheless, he was eventually able to cut away the fibers that bound his other arm.

Granted the use of two hands, it was relatively easy. Soon he was flaying the shroud from his face. He looked about. His vision was somewhat blurred— also due, no doubt, to the bane he had been injected with. As nearly as he could determine, he was hanging in a cocoon anchored to the vast gray wall of the funnel. Below him and to one side was the bridge spun by countless spiders to provide an arena for the battle. He had left his cloak there, but there was no sign of it now. He could dimly make out something multicolored lying on the arc, and after a moment he realized what it was: Tahrynyar's feathered mantle.

Of the Marquis there was no sign. Doubtless events had proceeded as he had speculated, and Tahrynyar had also fallen victim to the Spider Lord. Kan Konar looked about him. There were hundreds of lumps of webbing containing the bodies of Zhormallion's prey within sight. In the nearer ones he could make out the dried skeletal remains of animals and men.

The Marquis might still live, paralyzed as he had been, but the chances of finding him were remote. Kan Konar continued cutting himself free, moving more carefully to avoid losing his grip and falling into the hellish depths. He glanced up—above was light the color of a bruise. Evidently the web opened onto Xoth's surface.

The loss of his cloak further demoralized him; for nearly twenty commonyears he had virtually lived within its sable folds. Woven of unicorns' manes and treated with distillates of exotic herbs and plants, it repelled water and retained body heat, yet was also loose enough to provide shade from the sun. More than a garment, it was almost an extension of the vital energy within him. Without it Kan Konar felt worse than naked—he felt stripped of his knowledge, his fighting ability, as well as his weapon.

But he had come this far; there was nothing to do

but continue. The cloakfighter dug his fingers into the smooth layers of webbing and pulled his boots free of the cocoon. His reaction to the venom had subsided now to a general malaise and weakness, and he wondered if he had the strength to climb out of the web.

It did not matter, he told himself. He would climb, or he would fall. It was all the same.

He climbed. The web was so striated with numberless crosshatchings of filaments, each laid down by a different spider, that hand and footholds were easy to find. The multitudes of vermin that dwelled there crawled over him, hung from strands and observed him, but made no attempt to bite or stop him. They ranged in size from smaller than the point of a dagger to as large as a glove, and once he glimpsed an obscenely bulbous body scuttling away from him that was easily the size of his head.

The cloakfighter did not try to avoid them. He simply climbed, until the endless struggle against gravity ceased to be an effort and became, instead, all that life had ever been or could ever be. He ceased to think, to speculate about what he was doing or why. He gave himself over instead to the instinctive drive for survival, and he let that urge take him where it would.

It took him, at last, to the mouth of the web, and the surface of Xoth.

At first he could not understand why he was not climbing any more. When his senses returned, he found he was lying full-length on a sheet of black obsidian that sloped gradually downward. The anchoring threads of the vast web were behind him. He was on the lip of what seemed to be a crater, some enormous fumarole blasted, perhaps, by the world's disintegration, and which now provided a home for Zhormallion and his brood.

The cloakfighter rolled over and sat up. He was atop one ridge of a series of basaltic megaliths that jutted high above the tangle of giant etiolate fungi that covered Xoth's surface. Overhead, filling nearly the entire sky and seemingly close enough to touch, was the dark, featureless fragment in whose shadow Xoth orbited. To one side, barely visible through the caliginous air, was a line of bright light. He recalled that Pandrogas and Ardatha had spoken of the Cliffs of the Sun, the one area on Xoth where light touched and seared the landscape.

He looked behind him; the spires and blocks of stone rose like a rudely built cyclopean castle. Kan Konar stood somewhat shakily and began to walk.

He did not know where he was going, nor did he particularly care. No doubt a cacodemon would find him soon and return him to the Spider Lord. He wondered why the thought did not frighten him.

He crossed an arcing sheath of rock in which openings like lava tubes were peppered. Rising from these he could faintly hear a hellish concert—cries, moans, shrieks, bellows of rage. He dropped to one knee before one of the openings and peered into it.

He was evidently atop a huge natural dome—the roof of a vaulted cavern. Below him, barely visible by some faint luminescence, he could see the columns and formations of a gigantic chamber. As he watched, a dim, batwinged form flitted across his field of vision as though fleeing some deadly danger. One voice rose above the cacophony—a voice deep and powerful, yet laced somehow with a crepitant undertone that made the cloakfighter think of snakes. Though the words were in Talic, the most common language of the fragments, the voice itself was no more human than the rumbling of thunder or the crash of surf.

"I have been beaten! *Defeated!* By a *human!*"

A rock the size of a barrel crashed against a column of stone and shattered it.

"There will be reparation! I *swear* it!"

Kan Konar leaned back and thought about what he had heard. The Chthon venting his rage on the hapless cacodemons below could only be the Demogorgon himself, Sestihaculas—and he felt fairly certain that the human who had evidently humiliated and bested him was none other than the sorcerer Pandrogas. The cloakfighter smiled faintly. He would have liked to have seen the battle. The last he had seen of Pandrogas, the master of Darkhaven had been weak and injured—yet somehow, evidently, he had contrived to triumph over one of the most powerful forces of evil in the world. His respect for the sorcerer was increased. He hoped the man had survived the encounter.

He stood, looking about him. When Balandrus the cacodemon had carried him here together with Pandrogas, Tahrynyar and the enchantress Ardatha, the warren-like cliffs had been teeming with scabrous life. Cacodemons had flitted from spire to spire, roosting in the dim light like huge ungainly bats. Now there were none. He wondered if they were hiding from the wrath of their master.

He did not know the reason, nor did he particularly care. He would escape, somehow, or he would not.

The cloakfighter resumed his wandering, climbing over blocks of stone that rose like gigantic irregular steps, sheered by long-ago geological convulsions from the world's crust. The physical exertion was helping to flush the last of the toxin from his system—he felt better, though still very weak and hungry.

He was making for the highest part of the jumbled cliffs, with some vague concept of charting his course from the vantage of a good viewpoint. Then he saw something out of the corner of his eye—something that clashed discordantly with the bleak stygian stone that composed the cliffs. A shape that was somehow familiar . . .

The cloakfighter turned and saw a dragonship moored to a nearby pinnacle.

It floated a few inches above the stone, the magic of its runestone counteracting, to some small degree, the attraction of Xoth. Kan Konar approached it, recognizing it as a chase boat from one of the huge hunting ships that sailed the Abyss in search of dragons. It was in sorry shape—the mizzen and main masts were missing, with only stumps indicating where they had been broken off, and one of the dragon-leather wings was ripped and tattered. It could not be maneuvered in the Abyss.

He swung himself over the low gunwale, feeling a momentary disorientation as he put himself within the range of attraction of the boat's runestone. The stores were intact—he found rations of dried jerky and fruit, some of which he devoured. Then he considered his options.

He could not launch the small craft—the pull of Xoth was far too great for the ship's runestone to overcome. He would have to somehow get the boat to the edge of the fragment—and that, of course, was impossible. And even if he were to somehow accomplish it, he would merely be condemning himself to a slow death by starvation in the Abyss. The chances of his being picked up by another craft or landing safely on another fragment were much too small to be worth considering.

It seemed that his luck had indeed run dry. He could either wait here for inevitable capture, or attempt to survive as long as possible in the jungle that surrounded the crags. Neither concept held much hope.

It was then that he heard the sound of approaching footsteps.

The cloakfighter's reaction was instinctive—he dropped below the level of the gunwale, sprawling flat on the deck, and pulled a tarpaulin over him. Then he lay still, breathing shallowly.

Through a hole in the sheet of dragon peritoneum that covered him he could see the clouds and part of a glistening spire. The footsteps—there were two sets of them, one light and almost human, the other shambling and heavy—stopped beside the boat. Kan Konar could smell a faint stench of brimstone. There was a long moment of silence.

"The humans are clever in their craftwork," a voice finally said. Kan Konar's eyes widened slightly in surprise—the tones were female, dulcet and light, but still with that feral undertone that marked the owner as a Chthon. Though by no means as thoroughly and terrifyingly alien as the voice of Zhormallion had been, the sound still washed over him like a drench of cold water.

The speaker moved into his limited field of vision. He could see her quite clearly. She was beautiful in a totally inhuman way—a woman's face and form, covered with dark fur, the nose and mouth jutting forward in a short muzzle, the ears large and pointed. Black lips smiled, revealing sharp fangs. Behind her, folded membraneous wings arched to spires over her shoulders. The cloakfighter had seen her image many times in the studies he had done to prepare himself for his journey to Xoth. She was Trisandela, Lady of Bats.

The boat suddenly rocked, and Kan Konar heard a cracking sound. Something with enormous strength had seized the craft. A voice, rough and grating: "Lord Sestihaculas has commanded that we destroy it." The voice of a cacodemon.

Trisandela laughed—a sound no warmer than ice cracking in the sun. "Clod, have you no aesthetic appreciation? This ability of mankind to change and distort the shapes of nature has always fascinated me. I would see this artifact perform its function. Tow it beyond the edge of Xoth and set it adrift in the Abyss."

Kan Konar could sense the cacodemon's uncertainty. "But the Demogorgon's command—"

"Will be as good as fulfilled. He does not desire to look upon anything that reminds him of his recent defeat by the sorcerer, and that includes this thing that brought the sorcerer's woman to Xoth. Very well—we shall remove the offense." The soft tones now grew hard with command. "Do as I bid you, Daimar!"

The chase boat trembled again, and then Kan Konar felt a sudden lurch as the cacodemon called Daimar lifted it. He could picture the rough-hewn musculature of the creature as it raised the craft overhead. Then there was an explosion of sound—after an instant, he recognized it as the beating of the cacodemon's wings. The smell of brimstone was momentarily unbearable—and then, just as suddenly, it was gone.

It was impossible to tell, with the runestone's magic providing him with a stable weight, whether or not he was still on the ground. Kan Konar assumed, however, that he was not—that the cacodemon, acting on Trisandela's command, had hurled the chase boat and him with it into the Abyss.

He counted slowly to one hundred, then lifted a corner of the tarpaulin and looked out. He could see nothing but the blue of the sky. He sat up cautiously.

The boat was adrift in the Abyss.

It floated at an angle to the fragment below him; he could clearly see the glistening dark towers. They appeared impossibly canted from his point of view.

He was still in the shadow of the shielding fragment, and drifting slowly toward the sunlight.

And so he had accomplished the impossible—he had escaped from the Spider Lord's web, and from Xoth itself. But the price of that escape, ironically, would be starvation in the Abyss. The cloakfighter turned toward the stern to check the stores of food. He knew it was a futile gesture; he could be adrift for years in the void between the world's fragments—

He stopped, staring. Perched on the broken shaft of the mast was the Lady of Bats.

Kan Konar felt his fingers grope uselessly for the edges of the cloak he had worn for so long. The Chthon was hunkered in a squat, arms wrapped around knees, wings shrouding her. The lambent eyes regarded him with amusement. He saw her fangs, startlingly white against the darkness of her face, as she smiled.

"I knew of your escape," she said, "before you crawled from Zhormallion's web."

Kan Konar said nothing. If she intended to kill him, she would do so—he honestly did not know whether he would attempt to defend himself or not. To what purpose would it be, after all? Was not a quick death at the hands of the Chthon preferable to a wasting one in the Abyss?

Trisandela stood and stepped down from the ivory stump. She stretched languidly; he could see muscles moving beneath her pelt, could see the tiny dugs she had instead of human breasts lift with the movement of her shoulders. Her wings extended to their full, amazing length, and the clouds and land about them shifted as the wind caught them and moved the dragon boat. The boat was, he noted, not far from the boundary of sunlight and shadow— whatever her intentions, Trisandela would have to implement them soon or be destroyed by the searing radiation that was anathema to her kind.

"I knew you would find this craft," Trisandela continued, "and so I made certain I would be the one to see that Sestihaculas's order was implemented."

The cloakfighter said, "Why?"

Trisandela smiled again. "I have heard that all humans are impudent—it appears to be so. Nevertheless, I will answer. Rivalries and jealousies exist between Chthons just as they do between humans. Zhormallion and I have long been in conflict over matters beyond your poor comprehension. It pleases me to see one of his prey escape. I would not have dared to venture into his web to rescue you, but I was able to see you off Xoth."

"And what happens now?"

The Lady of Bats laughed. "Now you will undoubtedly starve to death in the Abyss—but that is no concern of mine. My little game, of which you are the pawn, is ended," and with that, she hurled herself from the chase boat, wings catching the air and stabilizing her while the attraction of Xoth drew her slowly down. In a few moments she was lost against the black backdrop of the crags.

The cloakfighter stood for several minutes watching Xoth recede, until at last the boat drifted beyond the realm of shadow. The sunlight struck at him like a physical blow. Xoth and its parent fragment were much closer to the blazing orb than most of the other fragments—at times, he knew, its orbit brought them near enough for the burning rays to ignite fires. The sunward surface of the nameless fragment that shielded Xoth was, by all accounts, a blasted expanse of naked rock.

He could tell from the sensation on his skin that he would not long survive exposure to such intense light. Trisandela had condemned him to a death only slightly less cruel than the one he had escaped.

Kan Konar nodded and sat down. He would not starve to death, then—he would be dead before the meager store of food the dragoneers had put in the chase boat ran out. So be it—he could face his death, dishonorable though it might be, with equanimity, as long as it was not by the fangs of the Spider Lord.

If it was his fate to survive this latest ordeal, he would. If not, then his sunbaked corpse would be prey for the vultures and vampires that flew between the world's pieces. He had abdicated any say in the matter. As far as he was concerned, he was already dead—all that remained was to learn the matter of his passing.

CHAPTER II

Aftermath

For the majority of the long Rhynnish day, nearly a commonweek in length, she had floated, clinging to the log. The furious waves and storms caused by the impact of the aerolith had subsided finally, leaving a steady iron-gray rain that was filled with silt from the ocean's floor.

Mirren had survived by eating the dead and stunned raw fish that had been one of the results of the cataclysm. That source of food and water had dissipated quickly, however, and for the last few commondays she had had nothing in the way of sustenance. She drifted in and out of delirium as aimlessly as she floated on the limitless expanse of the Ythan Sea, and in her occasional lucid intervals, which came farther and farther apart now, she knew she could not last much longer.

The *Elgrane*, the ship upon which she and the rest of Cardolus's carnival had booked passage, had gone down swiftly in the initial chaos. She had attempted to save herself and her companion, the dryad Ia, by trying to climb onto the back of the gryphon that Beorn the thief had liberated from its cage. But a wave had washed her and Ia from the deck, and a moment later, foundering in water wracked by the impact of the fallen fragment, she had seen the thief and the woman with him borne aloft by the gryphon's mighty wings.

Providentially, a log that came from the dryad's forest and which Cardolus had kept to control her had also fallen into the sea. Holding onto the sustaining wood had been all that had kept Ia alive for the next few commondays, for the dryad could not eat raw fish. Eventually, however, her overall frailness had combined with her hunger and exhaustion to overcome her. Mirren did not know when it had happened—she had come out of the dazed, soporific state which passed for sleep to find herself alone. Ia had disappeared silently into the bathyal depths.

Mirren had been stunned by the loss; though she could not have said that she considered Ia a friend, she had felt sorry for the pitiful childlike creature, wrenched from her home in the woods of Prasan by an enchanter who had sold her and her wood to Cardolus. They had been close in that manner that only two utterly dissimilar people who share a common misery can be.

She knew that she would not long survive the dryad. It amazed her that she had managed to last this long; she attributed it to the beast within her, the wolf that possessed such a driving will to live. Weakened by exposure and hunger, she could hear the feral creature howling at the gates of her reason, demanding to take over, to transform her into a panting, lupine form that would swim in search of land until its lungs filled with salt water.

She had never had to hold back her metamorphic urges before. Beorn the thief, who had also been a shapechanger, had told her that he dreaded the bear that lived within him, that he fought against each transformation until the creature that shared his form could be denied its temporary dominance no longer. He feared always that the savage mind of the bear would subsume and subdue his human personality forever.

Mirren, on the other hand, had never had that fear. She had lived in peace with her bestial symbiont since that long-ago day when she had bought the spell that implanted the wolf within her. More, she had gloried in the knowledge that it was there. It was her secret; it made her special, unique. The knowledge gave her comfort and security—a spurious security at times, she was well aware, but nevertheless the wolf within her warmed her like its furry pelt might on a cold day. Its first task had been to rip out the throat of the seignior who had taken her from her family and raped her, and from then on she had lived in fear of no man.

It was true that the physical stress of the transformation was far greater now than it had been when she was young, and at times she grew uneasy dwelling on what it would be like as she entered old age, when her bones would grow more brittle and her skin less elastic. But that was a worry for the future, and Mirren had never been one to ponder overmuch on that. It was still immensely gratifying to give in to the burning need, to feel the lithe power and ferocity of the wolf, to race through the woods in pursuit of prey, to taste coppery hot blood . . .

A pity, she thought now, that she would never know that pleasure again. For it was obvious to her that she would soon join Ia at the bottom of the Ythan. She was very weak, and her throat ached with thirst. At times she could no longer feel the smooth wood over which her arms were draped. She was spared the devastation of the sun as it moved in its imperceptible crawl overhead, for the clouds blocked it, but in its place she had to endure the endless rain. At first it had been hot enough to blister her skin; now it was cold, and the mud it carried had caked in her sodden hair, making it a burden on her neck muscles. Stones and sand-fused glass, hurled high into the air by the impact, had fallen from the sky as well in those first few hours. But now it was only the eternal, filthy deluge. Mirren could not even drink it, for the dirt and salt carried aloft made it unpotable.

She had been only barely conscious for an indeterminate time—images chased themselves at random through her brain. She remembered the first time she had seen the thief, standing stocky and redbearded in the morning sunlight on the deck of the caravel. Cardolus's troop, which had consisted of herself, Ia and Saade the dwarf, had just trundled the wagons on board, bound from Althizar to Cape Uloth, on the continent of Quy. The two of them had known in the same moment that they were kindred spirits—both metamorphs with animalistic sexual fury pent in their souls. It had taken only an instant for her to decide that she wanted him.

They had attempted to make love in a storage locker in the steerage, and there the thief had gone mad. There was no other explanation for it—he had hallucinated that she had been turning into a wolf, even as he, unbidden, started to become a bear once more. It had not been true, at least not on Mirren's part. But Beorn had accused her of attempting something perverse and unnatural with him, and had stormed onto the deck. And then the fragment, or whatever it had been, had fallen . . .

The wolf was surging stronger within her now, and Mirren did not know if she had the strength to resist it much longer. To give in now would be to drown, she knew—she would not be able to hold onto the log while writhing and twisting in the throes of the transformation.

She was not really sure why she continued to cling to the log, to life, with such obduracy. There was no hope of rescue, after all—she was leagues from land, and the chances of her encountering another boat seemed too absurd to contemplate. Why not release her palsied grip, allow the ocean to claim her? It would be a kinder death, she knew, than the lingering expiration she was enduring now or the brutal attack of some sea creature such as a kraken or an ichthyocentaur. Heretofore such dark speculations had seemed abhorrent—Mirren loved life too much to admit the possibility of death, even though it seemed certain. But now she could no longer deny the truth—that she was in effect dead already, and only prolonging her suffering, not her life.

So be it, then. She could hear the thunder of her heart, loud in her ears, as she prepared to let go of the dryad's log and sink. Instinctively she started to take a deep breath, then actually smiled slightly with salt-cracked lips as she realized what she was doing.

Her fingers would not obey her at first; when she did release the log they drifted over her head, numb and useless like her hair, as her waterlogged garments pulled her down. She opened her mouth to let the chilling, alien element rush in and numb her lungs . . .

And felt her feet touch smooth rock.

At first the wolf woman had no idea what the unexpected sensation meant. Her surprised reaction nearly caused her to gasp and so suck water into her lungs, but something—perhaps, again, the animal cunning of her coeval—kept her from doing so. Simultaneously she felt herself pushed forward gently, and realized that what she had thought was the pounding of her heart had been the sound of a gentle surf.

Revitalized, she thrust herself ahead, kicking

toward the surface. Her lungs, nearly empty, were already screaming for air, and she very nearly passed out as she came out of the water and stumbled forward.

It was not, properly speaking, a beach she found herself on—the waves stroked gray, striated rock instead of sand. Mirren was only vaguely aware of this as she staggered, moving now by sheer willpower, up beyond the reach of the breakers, through the driving rain. Her waterlogged clothes felt as heavy as chain mail. Before her was a tangle of wet, reeking seaweed; a cloud of flies exploded away as she collapsed onto it, and into oblivion.

Mirren awoke coughing; she had been lying on her back, and the brackish rain had trickled into her open mouth. Slowly she sat up, every muscle knotted and cramped. She was appalled by how weak she felt. If she did not find food and water very soon, she would certainly die.

The omnipresent cloud cover made it difficult to gauge how long she had slept, but there seemed to be a slight change in the quality of the light. The long night was approaching; she had to find food and shelter before it arrived. The wolf woman stood, balancing carefully on legs that felt like they belonged to someone else, and looked around her.

The islet she was on was small and rocky, and appeared to offer little in the way of protection from the elements. Mirren turned—and gasped in astonishment. She had expected to see only the gradual slope of barren stone up to a small apex before it plunged back into the water—instead, the rock rose steeply before her, gathering into a natural tower of fluted gray stone that loomed far overhead, its peak lost in the mist. Mirren could see dark cracks and slits in the sheer curving wall. Before her, rude stone steps led toward a wooden door which now hung by one iron hinge.

Seaweed and the remnants of dead ocean creatures were everywhere; she could see kelp hanging from spires and crevasses high up the side of the pinnacle. The gigantic waves following the impact had struck here with devastating force. She wondered vaguely if whoever had dwelled here had survived.

At the moment, however, her overriding concern was finding food and water. She made her way up the steps and past the broken door, to find herself facing a spiralling stairwell cut from the living rock. Pools of water shone blackly in the faint light.

She did not know if she had the strength to climb the stairs, but there seemed to be no alternative other than to sit down and wait for death. She had given into that urge once; she did not intend to let it overcome her again. She shed her clothing; the air was chill against her bare skin, but she preferred that to the weight of the sodden cloth. Slowly, feeling as if she bore the weight of the entire hollow spire on her shoulders, Mirren began to mount the steps.

As she climbed them she wondered at what force had raised this spire from the Ythan's floor. Had it been a natural phenomenon, a result perhaps of the Shattering? Or had some incredible spellcasting shaped the rock?

The stairs rose remorselessly, the curvature of the wall seeming to mock her, revealing an endless succession of wet steps. An occasional starcrystal rod, set against the Rhynnish night, thrust from the wall. The stench of rotting fish and seaweed was stronger in the tower than it had been outside—at times it seemed that she must pass out from its power. Occasionally she passed other wooden doors, all securely locked—the flood of water evidently had not been strong enough to burst them open. Her leg muscles trembled with fatigue. It would almost be preferable, she thought, to be back in the water, hanging onto the log . . .

When finally Mirren found an open door on one of the landings, she very nearly passed it in her ataractic state. She stood, swaying, and stared at the sunken chamber, half-filled with water, before her.

It had evidently been the laboratory of a magician of high rank before the deluge; she could see, half-submerged, tables and shelves filled with ancient volumes, decanters and repositories of various salts and liquids, and other magical impedimenta for which she had no names. Few of them were still intact; the flood had overturned bookcases and cabinets, and a potpourri of various ingredients for spellcasting floated before her. Oils stained the water with rainbow colors in the light from the single window.

Mirren turned away; there was nothing that would aid her in this room. Across the stairs, however, was another chamber, this one much smaller and set on a higher level, and consequently not as damaged by the water that had raged through the spire. It was a larder, and in it she found stone shelves on which sat earthenware jars filled with preserves, loaves of stale, coarse-grained bread and salted fish.

After a time, she felt better. She had attempted to eat too much too fast initially, and her shrunken stomach had rebelled. A more careful consideration of her condition had enabled her to ingest some dried fruit and bread, as well as some water and even a little wine. Where the water had come from she had no idea—perhaps there was a spring somewhere on the islet, or—more likely—it had been distilled by magical means from the sea. At any rate, it had been sweet and pure, and Mirren felt remarkably rejuvenated.

Another closed door which had also resisted the flood led to a bedchamber. The mattress was a simple one of tick, the woolen blanket scratchy, but they felt to Mirren's weary form as she imagined the finest eiderdown beds that comforted royalty. She slept long and deeply. When she awakened, the protracted night had come; she dined again by starcrystal light, and returned to dreamless slumber.

After a few commondays of resting and eating, Mirren felt her strength returning. It was still raining; she wondered if it would ever stop. She managed a sponge bath of cold water and afterward found a robe that was reasonably dry. The salt-caked tangles of her hair reluctantly yielded to her fingers' tugging. Afterward, she explored the spire's rooms, learning from waterlogged notes on parchments and scrolls that it was called Graystar Isle, and had been the provence of a sorcerer named Thasos. He had been a member of the Circle, the coven of magicians who believed strongly in the reunification of the world's fragments in order to obtain grace once more from the One God they worshipped.

She also learned that there was no way off of the islet; apparently the sorcerer had kept neither dragonship nor seafaring vessel. Mirren resolved not to worry about that just yet; after all, there was food enough to last for a few commonweeks, and she was infinitely better off than she had been.

She took no undue advantage of her absent host's hospitality—it seemed wise not to unduly antagonize a sorcerer. Only one small indulgence she allowed herself; when she found a ring containing a sliver of faintly glowing stone set in resin, its beauty induced her to wear it. The small feminine gesture comforted her, made her feel somehow less a homeless castaway.

The topmost room of the pinnacle had evidently been the lair of some sort of beast, to judge by the remnants of straw and crut the waves had left undisturbed. It was a large, open space, quite suited for Mirren's particular needs.

She had to release the wolf for a time; it had been caged much too long. Standing in the center of the

room, looking out through the open wall at the dark
sky and sea, the lycanthrope let fall the robe she had
found in Thasos's bedchamber and stood naked in
the cold humid air. She shivered, feeling a thrill of
anticipation as she relaxed and let the wolf have its
way.

The transformation was swift, as though the beast
within her were quite eager to manifest itself. She
dropped to all fours as her limbs began to twist and
change. The pain as joints reformed and ligaments
stretched was intense, but also somehow enjoyable—
like the exhilarating ache that accompanies a strenu-
ous bout of exercise—and also decidedly sexual.

Thick, wiry hair sprouted swiftly, coating her skin
with a luxuriant dark pelt. Her breasts shrank, and
dugs formed along the ridges of her belly. Her coc-
cyx lengthened, forming into a tail that twitched and
lashed against her legs. In a matter of moments the
change was complete; where Mirren had stood, a
gray she-wolf now crouched.

At first it was enough simply to leap and run about
on the wet stone, tail held high, exulting in the
power and the swiftness of her animal form. She
threw back her head and bayed, listening to the
clash of echoes. Within her she could feel the wolf's
savagery prowling her soul, snapping and snarling at
the human mind that still dominated it. She enjoyed
the war of wills; the sensation of danger, the tug of
animal ferocity was stimulating. Mirren padded swiftly
down the spiralling length of the stairs until she
stood outside in the darkness. Only one thing was
missing—the opportunity to hunt. Save a few inver-
tebrates in tide pools and some gulls that wheeled
overhead, the tiny bit of land was lifeless. She longed
to feel her claws digging into the forest floor as she
hurtled in pursuit of a stag or unicorn; she wanted to
feel neck bones snap and crunch between her jaws
and taste the jetting lifeforce.

With a growl of frustration, she prowled over the slippery, rain-washed stone. She was growing hungry again, and though as a human she could exist on the meager fare she had found in Thasos's larder, the digestive system of the wolf needed red meat. Mirren could feel the beginnings of animal panic stirring within her. Firmly she closed off the instinctive fear of starvation, keeping her rational mind fully in control. It was unpleasant, for she would have to let the wolf run free for at least a few hours before attempting to subdue it again. And, once that was done, she would have to address herself seriously to somehow leaving Graystar Isle. A bonfire, perhaps, constructed in the highest room, might attract rescuers, if she could find anything dry enough to burn. . . .

The problem was that the isle was no doubt well known to sailors as the citadel of a sorcerer, and thus probably avoided with superstitious fervor. Perhaps supplies were delivered on a regular basis, but she had no idea how much the storms and waves had disrupted shipping.

Mirren felt exhausted again, abruptly; whether it was due to the apparent hopelessness of her situation or to taxing her lupine form so soon after her ordeal she did not know. She only knew that she needed to sleep. She entered the spire again. She had no need, as a wolf, of a mattress and quilts to sleep comfortably, and so she curled up on a dry patch of rock near the door. Almost immediately she was asleep, and her dreams were of the pursuit of prey through a nighted forest.

She awoke instantly, all faculties alert and aware. The unfamiliar sounds came again—the creak of canvas, rope and timber, and the faint sounds of human voices. Her nostrils flared as the breeze brought her additional confirmation. She did not need her nearsighted vision to tell her that a ship had arrived. She arose, slunk quickly toward the shadows at the base of the stairwell, and listened.

The murmur of voices resolved into words as they approached. "—looks deserted; I *told* you it was a fool's journey! The waves no doubt drowned him."

"We'll find out soon enough. He's a sorcerer, after all; if anyone could've survived it, it's him. And it's sure worth it for what he'll pay . . ."

Mirren quickly considered her options. She would have to greet them as woman rather than wolf, obviously. That way she could keep her savage alter ego a secret until it might be needed. But would the wolf willingly relinquish its form after so short a freedom?

There was only one way to find out. She leaped up the stairs, trotting swiftly back to the chamber where she had left her clothes, and there instigated the metamorphosis again.

It was hard; harder than it had ever been before. The wolf was reluctant to be caged within human flesh again so soon. When at last she saw in the mirror her own face and body, skin shiny with perspiration, Mirren felt as if she had been beaten with staves. For the first time she understood some small measure of the fear of which the thief had spoken.

There was no time to rest, however; she could hear the bootfalls of the sailors on the stairs. Quickly she dressed, using the edge of a blanket to blot a trickle of blood from one nostril. She had been an actress in Cardolus's troupe, and now she had a part to play. She had no doubt that she would play it well. Her costume was simple—it consisted of another ring, this one a simple band of silver which she had found in the sorcerer's laboratory. Mirren slipped it onto the fourth finger of her right hand.

Then she went out to meet them.

There were two men, and Mirren knew immediately that they were thieves. They were not nearly as consummate in their artistry as Beorn had been, either—these were simple footpads, cutthroats, willing and ready to cave in a skull for a purse containing a few crystal coins. She had encountered their kind often enough in her travels to recognize their type.

"Why have you come to Graystar?" she demanded, assuming control of the situation immediately and easily.

The taller, blackbearded one glanced quickly at his compatriot, a stocky man with one cast eye. Mirren read volumes in that glance. She brushed a stray lock of hair back, making sure that the ring that named her an enchantress was visible to them.

Casteye said, "B-beg pardon, Ma'am—we were looking for the sorcerer Stonebrow."

"It's known he pays good crystal for runestones," Blackbeard added. "We've brought him one."

Mirren almost let her surprise show. Thasos, or Stonebrow as he was evidently also called, must have been in the habit of paying well indeed for such as these to risk a journey through the Abyss and the theft of a fragment's most prized possession. They would be desperate to consummate the sale, and that realization sparked a plan within her.

"You are just barely in time," she said smoothly. "Stonebrow is no longer here; he has moved his base of operations to Cape Uloth in the wake of the disaster. I am his assistant, and I go now to join him. Let me see the runestone."

The thieves looked uncertainly at each other again, and then Casteye pulled an object wrapped in cloth from a pocket. He gave it to her; it was small enough to fit comfortably in the palm of her hand. Mirren unwrapped it and beheld, for the first time in her life, a runestone—the repository of enough ectenic force to sustain an entire fragment in its orbit, as well as providing those who dwelled upon it with weightfulness. It seemed impossible that so unassuming a thing as a small black stone etched with cabalistic engravings could be so powerful. But when she touched its surface with the tip of a finger and felt the galvanic tingle of power, she knew it was true.

At the moment, however, Mirren had no interest in the runestone other than as a prop for the role she was playing. She closed her hand and nodded. "Quickly, then—we must reach Cape Uloth before it is too late! Stonebrow needs as many runestones as possible for the spell he is casting."

Blackbeard hesitated. "Quy's a day's journey from here by boat. If speed's so important, why not just pay us and use your magic to summon a cacodemon to carry you there?"

She lifted an eyebrow, regarding the thief with mingled amusement and disdain. "I see no rings on your fingers, thief. Yet you think you know my profession better than I do? Should I summon a cacodemon, Lord Sestihaculas himself would not be far behind, and that would not bode well for Stonebrow's endeavors. There is no more time for questions—your choice is to accompany me willingly, or under a geas."

It was the threat of the ring on her finger that convinced them. They muttered imprecations and cast resentful glances at her, but they agreed to ferry her to Cape Uloth.

When Mirren saw their craft, however, she almost wondered if it might not be safer to remain on Graystar Isle. The thieves had braved the Ythan in a small fishing boat, hardly more than a skiff. Mirren looked dubiously at the patched sails and frayed ropes. She had no choice, however, and she knew it. Still, it was best to keep up appearances. She turned to the thieves and said, "You expect me to wish to risk my neck in such a frail scow? If I had the luxury of time, I would be more comfortable calling a selkie and riding him to Quy!"

"Your pardon, Enchantress," Casteye said. "It may not look like much, but it's a good ship, it is, stout and seaworthy. I've sailed her from Dulfar to Far Kaxol and back."

"I doubt that," Mirren replied. "Still, perhaps something can be done with it." She shouted some nonsense words she made up on the moment, and then continued, "Cardolus's Spell of Protection now envelopes your sorry craft. We should have no serious trouble reaching Quy."

She had been right in assuming they knew little of magic; they were quite grateful for the bogus enchantment. The blackbearded one, whose name was Junge, offered her the use of their cabin if she so desired; he and his companion, Vangik, could sleep on the deck in the rain. She indicated strongly that any other arrangement was out of the question.

Even though the two men seemed properly cowed, Mirren debated the wisdom of putting herself at their mercy for the seven or eight commondays it would take to reach Quy. She would have to walk a fine line, keeping them in fear of her without arousing their resentment. If the situation became serious enough, she could always let the wolf dispatch one of them—she would need the other to pilot the ship, as she had no knowledge of navigation or sailing.

They put out to sea quickly, after taking on a few extra supplies of food and water. Mirren stood in the stern, watching Graystar Isle recede over the horizon, feeling grateful to the mysterious Stonebrow for having inadvertently saved her life. If the gods were kind, soon she would begin a new life in Quy, free of Cardolus's carnival. She smiled. Perhaps the sun might even shine again, some day.

CHAPTER III

Castaway

Within the vermicular tunnels and chambers that honeycombed the cliffs of Xoth, Trisandela, Lady of Bats, stood before Sestihaculas, Lord of Snakes. The Demogorgon looked down at his subaltern, the tentacles framing his ophidian countenance writhing slowly.

"You have disposed of the humans' craft, as I ordered?" he asked.

"I have, Demogorgon."

Sestihaculas lidded his eyes. "Good. There will be no contact of any form or source with the race of man until I so decree. Let no cacodemon answer a sorcerer's summons for whatever reason, and let no Chthon take sport with the crews of venturesome dragonships, or travel by incantory means to other fragments."

Trisandela waited, watching her master brood. The penile viper below the ridged belly plates slowly coiled and uncoiled; other than that, the Lord of Snakes was as motionless as one of his minions at rest. The cavern in which they stood was silent, save for the dripping of slime from black stone.

At last Sestihaculas said, "Pandrogas thinks he has won—but he has not."

"Your pardon, milord," Trisandela said cautiously, "but did not you admit as much to him? And did you not pledge—"

"To cause no harm to him or those with him, and to aid him in his quest," the Demogorgon interrupted. "The second part of that pledge is fulfilled—as for the first, I am bound to honor it.

"But you are not, Trisandela."

The Lady of Bats gave no reaction to this, save to draw her wings more tightly about her.

"Talorath the cacodemon has borne the sorcerer and his woman to Nigromancien. I cannot order you to follow them there, nor can I suggest that you interfere or make what mischief you deem appropriate. Do you understand?"

Trisandela inclined her head slightly. "I do, Sestihaculas." She stepped back from him. "I will go now."

"I have no knowledge of your destination."

"Farewell, Demogorgon." Trisandela extended her wings to their full dimensions. A thunderclap and the stench of brimstone enveloped her, and she was gone.

Deep within the fragment called Nigromancien, Trisandela materialized. She was somewhat surprised that the apportation had been accomplished so easily; she had expected the final resting place of the Necromancer to be protected from casual intrusion, particularly by such as she.

The Lady of Bats looked about her. She stood within the crumbled ruins of a gigantic chamber. The ceiling had partially collapsed, and three of the olympian columns which had supported it had fallen as well. The fragments were scattered far and wide, almost as though some sort of explosion had taken place. Her clawed feet stirred clouds of gray dust when she walked.

At the far end of the chamber was a huge sarcophagus of onyx. It was open, and there was no sign of its lid. The Chthon stepped quickly up the steps of the dais and peered inside. It was empty.

Trisandela listened. Her ears, sharper by far even than those of the creatures she espoused, strained to catch any slightest sound that might lead her to her quarry. She heard nothing; the silence was complete.

She could sense the faint vibrations of magic recently invoked in the burial chamber. Pandrogas and Amber had been here—perhaps only a few moments before her arrival. Talorath had brought them, and from here he had ferried them to a new and unknown destination. But the cacodemon's path, though indetectable to all but the most powerful of sorcerers, was easily discernible to her. The astral pathways coterminous with all fragments that were open only to her and her kind kept a residual evidence of passage for some time. By this she quickly learned Talorath's destination—the castle called Darkhaven.

As far as she knew, Darkhaven was on a collision path with its parent fragment of Oljaer, due to the theft of its runestone by the thief Beorn. She looked at the vault again. If the Necromancer's body had rested within it, it was not there now. Had the sorcerer and his student exhumed it and carried it with them to Darkhaven, perhaps hoping to revivify it in hopes that the Necromancer could prevent Darkhaven's fall?

There was no way of knowing. Even with the castle's runestone gone, the spells Pandrogas had invested it with as protection against the Chthons were too powerful for her to breach. If Pandrogas had returned to Darkhaven, he was beyond her reach.

But Trisandela knew that she dared not return to Xoth with news of failure. Sestihaculas had given her an order—indirectly, but no less emphatically for that—and she had no desire to face his wrath by returning without fulfilling it.

She would have to wait, then. It might take a commonmonth, or a year, or longer, but that did not matter. The Chthons viewed time from a different perspective than did the ephemeral humans. And perhaps it might be better for her to be absent from Xoth for a time—Zhormallion would have no doubts as to who had helped the cloakfighter escape from his web. While Trisandela did not shrink from a confrontation, neither did she relish the thought of one.

She would have to prepare an enchantment that would alert her to the sorcerer's movements, however. There were several ways to go about this. Trisandela enfolded herself in her wings and began to give it thought. There was no hurry. Sooner or later Pandrogas would leave Darkhaven, and when he was beyond its walls and out of the deadly sunlight, she could strike.

Mirren and the two thieves had been bound for Quy for the majority of the long Rhynnish night when Junge began to make advances toward her.

Of the two of them, she feared Junge more; not because he was larger, since either of them could easily overpower her, but because he was the more intelligent of the two, and thus more prone to suspicion of her status as an enchantress. Several times already he had requested her to use her powers to shield him and Vangik from the rain, or to summon a steady wind to speed them to their destination. For Vangik, the reply that she was conserving her strength to aid Stonebrow in his spellcasting seemed to suffice, but she could see suspicion gathering on Junge's sloping brow. Duplicitious himself in all things, he expected duplicity from others as a matter of course.

She remained below as much as possible, for she had grown to detest the unrelenting rain. Though most of the silt that had been carried aloft by the fragment's impact had precipitated out of the clouds by now, the downpour itself was depressing, particularly so when coupled with the week-long night. Mirren was not a native of Rhynne, and so had not become used to the odd fluctuation of day and night— her own fragment, Pandor, was a land of fairly normal rotation. And the weather had grown cold, enough so that she could see her breath. She had to keep herself wrapped in blankets that were filthy and smelled of fish.

Because of this, even though she was cold, there were times when she felt the need to remove her clothes and wash herself down with cold seawater in a somewhat futile attempt to remove the accumulation of grime and sweat. It was while she was in the process of doing this, standing naked and shivering in the cramped cabin, that she heard the door open.

Mirren knew it was Junge even before she whirled about. She glared at him, hoping that only rage and not shock or fear showed, resisting the temptation to grab a blanket or her clothes. She had to stay in control of the situation.

His look of surprise was unconvincing—no doubt he had hoped and planned for just such an occurrence. "Your pardon, Enchantress," he said throatily. "One forgets, at times, that magicians are human too."

"You are pardoned," she replied haughtily. "And you will do well to remember that, human or not, I *am* an enchantress."

He hesitated on the topmost step, and she could see quite clearly desire warring with caution in his expression. "Stop!" Mirren commanded before he could speak again. "I know your thoughts, Junge. I know what you are contemplating, and I tell you most sincerely that, should you attempt it, there will not be enough left of your blasted corpse to feed the fish."

Such an ultimatum, she knew, would either cow him or drive him to attack. If it were the latter, then she had only one recourse left to her. It would be dangerous, but—

Junge interrupted her thoughts by leaping down the rest of the stairs. "We'll see about that!" he shouted, and then he was upon her.

It was not that the thought of bedding with a man to further her plans was that repulsive—as long as it was her choice. But she knew that once she bowed to their will, it would not stop there. She knew the kind of men they were, and that there was no limit to the degradation they would subject her to, including killing her. They could never view her as an equal—only as either a superior or as chattel.

When Junge seized her, she had already willed the metamorphosis to begin.

She saw him release her as he felt her bones twisting and shifting beneath his hands; he staggered back in shock. Now was the crucial moment—she could not afford to make the full change, for by that time he might gather his wits enough to attempt to kill her while she was relatively helpless.

In a cracked mirror hanging from a nail she caught a glimpse of herself—a terratoid horror, half wolf, half woman. Her skin was already covered with sparse gray fur, and her face had begun to elongate into a muzzle, her lips blackening and her teeth lengthening into fangs. Her nails were thickening into talons, and her legs were beginning to reform into the stifles and hocks of a wolf's limbs. She could feel her spine shortening, attempting to pull her down into a quadrupedal position.

The wolf, having been granted only a short period of dominance in its last incarnation, was emerging fiercely and quickly this time. Mirren would have to do what she had never done, never even attempted before—she had to stop the metamorphosis *now*, and reverse it before it was completed. And she would have to do it quickly, surely, giving no indication of the pain it caused.

She exerted all of her will power, concentrated every fiber of her body and focused her mind completely on what had to be done. She could *hear* the wolf howling in anger and frustration. She forgot about Junge, about everything but overcoming the awesome inertia of the transformation. She came perilously close to blacking out—but when she opened her eyes again, she was human once more.

Vangik had joined Junge at the door, and both of them were staring, white-faced, at her. Mirren did not move, for her heart was pounding so fiercely and her brain so drained of blood that to do so would have made her collapse—and that she could not afford to do. She stared at them as though down the length of a long tunnel, hoping that her dazed look would be misinterpreted as disdain. Faintly, she heard herself speaking:

"Do you dare embrace me now, Junge? Attempt such familiarity again, and I will tear your throat out!"

Both thieves turned and scrambled for the deck, falling over each other in a haste that would have been comical any other time. Mirren waited until she was sure they were gone, then collapsed wearily into a bunk. She could sense her animal counterpart snarling within the pathways of her mind, enraged at being teased thus. She wondered if she would be able to keep the beast pent for the remainder of the voyage.

But she had done the right thing, she knew. To

evince only a glimpse of the creature within was far more frightening than allowing the transformation to complete itself. A wolf was, after all, a relatively familiar beast, and not that hard to kill with a boathook or a sword. And there was always the possibility that they knew that most magicians preferred to use illusion instead of actual shapechanging.

But by giving them only the glimpse of some monstrous *thing* that dwelled within her, she had terrified them. And with any luck, that fear could last until they reached Cape Uloth.

The cloakfighter sat in the prow of the small chase boat, eating an apple and contemplating the infinite blue gulf before him. The sun was at his back and slightly beneath him at the moment. It appeared he would not die from its searing rays after all; the random air currents of the Abyss had chosen to send him back toward the main group of fragments that whirled in intricate paths about each other.

He could see no sign of them; though a close-knit arrangement in comparison with the fabled stars that shone in ancient nights, the shards that made up the world were still much too far apart to be viewed more than a few at a time from any particular vantage point within the Abyss. At present he could see none of them, not even Xoth and its parent; the blinding rays of the sun concealed them. The fathomless azure depths, broken only by a few cloud banks in the distance, were hypnotizing; he had to blink and turn his eyes away from contemplation of them, to reassure himself of reality by looking at the derelict that carried him.

He dropped the gnawed core of the apple to the ivory deck, where it struck with a thump. The runestone the boat carried made the craft, in effect, a tiny fragment; standing on it, the cloakfighter was as solid and heavy as he had been on Rhynne, the largest of the world's pieces. It was quite marvellous, really, Kan Konar thought, how the magicians of the ancient world had managed to save its broken remnants from complete destruction by the Necromancer's final spell. As well as creating the runestones, they had invoked thaumaturgies that kept winds moving through the Abyss, providing weather and climate. They had done the best they could, but they had known, even then, that their efforts could only prolong life another millennium at most. So Pandrogas had said; the sorcerer had been devoting his efforts to finding a basic force that would unite the disparate systems of magic prevailing on various fragments. Had he succeeded, life might continue precariously for a few hundred more years. But eventually the spells would die, and the unending frozen night that scholars thought pressed hungrily in from all sides would claim everything. That was the true Abyss, Kan Konar thought—not a warm and friendly blue gulf lit by the sun and dotted with green and hospitable fragments, but instead a black, eldritch cosmos that negated all life, all substance.

He did not find such thoughts depressing, for they had nothing to do with him; the void in which he drifted, forgiving though it might be in comparison with the outer one, would engineer his undoing easily enough. He estimated that the chase boat carried enough food and water to last him a commonmonth, if he used them sparingly.

He had no particular intention of being usurious; death would come when it would, and the event was no more to be feared than it was to be welcomed. He had dishonored himself and, as Shadowmaster had often told him, "Dishonor is as a scar on the face of a tree; instead of vanishing with time, it only grows larger."

As he drifted aimlessly in the limitless vault of heaven, it seemed to Kan Konar that he could almost hear the voice of his instructor, could almost see the small, lean body, shrunken with age but not bowed, surrounded by the cavernous folds of his cloak. Those had been times of privation and hardship, as he had slowly learned as a small boy the way of the warrior he was to become . . .

It was not easy; at first, to the lad of less than ten commonyears, the tasks did not even make much sense. His duty was to carry water from the spring to the old man's hut, and to chop wood for the fire. The old man ordered him to keep the fire burning constantly, and had also decreed that the water barrel never drop below a certain level. For months the lad did as he was bid, wielding the axe and shouldering the yoke and buckets with a will, confident that soon Shadowmaster would begin teaching him the secrets of the cloak. But as time passed, and nothing happened save that his hands grew callused and his shoulders broad and hard from the labor, the young Kan Konar began to resent the wizened old character who spent most of his days silently writing on scrolls of rice paper. He wished he knew what Shadowmaster was writing, but since he could not read, and since the old man either ignored or ridiculed his questions, he had no way of learning.

One day he worked up the courage to ask his instructor when his lessons with the cloak would begin. Shadowmaster merely held out one of the small slivers of dragon ivory that lined the cloaks' hems and provided the deadly cutting edge, and said, "When you can catch this without moving your hand." He held it between the latter's thumb and fingers, then dropped it. No matter how fast Kan Konar closed his fist, no matter how carefully he watched Shadowmaster's expressionless face and eyes for some hint or clue, he was never able to seize the tiny sliver before it fell beyond his grasp.

It was maddening. The boy sulked and contemplated running away. But he knew that to return to his parents would be to cast shame on both them and himself, and so he resolved to stay and see it through, though privately he was convinced that the ancient had entered his dotage. This conviction was markedly strengthened one day when, as he was pursuing his chores, one of the weighted ends of Shadowmaster's cloak suddenly struck him from behind, knocking him over and eliciting a howl of pain. He scrambled to his feet, confused and hurt, but the old man was already stalking away, his deadly garment wrapped about him.

Thus a new element was added to the game, and Kan Konar never knew when the flickering cloak would strike. He was never cut, only bludgeoned by the bone knobs that snapped against his back and legs with whiplike quickness. At first it seemed impossible to avoid them, but gradually, by always watching the instructor when he was within sight and by learning to keep a certain part of his mind constantly alert for the sound of the cloak's passage through the air, he began to avoid some of the blows. Slowly the constant awareness became just another part of his life. He learned to make judgments instantaneously, based on the knowledge that even an action so innocent in appearance as entering a hut or passing a tree could have immediate and painful consequences. His reactions became quicker as he learned to move with animal swiftness and cunning.

And, at last, there came a day when his fingers closed upon the thin oblong of ivory before it passed his hand.

It was then that the difficult part of his training began.

One morning when he awoke, Kan Konar found lying beside him his own cloak. Cut to fit his young frame, it was white as a cloud in the sun, silken and strong to the touch, its edges sharper than steel. In a burst of joy, forgetting all else, he leaped to his feet and donned it. For the first time in his life he knew how it felt to be nestled within a warrior's cloak, a garment that would eventually become more intimately a part of him than his own skin. The cloak was considered to be the very soul of a cloakfighter, an extension of the vital energy tamed and tempered within him. He gripped its folds and whirled them around his head—

And felt Shadowmaster's garment snake about his legs, pulling them out from under him. The lad fell in an undignified heap.

He had gained his first cloak, and now he learned the price of keeping it. Shadowmaster initiated the duels—if they could be referred to as that; slaughter was perhaps a more appropriate term—at his discretion, anytime and anywhere, and they consisted simply of a few futile passes and dodges upon Kan Konar's part before the edge of the other's cloak lightly caressed his throat, or the heavy corner grazed his temple, or the instructor indicated in any of a hundred and one other ways that, were his own control not perfect, the student would now lie dead at his feet.

The boy practiced assiduously every spare moment with his cloak, inventing forms and perfecting them, only to see them brushed aside like ineffectual leaves by the master's weapon, or to find himself suddenly blinded by the sun glancing from the lining of reflective phoenix feathers within the cloak. He watched his mentor, studying his movements, watching for subtle tensings of his limbs an instant before he moved, trying to read his gaze. It did not help; the most he was able to do was put off the inevitable for a few more precious moments.

Slowly he learned to look deeper than just to the infinitesimal twitch of facial muscles or the subtle shift of stance that might or might not signal an attack. He learned to put himself in the old man's place, to *be* Shadowmaster, for the length of the battle. And, at long last, he was able to land a blow of his own.

The next morning, when he awoke, a new cloak was lying at his side, and its color was the gray of a thunderhead.

And so the years progressed, and the young man learned. In addition to his growing skill with the cloak, he was taught other things as well, including the mastery and understanding of calligraphy, which unlocked secrets hidden in the old man's cache of scrolls. From them he gained knowledge of character and moral obligations as well as skill. "Learning without thought is useless," Shadowmaster told him; "and thought without learning is perilous."

He learned to control his emotions, to keep them hidden behind the mask of his face and eyes. He was never without his cloak; he slept in it, and even when he washed it in the clear mountain streams he used the opportunity to augment his skill by practicing with the sodden, heavy mass until it was dry again. He learned to know every fold and wrinkle in it, and saw it as an object of surpassing beauty, its weave immaculate, its movements as awesome as the stroke of a dragon's wing. Shadowmaster cautioned him against being too taken with its appearance—he did not want to run the risk of valuing the artistry of his technique over its practicality. The time spent admiring it would be better used in practicing.

His master did, however, urge him to take pride in his appearance—to keep his weapon as well as his body neat and clean, for to do so would reflect well upon his master when he gained one. And so he took care to shave his first few wisps of beard every day, wetting his skin with water and scraping it with the slivers of bone to toughen the skin. Similarly, he kept his hair trimmed and bound. He would be a warrior in appearance as well as action.

He learned to move wraithlike through the forest, so that no leaf or twig protested his feet; how to turn the blow of a knife or sword with a precise movement of his cloak; how to whip the garment from his shoulders by grasping the chain clasp and imparting a deadly spin to it.

Kan Konar did not know when he first realized that he was holding himself back to avoid injuring Shadowmaster in their duels. Realizing it, however, he knew that he had been cautious in that manner for some time, and that Shadowmaster knew it as well. He knew also that he had become a man—and that it was time to return to the city he had left so long ago, to seek employment as a retainer in a Daimyo's house.

He said nothing of this to Shadowmaster. Nevertheless, when he awoke on the morning he had planned to leave, lying beside him was a new cloak, and this one was the color of one of the nights of the legendary whole world.

The cloakfighter smiled slightly at the memories. Staring into the Abyss made it quite easy to visit other times, other places. Perhaps this is how he would pass his final moments, lost in a delirium of the past. There were, he knew, worse ways to die.

And so he pursued his lonely, aimless way, making no effort to direct his course, watching his meager store of supplies dwindle steadily. There was no day or night in the Abyss, and the only way he could judge the passage of time was by the growth of his beard—when it came time to shave again, he knew another commonday had passed. He kept track of them, marking them into the bone gunwale.

The Abyss was capable of driving strong men mad with isolation, but Kan Konar felt none of this—he had been alone all his life, and preferred his company to that of any other. He had been taught from an early age to be self-contained and self-sufficient. And besides, dead men have no need for company or conversation, and Kan Konar considered himself no more than that. Soon he would be brought to his final resting place, and there he would lie down.

He had been drifting for nearly three commonweeks when he saw the fragment in the distance.

At first he thought it was a cloud bank—then he could see steep peaks rising from the white fog. The winds ushered him slowly closer over the course of several commondays, until he could make out forests and rivers. It was a mountainous shard, large enough to be home to a small town or village, though he saw no sign of such on its surface. Many of its valleys were wreathed in clouds, however, and so concealed from him.

It became obvious that this was his destination. The boat's runestone counteracted to a considerable degree the fragment's attraction, but the greater mass of the latter slowly drew the boat down to the surface. It landed as gently as a bird on one of the higher peaks' declivities.

Kan Konar stepped from the craft onto the short, scrublike grass. It was twilight, the sun barely riding the tip of the close horizon. The air was crisp and laced with the scent of pine. Below him he could see a beautiful vista of evergreens sweeping into a cloudmasked valley. A stream tumbled down the slope nearby. Behind him, a cave—little more than an eroded lacuna—pocked the side of a sheer cliff. It was deep enough to provide protection from storms.

Kan Konar nodded to himself. This, then, was his fate—to be a cenobite on this nameless fragment. Obviously whatever gods that still took interest in the broken world had decreed this, providing him with the boat and the cacodemon to hurl him into

the Abyss, and now bringing him to this sylvan locale. Instead of being granted an honorable end in
battle, he was banished to a living death.

It had been a most stirring adventure, all in all. A
pity it had to end so poorly, he told himself, but
adventures were often like that in real life. He would
not question the will of the gods. Here he would stay,
and meditate upon what he had learned, and wait for
his death to be complete.

The cloakfighter turned and entered the cave that
was his new home.

BOOK TWO

Tamboriyon

And besides, a fresh reality will perhaps make us forget, detest even, the desires on account of which we set out on our journey.

—Marcel Proust,
Cities of the Plain

BOOK TWO

Transformation

CHAPTER IV

The Voyage

Far and wide across the broken remnants of the world, the fragment of Tamboriyon was synonymous with Heaven. A place of ideal climate, emerald meadows and forests, and gentle, civilized people, it was the land of milk and honey to which many aspired to journey.

But to Amber, at the moment, it felt closer to Hell.

Amber Jaodana Chuntai Lhil, late the Marquise of Chuntai, stood near one end of a large atrium in the temple of Taggyn Saer. She was breathing heavily, and her loose robe was damp with perspiration. Behind her, arrayed on either side of the small impluvium, the other members of her class watched her intently. Before her stood her instructor, Ratorn, sorcerer of the fifth rank in the Taggyn Saer system, his hands upraised in poses of power.

"S'en yai, palis tanyak!" he shouted suddenly, ac-

companying the Payan spell with a complicated gesture.

Amber recognized the cantrip—Kahnya's Spurious Demon, or the spell of False Invocation. With a thunderclap, what seemed to be a ravening cacodemon appeared before her. There was no telltale accompanying scent of brimstone, however, and the monster stood without discomfort in the shaft of sunlight from the conpluvium above; either of these facts would have alerted her to the hoax even if she had not been familiar with the spell. The phantasm leaped toward her, rugose muzzle wrinkled in a snarl, talons gleaming.

Amber stood her ground and spoke three words quietly. The image of the cacodemon vanished in a wisp of smoke—and simultaneously she was seized in a python-like grip by bands of maroon fire that pinned her arms to her side. She realized in an instant her mistake—while she had allowed herself to be distracted by an illusion, Ratorn had trapped her.

For one brief instant she felt panic—but then the proper counterspell came to her. Since she was unable to use any accompanying form to enhance its power, it had to be spoken with precisely the right intonation. *"Diton keph lahn—"* she began, and found herself dazzled by an incanous flash of light from the sorcerer's left hand. The burst left her momentarily blind, but she did not falter in her incantation: *"—tula mosth zeyat!"*

Her pronunciation was true, and the imprisoning bands dissolved from about her. Amber stepped back, raising both arms as she prepared to counterattack with Malrai's Lance of Light—

"Enough," said Ratorn. He was smiling, his arms at his sides. Amber hesitated somewhat uncertainly— was it another trick? But no—there in his hand was the golden ring. He stepped toward her, took her left hand in his right and slipped the ring on the middle finger, removing as he did so the band of polished jade that had adorned her index finger.

"You have proven yourself worthy of advancement," he said. "I grant you the rank of Conjuress in the Taggyn Saer system."

The formality of the class precluded Amber showing any sign of the joy she felt until after Ratorn had dismissed his students. Once that had been done, however, the others gathered around her enthusiastically, offering congratulations. She was the first of them to reach this higher rank, and if any of them felt any jealousy at the rapidity of her advancement, none showed it.

Amber felt elated, despite the exhaustion that was the result of the rank test. The gruelling combination of physical exercise and spellcasting had taken over three hours; her muscles were trembling and she felt weak and dizzy. Zerrad, one of the first students she had met when she had arrived at the school nearly a commonyear ago, offered her a draught of fruit nectar. After only a few sips she felt revitalized, though still tired.

He walked beside her down the megaron, past the colonnade and out into the open air. The cenacle of Taggyn Saer stood on a hill at the base of snow-capped mountains. Facing them was the magnificent sculptured peak of Borea, carved by generations of laborers into the image of a robed woman seated on a throne. Though Amber had seen the vista nearly every day since arriving at the temple, it never failed to take her breath away.

"It is beautiful, isn't it?" she murmured to Zerrad, who had stopped by her side.

"Not nearly as beautiful as you," he replied, putting his arms around her waist.

There had been a time, after she had first come to Tamboriyon, when his compliments had both amused and annoyed her—the amusement came from his earnestness and almost painful naivete, and the annoyance from his perseverance after she had told him of her commitment to Pandrogas. But Zerrad had persisted, and slowly Amber had come to be uncertain of just how she felt toward him. He was three years her junior, a shipping merchant's son from Xhrann—well-educated, intelligent and quite handsome. He was obviously smitten with her, and she had reluctantly admitted to herself as the commonmonths passed that she found him attractive as well.

She had spent her first few weeks on the empyrean fragment simply recuperating from the headlong nightmare that had engulfed her for so long. The events that had begun with Beorn's theft of the Runestone of Darkhaven and the crippling of Tahrynyar, her husband, and the subsequent mad flight from fragment to fragment that had eventually culminated in the confrontation between Pandrogas and the Necromancer had exhausted her both mentally and spiritually. She had needed time to heal, to become acquainted with the new Amber who had been forged in the fire of that time—a woman possessed of innate magical ability surpassing even Pandrogas's; a woman who had lost a husband and gained a lover, only to lose him, too, for a time.

For those first few weeks she had awakened with a pounding heart from incredibly vivid nightmares: visions of the dungeons of the Chthons; of Beorn as the bear, battling the deadly chimera that guarded the Necromancer's tomb; of the terrifying journey through the gauntlet of the Labyrinth that had ended with her face to face with Ardatha Demonhand. These dreams, and others, had gradually subsided in intensity, though even now they sometimes returned to her with sufficient force to cause her to start upright in bed.

Oddly enough, the stark reality of the horrors that she had faced existed only in her nightmares now;

her waking memories of them seemed dreamlike and vague. It was as if her mind was attempting to shield her from their effects by removing them to the realm of the fantastic. It had become harder and harder to really accept that any of it had happened—and that included her love affair with Pandrogas.

"Is anything wrong?" Zerrad asked, taking his arms from about her. Amber realized that she had been staring wistfully into the distance for several minutes. She smiled and shook her head, running a hand through her heavy dark hair—it had been honey-colored when she had been born, prompting her descriptive use-name—and continued down the winding path that led from the temple. The warlock hurried to keep up with her.

When Amber had first met Pandrogas during the tumultuous storm that had hurled Tahrynyar's dragonship against the roofscape of Darkhaven, he had seemed almost godlike to her—a sorcerer of the tenth rank, the master of a castle the size of a small city that floated, serene and aloof, through the sky. Initially he had been remote as well, which only increased her fascination. Then, gradually, she had come to see and know the man behind the sorcerous mask—to realize that he was lonely and in need of someone to understand his complexities, even as she felt herself to be. She had never, it seemed to her now, really loved Tahrynyar—or, rather, the woman who had felt that love seemed now as remote to her as the farthest fragment. What she had felt for Pandrogas had been a passion new, exciting and consuming, and she had given herself wholly to it, willingly cuckolding Tahrynyar.

And now—like everything else, it seemed—that passion too had passed.

Amber thought of the gradual disillusionment that had accompanied her trek with Pandrogas from Darkhaven to Rhynne, and later from Xoth to the

eponymous cenotaph of Nigromancien, and thence
to Darkhaven again. To learn that, sorcerous abilities
notwithstanding, he was only a man after all, with
human frailties and shortcomings, had not been the
worst of it. And to realize his uncertainty—even
jealousy—regarding her and her burgeoning magical
ability had been painful. But that had not been the
whole of it. Amber had tried for nearly a commonyear
to sort it all out, to understand her feelings for the
master of Darkhaven. They seemed no clearer to her
now than when she had stood on the grassy knoll at
the edge of Tamboriyon with him, and they had
watched the bear that had been Beorn investigate
the meadows and forests of his new home.

They had agreed to return to that knoll in a
commonyear's time, she from the school of sorcery
on Tamboriyon and he from the musty corridors of
Darkhaven, to see if it were possible or desirable to
continue their relationship. And now that year had
passed. Tomorrow was the day of reunion and possible reconciliation.

She had worked hard to reach the rank of Conjuress,
that she might stand before him with a new ring of
rank on her hand. There had never been any doubt
that she would meet him—but now, suddenly, she
was filled with uncertainty. She was so very different
from the woman who had made that promise so long
ago.

She felt Zerrad seize her by the shoulders, gently
stopping her. He turned her around to look at him.

"Are you too advanced now to be bothered with
one of a lower rank?" he asked, his smile taking the
sting out of his words.

Amber gave a rueful little laugh. "I *am* sorry,
Zerrad. It's just that I have so much to think about—"

"I know," he interrupted gently. "You aren't the
only one who has made note of tomorrow's date. I've

been dreading your assignation ever since you told me about it, months ago."

She suddenly realized that, by spending the night with him, which she had done more than once, she had been terribly unfair to him. "I have been honest with you," she began, but he silenced her with a quick kiss.

"I am not accusing you of being otherwise—but you have to admit that I've a right to be disappointed. I've tried very hard to woo you away from the memory of Pandrogas. I guess we won't know whether or not I've succeeded until after you face him again."

Now it was her turn to put her arms around him. He was tall and asthenic, with a craggy face partially hidden by a beard that made him look older than he was. Amber felt him against her, listened to his heart beat beneath his robes. He was a good man; young and impetuous, but with a talent for magic and a desire to learn. And he was real, and here, and she knew he loved her. How much of the Pandrogas she remembered was real, she wondered, and how much a fantasy?

The sun was setting. Suddenly, without speech or any movement between them, the question was there—what would she do with her last night before she faced the past again?

Amber watched the sun touch the brow of Mount Boreas, crowning it with fire. Though the air was warm, she abruptly found herself shivering—and Zerrad's embrace seemed very much a safe haven.

The journey from Darkhaven to Tamboriyon by dragonship was a matter of nearly three commonweeks at this time of year; the two fragments were not at their closest approach to each other. It was not a particularly difficult or dangerous voyage; the dragons which had once roamed the Abyss so freely were all but extinct now, and the vampires and other raptors could be easily dealt with by a sorcerer of the tenth rank. It was certainly not fear that had almost kept Pandrogas from undertaking the voyage—at least, not fear of the Abyss.

Pandrogas stepped from the small cabin of the dragonship onto the deck, blinking against the eternal sunlight. In the distance he could see Tamboriyon, floating like a green and azure jewel against the cloud-dappled welkin. He was approaching on a fairly level plane with it, and so the full impact of its beauty was somewhat lessened, but even so he found himself entranced by the sight for several moments. In a day's time, if all went well, he would be standing on that knoll once again, and once again he would hold Amber in his arms.

He had very nearly decided not to come. Several factors had argued for that decision . . .

When he had returned to Darkhaven a year previously, the sorcerer had dwelled for some time in total isolation, meditating on what he had learned. His world view had been overturned by the realization that Necromancy, long regarded by nearly every mage alive as the ultimate abomination and the force responsible for the Shattering, had saved Darkhaven from destruction and was in fact the one hope of the world's salvation. This had been a numbing understanding. In common with most others, the sorcerer had always considered the Necromancer to be the personification of evil. But now, having communed with the latter's shade, he felt that such was not the case. The power of the dead was not necessarily a force for evil. In his one experience with it, Pandrogas had been no more than a channel for it, a conduit that had focused, but not directed, the overwhelming power.

Ever since he had first acquired tenancy of the

insular castle, Pandrogas had searched among the tomes and volumes of its libraries for the way to unify the disparate schools of magic that had sprung up after the Shattering. He had long been convinced that the ectenic force common to all systems of thaumaturgy could be manipulated more effectively and efficiently if an overriding set of axioms could be established.

Pandrogas thought of this synthesis as metamagic. He was convinced that, could he but discover a commonality to all the various concepts, he would be able to wield sufficient power to stay the slow, inevitable decline of the fragments' orbits.

But for years this unification had eluded him—he had been unable to find a single underlying precept that applied equally well to all forms of magic. And now he knew the reason why—he had ignored in his search the study of Necromancy.

Once he had dared to open such forbidden volumes as *The Book of the Black Skull* and other librams that had been chained to the shelves ages ago, Pandrogas had found that the ancient crumbling pages were the sources he had been searching for. Though eisegesistic and contradictory, the information within seemed to establish Necromancy inarguably as the set of universal theorems he sought.

The irony of it did not escape the sorcerer, and he wondered how he could have been so blind for so long. During the course of the next commonyear Pandrogas had delved deep into the secrets of the dead. Possessed now of the map that showed the only safe route through the Labyrinth, he had spent many hours in the catacombs that lay beyond it, deep in Darkhaven's heart. He had communed long with the wraiths that could be summoned by the revivifying spells, and he had learned, finally, the secrets of Darkhaven.

He spoke with revenants who had lived before the

world's destruction, and they had described to him what Darkhaven had been—the gigantic seat of power for a nation whose boundaries had been the largest continent on the globe, and which had subjugated every other nation and kingdom known. Ketra, it had been called, the Shining Empire; it had ruled for ten thousand years before the Shattering. Virtually all knowledge of it had been lost, save for isolated legends and myths, in the barbarism that had followed the impact of another world with their own.

Pandrogas had learned all this and much more in his year of study. At last he had felt confident enough to open the doors of the castle once more to students—those who were willing to accept the possibility that Necromancy might save rather than destroy. He had contacted the Cabal, that conclave of mages responsible for maintaining the precarious state of the world, and told them of his findings. Their response had not been completely enthusiastic.

The sorcerer sat crosslegged in the bow of the small ship, feeling the sun warm him and the breeze soothe him, thinking ruefully about the events of the last few commonmonths. Nion, a sorcerer of the Balisandra style who had replaced Thasos, had been shocked to learn of Pandrogas's studies in the forbidden power of the dead, and had urged the Cabal to repudiate him. Fortunately, others had been more receptive. The Cabal had been growing more and more desperate since the collision of the aerolith with Rhynne. There had been other impacts, though none so disastrous, and a score of near misses. It was becoming obvious that the ectenic power which kept the fragments' orbits stable was waning fast.

And so several of the members of the Cabal had elected to come to Darkhaven and investigate the possibilities of Necromancy. It was for this reason that Pandrogas had felt he could not, in all conscience, leave. The research they were engaged in was vitally important—nothing less than the fate of the world depended on it.

Another reason he had felt reluctant to go was the spherecasting he had made just before leaving. The interpretation of the scattered ivory fragments had not been encouraging: *It does not further one to cross the bright void.*

And yet, despite these reluctances, Pandrogas had left Darkhaven for Tamboriyon. His reason for doing so was simple—he still loved Amber.

He had thought of her virtually every day he had spent in the musty vaulted chambers. He would be pouring over a yellowed page of text, then realize that his mind had drifted, and that he had been dreaming of her smile, the way her hair fell across her shoulders and breasts. He could hear her laughter in the sound of running water, the music of her alicorn flute in the wind that sighed over the crenels and merlons of the walls. Though he had been unsure of his feelings for her during the adventures they had shared, his year of separation had left him with no doubt concerning the perdurability of his love for her. Not even duty could keep him from his tryst with her.

Pandrogas sighed and rose to his feet. His stomach was beginning to growl, and he had yet to perform his ritualistic spellcasting and exercises that he put himself through religiously every other day in order to keep his mind and body attuned. He started to turn toward the darkness of the cabin behind him—

He stopped, brow furrowing, pretending to study something in the bright blue distance. There was nothing in fact to be seen—he peered into the depths of the Abyss to gain a moment's time in which to deal with the sudden feeling of danger that had fallen over him like a cloakfighter's mantle. In an instant, though he still stood in the clean sunlight, the sorcerer felt a chill of dread. Something was not right—

It was the ship's cabin. *Something* now lurked within the dark interior, something which had not been there a moment ago. Pandrogas's nostrils flared slightly as the crisp breeze brought the barest scent of brimstone to him. He felt his soul contract within him, seeking to hide in the deepest recesses of his flesh, curling up into a small, protective nut.

A Chthon waited for him in the darkness.

I should have heeded the sphere's warning, he thought.

Quickly he reviewed his options. They were very few. Though his power had been revitalized when Darkhaven's runestone had been returned to its full power, and though he had learned much since in his dealings with the dead, still he knew that to face a Chthon in battle one on one was suicide. As long as he remained in the light, he was safe from a direct attack . . .

Who could it be? He had expected a pledge from Sestihaculas that prevented the Demogorgon from raising a hand against him, but this did not preclude one of his minions attacking. Had Endrigoth, the Lord of Rats, or some other decided to avenge his liege?

It did not matter. All that mattered was that the danger existed. Pandrogas could see only one choice open to him—to throw himself into the Abyss and trust his powers to bring him safely to Tamboriyon.

Even as he prepared to leap, however, he heard something behind him—a sound resembling the fluttering of a pennant in a gale. It multiplied rapidly. The sorcerer whipped around—to see a horde of bats pouring from the black entrance of the cabin. Beyond, within the breathing darkness, he caught a glimpse of two mocking red eyes.

Now he knew who his enemy was—and now it was too late.

Before he could speak the spell that would surround him with the Armor of Light they were upon him—their wings beat against his face and arms like whips, and he felt his skin scored by hundreds of razor-sharp claws and teeth. Their high-pitched squeaking deafened and confused him. He dropped to his knees, trying to shield his eyes. He opened his mouth to shout another spell of defense, then gagged in revulsion as a hot, squirming body forced itself between his teeth.

They were behind him now, forcing him to crawl forward on all fours. Pandrogas knew they were herding him toward the cabin, into the tiny pocket of night where Trisandela awaited him. He knew, but he could not stand against the living tide that urged him onward. He felt the cold shadow fall across his hands, and then his arms.

Trisandela said, "The Demogorgon sends greetings, sorcerer." And her laughter was one with the chittering of the bats that filled his ears and drove him into unconsciousness.

CHAPTER V
The Assassin

Through the twisting streets of Sarkeet, in the last hour of night, the assassin made her way. She moved silently, treading in boots of supple basilisk hide, her lithe form concealed by a short cloak and loose clothing of the same color as the night. Few others were about at that hour, and those who were hastily gave her as wide a berth as the narrow, cobbled lanes would afford. Though none might recognize her as a member of the Guild With No Hall, something in her carriage and the set of her face kept anyone from approaching too closely.

The night of Zarheena was darker than most, since the fragment orbited partially in Calamchor's shadow. Kyra could see dimly the other side of the constrictive street, lined with crowded shops and, above them, the rickety wooden dwellings of the proprietors. In a very few of them candlelight still burned. An occasional starcrystal rod gave a cold blue tint to the darkness. A cat leaped from one damp stone post of a balustrade to another, then watched her pass, its green eyes luminescent.

As Kyra passed the cat and reached the end of the lane she heard the tolling of the predawn hour, the sonorous tones sounding muffled and far away, as though the night were wrapped like cotton around the clappers. She nodded slightly in satisfaction. She was exactly on schedule—neither ahead nor behind. That was as it should be. All would go according to plan, as it had hundreds of times before. Thrisus, the Guildmaster, expected no less; nor could she give any less.

And yet, deep within her, she could not deny the tiniest stirrings of nervousness, as though some small insect moved within its silken womb, preparing to burst forth in a flutter of wings. She was one of the best assassins in the Guild; she had always killed as she had been instructed to do, without question or qualm. A colorful variety of souls had fled from her ministrations: souls belonging to, among others, a wagonwright, a seneschal, a gemwood merchant, a jewel smuggler and a slaver. All of these Kyra had dispatched with the utmost professionalism, with no doubts or uncertainties. She was one of the best; her ambition was to be *the* best. One did not achieve this by shrinking from assignments.

Not even when the assignment was to kill an enchanter. . . .

She turned onto that wide avenue known as the Verge, moving quickly despite flagstones made slippery by the wet air. To her left the Abyss gaped. As a child she had ofttimes climbed onto the low blockage wall and walked its length, like all the other children she knew, as much to distress the adults who saw them as to dare the fates, to feel the thrill that comes only from traversing the edge of infinity. Only one child she knew of had paid the price—he had tripped on a protruding bit of mortar and fallen over the edge, away from the saving attraction that the fragment exerted and into the eternal depths.

Her friend floated out there still, most likely, she thought, glancing into the luminous depths. Probably a clean-picked skeleton by now. The fragment that came nearest in its orbit to Zarheena was Calamchor, the jungle land—by all accounts a limitless expanse of green, rampant growth and dangerous beasts. Had the lad somehow come to land there, he would not have lasted long.

And yet she had still dared to walk the wall, even going so far as to do handstands and cartwheels on its narrow width. Her father had beaten her repeatedly to discourage her. But nothing had made her feel so alive, so vibrant, as had this dance with death.

There were few things she had feared, even as a child—and there was nothing she feared now. She had conquered the terrors inculcated within her by friends and relations, both well-meaning and not. She smiled as she recalled now one of her great fears as a young girl—that, during the summer months when the nights were warm and her father would leave her window open, a cacodemon would appear on the windowsill and carry her away to the nighted mushroom forests of Xoth. Though she realized now that such creatures were only fabrications with which to frighten children, at the time they had seemed very real. Even now she could recall her vivid imaginations of how it would be—the thunderclap of wings, the choking stench of sulfur, the phosphatic glow of its eyes as it reached for her . . .

Even on Zarheena, darkness was not as deep and velvety as the legends of the whole world once had it, and dawn would make it lighter still. Ahead she could see her destination: the manse of the enchanter Visantes. A gabled and many-windowed structure, cantilevered over the edge of the fragment, it had earned the nickname of the Hanging House. Kyra stopped a few yards away. A single light burned in one of the top windows. Though nothing appeared out of the ordinary, she knew that the house was protected with spells that would instantly detect an intruder. She was not foolish enough to attempt an invasion of the enchanter's home. But she had studied his movements, his schedule, for the past several commonweeks, and she knew that he was an early riser who customarily took a walk just before dawn. Moving swiftly and agilely, Kyra swung herself over the wall that bounded the Abyss, next to the enchanter's house.

She was no stranger to this exercise either; there are no limits to what children will dare. She had located earlier a lip of mortar that provided a secure grip, and now she hung, weightless, over the gulf. She wedged a piton fashioned from a dragon's tooth into an interstice and tied herself to it. Her clothing would blend in with the night—and who, after all, would look for a threat from beyond the world's edge?

On the back of her left hand was the weapon she had chosen for this task—a tiny arbalest, its recurved bow scarcely wider than the span of her knuckles, securely fastened with buckled strips of leather. With her gloved right hand Kyra withdrew from a pouch a tiny quarrel no larger than a needle, which had been steeped for a week in concentrated venom from a manticore's tail. Moving carefully in her unaccustomed ethereal state, she fitted it into the shaft's groove, then pressed the lever that cocked the bowstring.

She did not have to wait long. The door opened and light, rich and golden, spilled over the street. She heard a voice, but it was not the one she had expected to hear:

"—you are going to Darkhaven, then?" A woman's voice—his wife, according to all research. But she had never accompanied him on his constitutional before . . .

"Yes," Visantes replied. "I can do no less. The research Pandrogas is attempting may be the only thing that will preserve the little of the world that remains. I was fortunate enough to be born with the power strong within me; now is the time to repay whatever gods granted me that boon."

"I do not want to see you go, of course," his wife said unhappily. "Still, I understand your motivation . . ."

The assassin heard the voices move past her. She took from a belt pouch a cowl of black silk and pulled it over her head, then peered over the edge of the wall. She could see the backs of the enchanter, a short, somewhat rotund man, and his wife. This was an unforeseen complication. She could proceed with her task as planned, leaving a possible witness, or she could kill the woman also. But the decision had to be made quickly, for in a moment they would both be gone. The crossbow was accurate only at close range.

She extended her left hand and flexed the thumb, triggering the arbalest. The sound of the bowstring could not have reached their ears; the tiny quarrel made no noise as it disappeared in the enchanter's back, leaving no sign of entry. The virulence of the poison was such, she knew, that he would scarcely have time to feel the sting of the wound before he fell.

The enchanter's wife saw him collapse, his head striking the stone with a damp crunching sound. She staggered backward, immobilized for a moment by shock. Now was the time to deal with her, Kyra told herself. While she crouched beside him, trying in vain to awaken him, unwilling to admit the truth, there was ample time to load another deadly dart.

Then she could pull herself back over the wall and take her leave.

She did not do it. Her assignment had been to kill Visantes only; not unless her identity was directly threatened would she take the further step. Instead she took off her cowl, untied the leather thong that anchored her to the piton, pulled it free and began to work her way cautiously along the wall, out of sight of the avenue. She could hear the sobs of the enchanter's wife giving way to cries for help. There was still no suspicion of murder—the enchanter had simply dropped as though felled by a stroke.

She reached the angled support beams of Hanging House and pulled herself across their wet surfaces like a swimmer navigating the pylons of a dock. The wall ended at this point, and she floated next to dirt and stone. Fortunately, there were still enough handholds to let her guide herself. She moved swiftly and surely—there was no telling when a stray updraft from the Abyss might catch her and pluck her free, tumbling her like a leaf into the endless depths.

Behind her now she could dimly hear other shouts and cries as neighbors, finally roused by the woman's screams, investigated. She reached the far side of the manse and drew herself up level with the wall. This was the tricky part—anyone who saw her climb out of the Abyss would surely raise a cry. Kyra peered cautiously over the top of the wall, then ducked back down with a muttered curse. The avenue was now full of curious onlookers, some still wearing night-clothes or hastily-grabbed robes, others dressed to varying degrees.

There was nothing for it but to continue to work her way across the face of the continental wall. But she faced a problem there as well—the marbled surface of dirt and rocks that had afforded her handholds now gave way to several feet of sheer, smooth granite, as though planed by a stonecutter's axe a millen-

ium ago when the Shattering had occurred. Even a
fly, she thought, would have trouble clinging to its
surface.

There was no hope for it; she would have to return
to the crossbraces beneath the house and wait it out.
It was an annoyance; most likely she would be there
until nightfall came again. Still, Kyra reflected as she
guided her weightless body back to the structure's
sheltering overhang, she did not regret her course of
action. Indiscriminate killing was unprofessional,
sloppy—such an action would have gained her no
points with Thrisus. To him, as to her, professionalism was all.

What an interesting trade I have chosen, she
thought—who would have predicted that the little girl
who used to dare death at the world's edge would
grow up to grant it so dispassionately to those who
had been marked by the assassins' guild? There were
those who did not understand the function the guild
served, who clamored for its dispersal and the im-
prisonment of its members. Kyra paid no heed to
such complaints. She did not question how or why
her victims were chosen—she saw herself, when she
gave thought to the matter at all, as a dispenser of
justice. It was not something that weighed heavily on
her; she was not given overmuch to introspection.

Her profession isolated her, kept her from forming
close relationships with others—which was also as she
liked it. She had no family and no lover. Once only
she had allowed herself, for a few days, a secret
liaison with another assassin, though such was strictly
forbidden by the Guild's bylaws. Roge, his name had
been. It had not lasted long. He had accused her of
gaining a perverse pleasure from her work, though
admitting that she never allowed it to affect her
neatness and accuracy. There seemed, he had said,
to be at times a great anger in her, contained as a
plug of rock might cap a mounting pressure of magma.

Roge had complained that there were parts of her past about which she had never told him. Kyra had come to be concerned that his lack of discretion might jeopardize her standing in the Guild, and so she had killed him.

If Thrisus had suspected anything, he had not spoken of it. Such intra-regimental slayings were rare, but they did happen, despite the fact that one who had gained the right to wear the black cowl had supposedly gained control of all emotion and feeling.

Kyra knew that she had; her decision to kill Roge had been based entirely on enlightened self-interest. She took no pleasure in killing other than the satisfaction of a task well performed. She was content to leave the decisions and the moral questions to others. She had found her niche, and she fit it well.

The assassin huddled between one of the huge corbels and the rock wall and settled in to wait, shivering slightly. Her clothes, though treated with various oils to repel the humid air, were nevertheless quite damp by now, and the stray breezes from the Abyss chilled her. She composed herself, attempting to slip into the fugue-like meditative state she had learned over time to cultivate when patience was required. But she was unaccustomed to this featherlight condition—when she closed her eyes, it was all too easy to imagine herself falling.

She wondered how workers had managed to build the house's foundation. She looked around herself, finding her surroundings unique and interesting. The child within her who had delighted in exploring dangerous areas was fascinated by this hiding place. Kyra could hear the slight creak of the timbers as the huge house above her shifted, responding to the warming rays of the sun, which was now slipping into view. She could see clearly the joists and wooden girders supporting the flooring. Then she squinted, peering upward. Something looked out of place above her . . .

She hesitated only a moment—then, gauging her movements carefully so as not to lose her balance, she pushed away and floated up toward the underside of the manse. Near the web of a large shadow spider, spun crazily in the ethereal environment, she saw a leathern pouch secured, like the egg sac of a cockatrice, to the flooring. There was only one thing it could be—a secret cache concealed beneath a tile or floorboard.

Kyra held onto one of the joists, anchoring herself, and thought about it. She was not a thief—in fact, she looked askance on burglary and those who practiced it. On the other hand, the evident clandestine nature of the pouch piqued her curiosity.

If she slit it open and took whatever was inside, the theft would be discovered, sooner or later. This might serve to confuse any assignation of motives regarding Visante's death. One of the earliest lessons she had learned was to confuse and bewilder the survivors in any way possible that did not compromise the mission. With that in mind, Kyra withdrew a thin, sharp stylus from her boot.

But as she was about to apply the blade, she recalled her earlier caution in not entering the enchanter's house. Might there not be some sort of spell laid on the pouch that could blast her in any of a thousand imaginative ways? Kyra smiled grimly; she had been about to make an amateur's mistake.

She could still hear the clamor of voices above her, and added to it now was a metallic clink and rattle that could only be the trappings of one or more of the Baroness's soldiers. Kyra felt a sudden surge of impatience. She had better things to do than drift like a vampire waiting in the Abyss while scandal-hungry townsfolk hovered ghoulishly about the scene of the crime. She looked about her once again—could she possibly work her way along the wall in the other direction, and take the chance of someone peering over it?

As she weighed the risks, she saw something—a darker patch against the dark wall—below her. Far down the side of the cliff was an opening—a cave, or a tunnel.

Kyra realized she was being reckless, but she was rapidly growing tired of her weightless state. Her head felt stuffy and clogged, and her stomach was beginning to rebel. Too, she resented the bungled mess she felt she had made of her assignment. Already she was late in reporting to Thrisus. If she could not find another way out of her dilemma, at least, once within the boundary of the cave, she would be able to tell up from down again.

Moving carefully, using the pitons and thongs to anchor herself to the wall, she made her way past the beams' anchorage and down the escarpment. This was indeed an adventure—she had never dared such a thing as a child. She had heard tales of intrepid explorers who, like perverse mountaineers, climbed down the sides of fragments to varying distances. It was due to their efforts, coupled with surveys made by dragonships, that had resulted in most of the fragments being well mapped. But no one, as far as Kyra knew, had descended into these depths before. She felt like a pioneer. It was a heady sensation.

It took longer than she thought to reach the cave, though she could not have said how long—weightlessness seemed to play tricks with her sense of time. She could no longer hear the crowd, and she was grateful for the thong and the line of pitons, for without them she would have no idea which direction was up. Reality consisted entirely of the rock and dirt before her—all else was a primordial nothingness.

Just as she was becoming convinced that she had

missed it, her questing foot found emptiness instead
of the cliff face. She felt the fragment tug at her leg.
Kyra changed her angle of descent, coming down
alongside the cave, then, carefully, eased herself into
it, allowing her body to adjust to the strange sensation of returning weight. She felt dizzy for a moment; when it passed, she was standing on a fairly
level stone floor at the mouth of a tunnel.

The dawning sun filled the interior of the passage
with a numinous glow that extended for quite some
distance. The effect was enchanting; it was like an
entrance into some heavenly afterworld. Perhaps five
ells ahead the passage canted gradually to the right
and into darkness. Her choice was now to wait here
in relative comfort for the advent of night, or to
explore the tunnel.

Still imbued with her sense of adventure, feeling
more in touch with the daring child within than she
had in a decade or more, Kyra chose the latter.
From her pouch she withdrew a sliver of starcrystal,
wrapped in layers of black muslin to absorb its intense azure light. She had removed the arbalest after
striking down the enchanter; now she strapped it
once again to the back of her left hand and loaded it
with another deadly needle. Though she no longer
believed in such things as cacodemons and Chthons,
she knew there might be other, more corporeal men-
aces to fear.

The light from the entrance was soon left behind,
and only the radiation of the starcrystal shard illuminated her way. At first Kyra had felt sure that she
stood in some sort of natural passage or lava tube,
perhaps somehow formed due to the cataclysm. But
as she probed further, she became more and more
convinced that this was, in fact, a corridor carved
purposefully from the living rock.

An escape route of some sort, then—no doubt she
would soon encounter stairs leading up to the base-

ment of one of the houses—perhaps even Visantes's. That would make sense. The tunnel was wide and high enough to permit the passage of a small dragon-ship, and the overhang of the cliff would insure that no casual eye would spot it from the wall above. An ingenious plan, though requiring considerable effort to complete. . . .

The corridor did not rise, however—instead it proceeded on a horizontal level, as best she could determine, turning and twisting. Something on the wall attracted her attention, and she held the light closer. She gasped in astonishment. What she had thought at first were the natural striations of the rock were, in fact, petroglyphic carvings: strange, curvilinear inscriptions that were oddly disturbing to view. Though the starcrystal's light was steady, they seemed nonetheless to waver somehow, as if seen through heat waves or the ripples of a shallow pond. Kyra stepped back from them. They were of no language she recognized, though that meant little, since she was proficient only in Talic. And the manner of their carving was odd as well. She could discern no evidence of chisel strokes; instead, the runic forms seemed almost to have been *gouged* in the rock, as might a human finger write in soft clay.

Kyra did not know why the sight of them brought a cold finger of fear to her spine, or why she found herself backing away from the wall. She was at another bend of the corridor, and when she turned, she saw that she had indeed reached the beginning of a staircase. But the steps did not lead up, as she had anticipated—instead they led *down*, beyond the pitiful radius of light the starcrystal cast, down into unguessed plutonic depths.

Stunned, unable to even comprehend in that first moment the implications of this, she stared into the pit, whose yawning darkness the starcrystal did not even begin to pierce. The slightest pressure of air wafted against her face from below—was it her imagination, or did she detect a faint charnel odor borne on it?

Her mouth suddenly dry with fear, she forced her gaze away from the darkness, looking up. She saw that the ceiling over the descent—huge groinings that joined in a vault—was carved as well. Kyra held the starcrystal high to better illuminate it—and then recoiled in terror, dropping the shard, which shattered into a thousand prismatic pieces at her feet. Darkness seemed to enfold her like a hungry cloud, smothering her, leaving her open and vulnerable to attack.

She turned and ran, colliding with walls, fleeing for what seemed an endless time, until at last she turned a final corner and saw the welcome gray light of the Abyss ahead of her. Even then she did not slow her pace, so convinced was she that what she had seen glowering down at her from the ceiling was pursuing her—it seemed that she could feel its volcanic breath on her back, hear the scraping of its talons on the stone. Her skin crawled in dread of a huge hand encircling her waist, searing her skin with its inhuman temperature. She very nearly ran headlong into oblivion, almost letting her momentum carry her beyond the lip of the opening. Barely in time she came to a halt, casting a frightened glance over her shoulder.

Behind her was nothing but the darkness of the tunnel.

Gasping for breath, her heart pounding, the assassin seized the thong that she had anchored to the last piton and once again carefully made the transition to the weightless environment of the Abyss. Then, at last, she breathed easier, for her memory of those childhood tales that had filled her with such terror assured her that she was safe in the light of day. A cacodemon could not stand the sunlight upon its skin—it would wither and die like a spider in a candle flame.

But what she had seen had not really been a cacodemon. It was only a statue—a carved likeness growing out of the overhanging rock like a guardian of some forgotten hell. It could not pursue her. But this belated realization gave her little comfort, because she remembered also the stories about how the Chthons and their demonic minions had lived beneath the crust of the world when it had been whole, and how the Shattering had driven them from their warrens, to settle at last on the sunless fragment of Xoth.

She had never believed such stories before—but now it seemed she had no choice. For what could the tunnel and the stone stairs at its end be but an entrance into that subterranean world? And how could she be sure that it was still deserted? Had all the creatures of the depths fled to Xoth—or did some still carry on their pre-cataclysmic rituals and ceremonies in the fragments' center? That whiff of decay she had scented—what had been its origin?

Gradually Kyra made her way up the precipice, her progress agonizingly slow from piton to piton. She was tempted to simply launch herself into the mist, to fly like a bird up the side of this piece of the world to the underpinnings of the enchanter's house. But to do so would be to risk injury, or worse, a slow death by starvation in the Abyss, were she to miscalculate by even the slightest degree.

Eventually she reached the timbers once more, and from there she topped the wall. She was past caring if anyone saw her now, but fortunately the crowd had lost interest, and the soldiers summoned had borne away the body. Only a couple of strollers were on the avenue, and none saw her.

Trying not to stumble under the burden of her once-again normal weight, the assassin hurried down the Verge and took the first side street inland. She was late for her report to Thrisus. She should be worried about his opinion of her performance. But instead, all she could think about was the passageway beneath her feet, and she wondered how many other hideous and unguessed secret ways wormed the ground beneath her—and where their exits might be. That cistern to her left, for example—could not, under cover of darkness, spatulate, taloned fingers slide back its stone covering, and nightmarish shapes, black against the stars, issue forth to wreak havoc and mayhem upon the sleeping populace?

Kyra shuddered and drew her cloak tighter around her. She did not know. She only knew that, for the first time she could recall in her adult life—certainly for the first time during her career as an assassin— she dreaded the coming of night.

CHAPTER VI

Into Mist and Darkness

Kan Konar did not keep a record of his days spent on the mountaintop of the nameless fragment, as he had in the chaseboat. He saw no need to; does a corpse, after all, seek to scratch tallymarks on the walls of his coffin? He occupied himself instead by focusing inward, by meditating on his life and on the circumstances that had hurled him here as flotsam is cast by the waves upon a strange shore.

"Repentance," Shadowmaster had told him, "is like upsetting a pot of water." Knowing a futility of self-recrimination, he nevertheless spent the first few months of his exile in vain regrets over his failure to avenge his Daimyo and, by association, over all of his past failures. Like a venesectionist carefully bleeding a patient, the cloakfighter opened the memories of his life, hoping that, by reliving the pain, he would exorcise it.

After a time, however, he came gradually to realize that such mental flagellation was useless. The world was as it was; all events that had led inexorably to his present condition and situation were not to be regretted, but simply acknowledged. His acceptance of this, however, did not grant him increased serenity. The dead know only one thing, after all—that it is better to be alive.

He had used the few accoutrements of the chaseboat to make the cave more habitable; the tarpaulin had become a curtain over the rocky entrance, and the sectioned bone planks of the hull provided flooring over the damp rough stone. His accommodations remained spartan, however; his warrior upbringing had made creature comforts foreign to him. His meals consisted of cloudberries and other viands gathered from trees and bushes, as well as fish seined from the nearby brook. His life was simple and utilitarian, and his mind, once the initial regrets had been stilled, became as pellucid as the deepest part of the sea.

His world was the high pass below the glacial whiteness of the peak; below him was the timber line, and a forest that disappeared into the mist of the clouded valleys. Sometimes he awoke to find the ground lightly misted with snow. The sun never rose more than a handbreadth over the tallest mountain and, save for the birds, the wind and the brook, all was silent. He never saw tracks of anything larger than a fox or badger. Once, at dawn, a shadow passed over him, and Kan Konar looked up to see a huge dragon, its scutate body gleaming in the sunlight, wheeling in accipitral curves high above him.

It was thus that his time passed. He put his mind firmly in death, and waited for its advent with the calmness of one who anticipates momentarily a knock on the door by an acquaintance who has business that must be dealt with.

Then, one day during a long twilight, a new sound invaded his small domain.

He was standing at the mouth of the cave, looking

down at the shrouded valleys, when he heard a long, slow, mournful note, like the despairing wail of some huge beast. Its echoes trembled in the air about him, so that he could not have said with accuracy when the sound truly ceased. A horn of some sort, but unlike any he had heard before—its tone was that of ineffable sadness and pain. Such a note, the cloakfighter thought, could well be the sounding of a convocation of the dead in any of a hundred hells.

It appeared, then, as if his land of exile were inhabited. He had seen no sign of humanity during his stay in the declivity, but that meant little. The sounding of the horn indicated that he was not alone. He made note of that, and thought no more about it.

He did not hear the horn again for many days. When its doleful rise and fall came again it was at the height of the short night, awakening him. He rose and looked past the hanging sheath of dragon leather, down into the darkness. Far away, a single light burned like a luminous snowflake in the mist.

Over the next few days he heard the dirge-like notes twice more. He tried not to allow curiosity about them to disturb his hard-won and fragile tranquility, but again and again he found himself speculating on the possible origins of the sounds. He ventured steadily closer to the perennial curtain of mist in his search for fruit and firewood, until one day, with a muttered curse of exasperation, he stopped not at the edge but continued into the cottony fog.

For the first mile or so he saw little change in the ghostly forest that surrounded him. The woods seemed to be lifeless—his own footsteps made almost no sound and, other than the condensed moisture dripping from branches, he could hear nothing. He felt almost as if he were a disembodied wraith walking through some netherworld toward an unknown ultimate fate. The cloakfighter smiled slightly at that thought.

At the same time, he could not deny a sensation of lurking excitement at this sudden break from his hermitage. He despised himself for having the feeling, but could not deny its reality.

The steep descent began to gradually level out. The mist showed no signs of thinning; if anything it became denser, until Kan Konar seemed to be moving through a luminescent sea. He had no doubts about his ability to find his way back to his eyrie, but he was beginning to question the wisdom of his course. When he had been a warrior, his way had always been to plunge ahead without thought for personal safety. But his new opinion of himself as one not worthy of life or an honorable death had, paradoxically, made him behave more cautiously than ever he had before. The taking of risks was, after all, the province of those who had something to lose, something to sacrifice for a greater good. Kan Konar had abdicated all such considerations.

Nevertheless, he continued. The oblique rays of the sun were barely sufficient for light now; he caught a glimpse of moist, lichen-covered cliffs no more than an armslength away. He felt a sudden certainty, though the brume was far too thick for his eyes to verify it, that he was at the bottom of a steep and narrow cloud-filled gorge.

He heard something move to one side of him.

It was the barest whisper of a rustle—a snake gliding over bare stone would have made more sound—but the cloakfighter's instincts caused him to whirl into an immediate crouch. He felt suddenly, nakedly vulnerable without his cloak, even though he had not worn it for several commonmonths at least.

The sound came again, marginally louder. Something faced him—it could be as close as ten feet in the thick fog.

Kan Konar had felt raw, unmanning fear only once

in his previous life—at its final instant, when he had fallen to Zhormallion's bite. Of course he could not feel anything close to such a shameful emotion now— why should the dead fear death? And yet a cold, damp tendril of the mist seemed to have somehow found its way beneath his tunic, where it caressed his spine. The silence and the suddenly claustrophobic atmosphere were abruptly, unbelievably malefic.

It was a warrior's duty to face his fear, however. And if Kan Konar was not a warrior now, still he had once been one. He straightened and stepped forward.

Five steps, nine, a dozen—he encountered neither man, beast nor ghostly apparition. The quiet seemed subtly mocking. He kept walking. An indistinct shape, bulky and curved, rose before him . . . a crude hut, constructed of wattle and daub.

The cloakfighter hesitated only a moment, then ducked into the low entrance.

He was not sure what he expected to find within— what he found was a tiny, empty chamber, its only sign of habitation a barely visible bed of yellowing grasses. The mist was puddled there, seeming almost solid.

He stepped back outside—all was quiet still, but it seemed now to be a waiting, breathing silence, as if the fog itself were gathering to rush upon him. Then, alerted by some subtle sense, the cloakfighter spun to face the doorway again—and saw, framed against its dark interior, the ghost he had known would be there.

On the morning of the appointed day, Amber stood on the edge of Tamboriyon, overlooking the meadow and stream where she and Pandrogas had released the bear a commonyear earlier. It was a day much like that one had been—the sky clear and blue, dropping away into the fathomless Abyss. The star-flowered grass gave a sweet scent to the air, and the rhythmic chuckle of the brook added the perfect final touch. Indeed, the intervening year might almost have not passed. In a burst of nostalgia, she had worn the same homespun skirt and blouse in which she had arrived on the fragment. Only two things marred the illusion—the absence of Pandrogas, and of Beorn, the bear.

She had come to this trysting point many times in the first few months; after that, with her increasing studies and acquisition of friends, she had come less often. Every time she had looked for the bear, but after that first day she had seen no further sign of him. She hoped that he still roamed the sylvan hills and vales of his new home—the home he had so often dreamed of as a man.

Amber looked down at her hands. There was one other difference—the ring of rank that she now wore. She wondered what changes the year had wrought in Pandrogas—it was so easy to envision him as he had been when they had parted, to think of him as having been frozen in time, unchanging, for the time they had spent apart.

She would know soon what those changes were, when he arrived. *If* he arrived . . .

She had tried not to let her hopes rise as her carriage had turned the final bend in the road and she had come into view of the land's edge. Still, she had been disappointed when she had not seen Pandrogas's dragonship tethered to the spit of land. But after all, she reminded herself, she had not been able to reach the appointed place until almost noon. She could hardly censure Pandrogas for being late.

A small stab of fear struck her then—what if he had arrived, found no one waiting, and left again? Immediately after the thought manifested itself, Amber smiled at the folly of it. He could not have changed *that* much—the Pandrogas she remembered, uncertain as he had been at times of their love, would have waited the day, and then sought her at the temple. His sense of honor and loyalty would have forced him to do that, even if his love for her had waned.

But as the time passed, and the trees eventually began to send their shadows groping over the grass, Amber began to feel at first disappointment, then nervousness, and finally real fear. She could not believe that he had not come out of choice—the only other possibility, it seemed then, was foul play.

Amber tried to reassure herself, telling herself that there were myriad reasons, all harmless, that would explain Pandrogas's absence. But the sense of uneasiness grew within her despite her attempts to rationalize, and despite the calming exercises and cantrips she had learned and now attempted to put to use.

She had learned, by bitter experience, to trust her instincts, especially the sense of dire portent that sometimes overcame her. As the sun touched the southern rim of Tamboriyon, Amber took from her pocket a small casting sphere. She found a flat rock near the land's edge, held the globe made of dragon ivory over it, emptied her mind of thoughts save for that single, all-important question, and dropped the sphere.

She heard it strike the rock, and for a moment was afraid to open her eyes and look at the results. When she did, the long hours she had spent studying the various positions and permutations of the fragments quickly interpreted the sooth. She was not completely sure she was correct—even the *Book of Stones* listed only a small percentage of the possible readings—but as nearly as she could recall, the oracular interpretation was not a good one.

The depths devour those who venture unwisely.

As always, the translation of spherecasting was aphoristic. Nevertheless, it seemed to forecast no good end to Pandrogas's journey. Amber felt cold despair wash over her. "The depths"—could it mean the Abyss, or did it have some darker, more sinister interpretation? She remembered how, well over a commonyear earlier, she had cast a sphere within the sorcerer's laboratory in an attempt to find him in the labyrinthine corridors of Darkhaven, and how she had been convinced that the reading postulated a threat from the Demogorgon Sestihaculas. She had been wrong—and yet she had been right as well, for had not Sestihaculas eventually confronted them?

Pandrogas had forced the ruler of Xoth to pledge never to attack them again. But the Lord of Snakes was wily. Had he found a way to maneuver around his promise?

Was the battle they had fought so long and so hard still unwon?

Stop it, Amber commanded herself. You are jumping to conclusions like some hysterical court wife. He may yet appear, and prove all your suspicions groundless and foolish.

But the sun slowly descended below the horizon, and luminescent night stole over the land, and still there was no sign of the sorcerer. And Amber, her heart heavy with unknown fears, returned to her carriage and began the journey back to the temple of Taggyn Saer.

Pandrogas awoke slowly and painfully. There was a vile taste in his mouth, and his face, hands and arms ached as though stung by hundreds of insects. He opened his eyes to total darkness.

At first his confusion matched the darkness, but then he remembered his last few moments of consciousness—the bright eternal day of the Abyss, the sudden realization that a Chthon lurked within the dragonboat's cabin, and the attack of the vermin that had named his adversary. He had been captured by Trisandela, Lady of Bats.

He sat up, slowly and painfully. He had been lying on wet stone, and the coldness of it had penetrated his bones, making his joints sore and stiff. He felt a rush of dizziness as he stood. All was silent. There was a gritty underscent of decay in the air.

He extended his awareness as best he could, probing the darkness without actually using a spell that might alert someone or something to the fact that he was awake. He seemed to be alone. Carefully he took a few steps, groping before him, and soon found a curving stone wall. He cleared his throat to make sure that his voice would be steady and sure when he spoke, then said, "*Limnus diam.*"

The small, simple spell worked—Pandrogas could remember a time when it had not. Cold golden fire enveloped his hand, illuminating his surroundings as he raised it.

He was at the bottom of a shaft of black rock, perhaps ten feet in diameter. He could not tell how far above him the opening was, if indeed there was an opening—he might, for all he knew, be sealed alive within a cist.

The sorcerer reviewed his options. There was a spell which would render him temporarily immune to the pull of whatever fragment this was—but if the walls of the shaft were too tall, he would find himself hurtling back down to a deadly impact. He could summon a cacodemon to bear him away, but since he was already in the clutches of a Chthon, such an action seemed foolhardy in the extreme. The best plan, for the time being at least, seemed to be to wait.

Pandrogas leaned against the wall, feeling suddenly and utterly hopeless. He had been a fool to venture outside of Darkhaven, a fool to assume that Sestihaculas would consider any word given to a human as binding. He would never rejoin Amber on Tamboriyon now—more than likely she would never know what had happened to him. And, without his guiding presence at Darkhaven, the knowledge of Necromancy would remain unfathomable to his students, and the world's fragments would continue their irrevocable spiral toward destruction.

A sudden explosive rustle of wings behind him, the stench of brimstone once more . . . the sorcerer turned quickly, and his upraised hand illuminated the Lady of Bats.

She smiled at him, her eyes glowing in the flickering light as an animal's would. "So you are the mighty sorcerer who humbled the Demogorgon," she said. "You do not seem a very formidable adversary to me."

Pandrogas did not reply; there seemed no need to. He rightly assumed that he could learn more from her taunts than from questioning her.

Trisandela stepped forward, regarding him with interest. "My lord Sestihaculas has waited quite a long time for his revenge, human. His only regret is that he will not be able to administer it himself—but he intends to respect his word to you, and take no action against you. Which is why he suggested that I have a hand in this."

"Mere sophistry," Pandrogas replied. "This is Sestihaculas's doing, whether he acknowledges his hand in it or not. He has broken his solemn vow, and no good will come of it."

"Certainly no good will come of it for *you*," and Trisandela laughed. "Yet you are right, sorcerer, though the Demogorgon does not yet know it. For a commonyear have I waited for you to leave your lair; waited outside the boundaries of Xoth, lurking in what night I could find, haunting the ancient caverns and tunnels in which we Chthons lived before the Shattering. I have studied ancient writings and runes that we left behind so long ago, and I have learned much. My exile has given me time to formulate plans of my own—plans in which you shall play a part."

Pandrogas stared at her in disbelief. "You seek to overthrow the Demogorgon? No Chthon would stand with you—his power is absolute!"

"Perhaps—perhaps not. We shall soon learn. Until that time, sorcerer, you will remain here, in one of our ancestral warrens, deep beneath the surface of the fragment you call Zarheena." Trisandela spread her ribbed wings, preparing to depart, but Pandrogas stepped forward.

"Wait! If you leave me here without food or water, I will die. Does that suit your plans?"

"At the moment, no. A cacodemon will visit you anon with sustenance. Until I have need of you, your time will be best spent sharpening your skills. You will have need of them, I assure you."

Pandrogas watched as a column of foul-smelling smoke enveloped Trisandela. The next instant he was alone again.

He felt the utter silence and oppressive walls bearing down on him. So he had been right—he was not done with the Chthons, nor they with him. But the last time he had battled them, it had been of his own free will. Now, it seemed, he was to be but a pawn in Trisandela's deadly game. And while she dabbled in her intrigues, the orbits of the fragments continued to decay, coming ever closer to the point where no amount of magic could restore them.

Pandrogas shook his head, extinguishing the fire that sheathed it, and felt darkness envelop him like his own despair.

CHAPTER VII

The Valley of Death

Kan Konar's first thought, upon seeing the ghost in the doorway of the hut, was that it had surely been in life the most beautiful woman who had ever lived. As the mists that surrounded it thinned momentarily due to some vagary of air currents, he saw her more clearly. It was then that he realized that she was not dead.

The woman who stood before him was definitely corporeal—he could see the beading of condensed mist on her skin, as well as the impression her feet—swathed in rags strongly reminiscent of cerement—made on the carpet of pine needles and dead leaves. But, though she was undeniably flesh and blood, she yet gave the distinct impression of one from whom the animus had but recently fled.

In common with most others, the cloakfighter knew the story of the Necromancer's powers to awaken and empower the dead. He had also heard enough from Pandrogas to know that there was truth in these legends. Did he then face, instead of an immaterial larva, a revivified corpse—a grotesque marionette that served some hideous, unknown purpose? The thought was even more unnerving, for some reason, than the possibility of encountering a ghost.

All of these speculations seared Kan Konar's mind in the instant of his confrontation with the other. Certainly the woman looked the part—there was no faintest indication of life or color in the visage shadowed by a hooded robe. The pallor was accentuated by the thin cheeks and sunken eyes. And yet, as the figure shifted slightly and Kan Konar was able to see her face more fully, he realized that the skin tone was not waxen and lifeless—that there was, in fact, a certain radiant cast to it. It was not the glow of healthy blood coursing just beneath the surface, however. Rather, it was a spectral vibrance, an almost numinous illumination, which had made it so easy for him to initially mistake her for a spirit.

The few strands of hair he could see beneath the hood also had that touch—blonde to the point of whiteness, they seemed like fine filaments of brass heated to the point of incandescence. And her eyes— they also were white, the iris distinguished from the lacteal sheen of the rest by the barest cast of blue. The pupils were like flecks of obsidian, startlingly black in contrast.

All of this in an instant's impression, before the figure stepped back, fear filling her face, then turned and disappeared into the mist which once more closed about him.

Kan Konar stood for a long moment trying to understand and accept what he had just seen. She had to have come from the hut—what he had thought was a particularly viscid area of mist within it had in fact been this woman, lying on a meager bed of grasses, her white skin and robes blending with the vapor. He took a step after her, then hesitated.

There was always the possibility of a trap. There had
been a time when such a thought would not have
mattered to him, but this strange, netherworldly
environment and the apparition within it would unnerve a stone statue. Nevertheless, he knew he would
have no inner peace again until he had solved this
mystery. Thus resolved, the cloakfighter followed
quickly, as best he could, through the mists.

For a long moment he could see nothing save the
looming dark towers of the trees as they appeared
before him and faded into the mist behind. The utter
silence in which this took place was perhaps the most
surreal aspect of it all. He was tempted to shout a
warcry just to break it.

Then, ahead of him, he caught the barest glimpse
of movement, white gliding through white. The
cloakfighter plunged forward. The mist thinned, revealing the green and gray canyon wall once again.
Kan Konar turned and faced the shifting fog.

At first, he saw nothing. Then another shape moved
dreamlike at the edge of his vision, and then another, and another.

At that moment it was very easy indeed for the
cloakfighter to believe that he had, all unknowing,
died in truth, and now walked the corridors of some
drear afterlife. He shook off the thought and stepped
forward quickly. His arm speared the fog, and his
fingers closed about cold flesh.

The sensation was almost enough to cause him to
release his captive—the wrist he had grasped was
not merely the same temperature as the ambient
vapors, but was icy—colder by far than the marble
its hue resembled. Kan Konar was equally unpre-
pared for the reaction of the one he had seized. It
was a young man, scarcely more than a boy, muffled
in shielding robes similar to the woman's. As he took
hold of his arm, the other screamed.

It was a sound that reverberated like a cry in the

narthex of a silent and empty cathedral—it seemed to set the cloakfighter's bones to vibrating. The youth fell to the ground, writhing in obvious and extreme pain. Kan Konar did not release his arm immediately—only when he was sure that there was no danger of reprisal did he let go. His eyes widened as he saw clearly, on the bare flesh of the youth's wrist, livid finger marks like brands.

He released the boy's arm and stood over him, unsure what to do next. And then, for the first time in months, he heard another's voice.

"Stand away from him, please. You have hurt him."

The soft, melodious sentences came from behind him; Kan Konar turned quickly. Before him, seemingly part of the luminous fog, stood the woman he had seen before the hut. Behind her he sensed, rather than actually saw, more swathed figures.

"Who are you?" he demanded, and saw them wince, stepping back from the sound of his words as though dealt a physical blow. His voice sounded harsh and grating compared to her murmurous tones.

"Please," she said; "speak softly. Have reverence, for you have entered the Valley of Death."

The dragonship skimmed an ocean of clouds which glowed like white-hot ore, lit from beneath by the rays of the sun. On the forward deck, Mirren leaned against the rail, enjoying the fresh, clean air and the spectacular view. She stretched languorously, feeling quite content and at ease with herself and the remnants of the world. And why should she not? After all, she had money in her purse, new clothes on her back, and the prospect of a new life before her. There were not many, man or woman, who could boast all these fortunes at once.

Aided by her shapechanging abilities, it had been an easy matter to elude the two footpads once they had reached land. Junge and Vangik had given her

no further trouble on the voyage after she had given
them a glimpse of the wolf. She had spent a commonyear in Cape Uloth, and the wolf had served her well
there. She had applied her special talent to thievery,
with laudatory results. Judicious listening and a few
friendly drinks in local taverns had taught her where
the richest moneybags were to be picked, and the
wolf could silently leap walls and enter houses by
ways that she could never manage. She had kept her
depredations few and far between, concentrating as
much on visiting merchants and nobility in the port
town as natives, and she had held her expenses
down, staying in a single room above a livery. By the
year's end she had amassed enough capital to pur-
chase new clothes, a ticket on a dragonship, and still
have a tidy sum left over.

Mirren had a plan. She did not care for the long
days and nights of Rhynne, and so she had booked
passage for the fragment of Zarheena. She had heard
tales for most of her adult life of the assassins' guild,
and it had occurred to her that her metamorphic
abilities ideally suited her to that line of work. It was
worth a try; if her application to join the guild was
rejected, she would be no worse off than she had
been.

She and the wolf within her had reconciled themselves once more to each other. Upon reaching Quy,
she had resumed her habit of granting the beast its
time to run and kill at frequent intervals, and felt
much the better for it. The transformations were
easier when done with greater frequency, and the
animal spirit, no longer pent within her for long
periods, was not so savage or hard to control when
set free. She had seen in Beorn what madness denying one's nature could cause, and she wanted no part
of that. She was a werewolf—very well then, she
would enjoy the fact, and use it to her advantage.

She listened to the shouts and colorful language of

the crew. There were few passengers on this ship—
its primary purpose was to ferry cargo. Confusingly,
all flying ships were referred to as "dragonships,"
even though relatively few of them now hunted the
huge firebreathing creatures. The name came from
the fact that the magic which made it possible for the
vessel to sail the Abyss only worked if every piece of
it, from the greatest of sails down to the tiniest of
lynchpins, were made from the skin, tendons, bones,
or other parts of dragons.

Though there were not many provisions for passengers, Mirren nevertheless travelled in luxury—the
captain of the ship was quite taken with her, and had
made an effort to see that her quarters were comfortably furnished and her meals the best that the galley
had to offer. She had been appreciative, but only
with words, knowing that there were enough passengers and other witnesses on board to keep her safe.
All in all, it had been quite a pleasant voyage. In less
than a commonday now they would dock at Zarheena.

She toyed idly with the ring which she had found
on Graystar Isle, and which she had forgotten to
leave behind. On rare occasions the fragment of stone
in the resin would glow, sometimes faintly, and
sometimes—as now—brightly enough to be seen even
in sunlight. At first it had worried Mirren, for it
smacked of sorcery. But when no harm seemed to
come to her from it, she had lost her fear of it.

She looked down at the incandescent cloud layer
"below" the dragonship. The stability provided by
the vessel's runestone made it difficult to accept the
fact that it was moving—it felt instead as if she were
standing still while the clouds rushed past her. Lances
of light occasionally burst in prismatic glory through
rifts in the cloud bank. It was a stirring sight.

As she watched, a shadow seemed to move between the clouds and the sun hidden below them.
She frowned in puzzlement. A thicker layer of cloud?

No, it was too dark for that; it had almost the appearance of some vast, subterranean creature gliding just below the surface of this vaporous ocean . . .

Mirren staggered back from the rail in astonishment as, almost directly ahead of the bow, a huge fragment broke through the cloud layer. Moving in majestic slow motion, the aerolith, easily the size of a small mountain, speared up, scattering milky crests of foam in its wake.

From all about her she heard the shouts and curses of the crew as they ran to their stations, shifting the ship's sails and wings in an attempt to change course in time to avoid a collision. The Abyss turned dizzyingly about them. The dragonship's momentum carried it toward the fragment, which seemed to rush at Mirren with alarming speed. She could clearly see small clumps of grass and gnarled bushes growing on the surface as it rotated. There seemed no way that they could avoid an impact. Mirren held onto the railing, bracing herself for the crash that would send her and everyone else on board tumbling helplessly into the Abyss.

The fragment turned beneath them. A fissure showed itself, running the length of one side—a jagged crack scarcely wider than the ship. They were moving parallel to it; she heard the screech of planked bone against rock as the keel scraped the sides of the fissure, felt the shuddering vibration. Then they were past it, and it continued on into the blue depths, spinning slowly and ponderously—a juggernaut of stone and soil.

Mirren sank to a sitting position as the reaction left her legs weak. Her heart was pounding. Around her, she could hear snatches of incredulous conversation:

"—impossible! The charts showed no fragment of that size—"

"—nearly ripped the bottom right out of us—"

"—would've lost our cargo, not to mention our lives—"

"—Hotath protect us from anything like that again—"

Mirren let the disjointed phrases and thanks to various gods wash over her. She was glad that this hairbreadth escape had taken place near the end of the voyage, rather than at the beginning. The Abyss now seemed, instead of a calming, serene place, to be a void full of danger of terrifying proportions. She devoutly hoped that Zarheena would be a city in which she would be able to find a living, as the idea of making another trek through the bright sky was not at all appealing.

Amber moved restlessly about her small monasterial room in the Temple. She had been unable to sleep, and now could see, through the single latticed window, the pale fires of dawn playing about the sculptured crest of Mount Boreas.

In the growing light, she looked about her chamber. Despite her occupancy of a commonyear, she had virtually no belongings; she had arrived with nothing but her clothes, and the life of an initiate did not encourage the accrual of material possessions. A bed that also served as a couch, a stool and table for writing or reading, and a chamber pot and basin were all that the room held. She wished now that she had taken some small memento of Pandrogas with her—not only for the comfort of having it, but because it might now provide her with some tenuous mantological link to the sorcerer.

She had no such connection, however. There was no way of knowing what had happened to her erstwhile lover and mentor. Her skill was not nearly such that she could communicate with him over the vast bright distance of the Abyss. She could only speculate as to what had kept him from making their appointed tryst.

Only two possibilities presented themselves, and neither she cared to think overly much on. The first was that someone or something had detained Pandrogas by force. The second was that he had simply not wanted to come.

In many ways, the second consideration was the worse of the two. As much as it grieved her to speculate on it, Amber could understand how Pandrogas might feel that way. That was the worst of it. After all, had she not also felt uncertainty about holding up her end of the assignation? A commonyear was a long time—an entire revolution of the cloud of fragments, some said, about the central fire of the sun. Many changes could take place in one during that time. When she had thought of him, it had always been as she had last seen him, standing on the meadowed cliff at Tamboriyon's edge, looking at her with love and pride in his gaze. She had not allowed him to grow and change in her mind's eye. It was very possible that he did not love her any more. She would not know, after all, until she faced him once more, whether or not she still loved him.

A decision had to be reached. She remembered a time, long ago, when she had sought him in the vast and byzantine maze of Darkhaven. She had let herself be drawn to him then, trusting, as he had taught her, the instinctive power within herself. She had to trust that same power now. She composed herself, sitting crosslegged on the bed and closing her eyes. She forced herself to breathe deeply and evenly, and willed herself to reach out, to sense what the situation was . . .

There was a soft knock on the door. Amber felt her heart miss a beat. Was it possible he had been merely delayed, and had come to the temple to find her—?

She opened the door and saw Zerrad standing

there. Her disappointment must have showed in her expression, for he looked surprised and hurt.

"I could not wait any longer to know the outcome of your meeting," he said. Amber saw him glance surreptitiously over her shoulder and register the fact that, save for her, the room was empty. "Was he—?"

She shook her head. "He did not arrive. I waited until sundown, then . . ."

His trepidation was replaced by concern. He stepped forward, putting his arms out to hold her, but Amber stepped back.

"No, Zerrad—I appreciate your concern, but I have decisions to make, and your presence will only make them more difficult."

"What decisions?" he asked softly.

"There is the possibility that Pandrogas is injured or in peril," Amber replied, her course becoming clear to her as she spoke. "Until I know for certain whether or not this is the case, I cannot remain here. I must find him and learn the truth."

His tone was incredulous. "You would leave Tamboriyon—leave your studies, at which you have worked so hard, on an unknown and dangerous journey simply because this sorcerer has not met your assignation?"

Amber nodded. The worry and fear had not left her, but they were tempered now by the sudden cool resolve that she felt. She knew what she had to do. She took her cloak from where it lay folded at the foot of the bed and donned it, then stepped past him and into the hall.

Zerrad followed her. They hurried past other students who were preparing for the morning lesson. "At least wait another day," Zerrad entreated. "Something could have delayed Pandrogas—a storm, or—"

"If that is the case, than perhaps you will be so

good as to inform him, when and if he does arrive, of my decision."

They emerged from the temple, and Amber started down the flagstone steps. Zerrad grabbed her arm. "You cannot do this, Amber. Completely aside from my feelings for you, I can't let you throw away your future as a sorceress because of this infatuation—"

She smiled slightly, and that unexpected reaction stopped him. He flushed, and she said quickly, before he could storm out in wounded pride, "It is not what you think, Zerrad. I am not acting out of love-lorn desperation. If Pandrogas does not care for me any more, than that is his choice, and my life will not be over because of it. But I feel quite strongly that such is not the case—the talent in me that you respect so highly tells me that it is not. And because of that I must seek him."

"I still do not understand," he replied slowly.

"We share a history, Pandrogas and I, that is much more than the sum of our love. Together, we faced the Demogorgon, and defeated him—we invoked the shade of the Necromancer." She had never spoken of these things to him before, and she saw the incredulity in his face, but pushed on before he could speak. "We witnessed and set into motion events that profoundly affected—and continue to affect—every fragment, no matter how far-flung. We thought—or I thought—that our parts in the drama were over, but I am beginning to understand that they are far from that. I cannot deny my role in this. That is why I must go—not because I love him." She made a half-wry, half-wistful expression. "That merely complicates matters."

"At least cast the sphere—seek its counsel." He was pleading with her now, and she suddenly felt a great sympathy for him. He was scarcely more than a boy, with only the faintest knowledge of the vast and inexorable forces that had so much to do with the shaping of lives and destinies. At that moment, Amber wished very much that she could simply stay with him, enjoy the easy infatuation—for she knew now that it was no more than that—that he had for her, and that she had for him. The way ahead was suddenly very dark and parlous, and she did not want to make her way down it—not even for Pandrogas's sake.

But, if her premonitions were correct, there was much, much more at stake than simply the life of the man she loved.

She kissed Zerrad lightly on the cheek. "Tell Ratorn that I am sorry," she said. "I think that he will understand. He is a magician of no small perception." Then she turned and hurried down the path, pulling her cloak tighter about her as she went, for the rays of the morning sun served only to accentuate the coldness she felt within.

CHAPTER VIII

The Crystal Sarcophagus

Trisandela had been true to her word insofar as sustenance was concerned—twice now had a cacodemon appeared, filling the cist with the choking stench of brimstone, to leave Pandrogas what seemed to be steaks from one of the giant mushrooms of Xoth. They were crudely grilled, half raw and half burnt. Pandrogas was barely able to choke them down, and their nutritional value seemed minimal—very soon after eating them he felt hungry again.

The cacodemon also left a rude clay pot filled with brackish water. The sorcerer washed down the last bite with a swallow of it. Then there was nothing to do but sit in the blackness and contemplate his fate.

He had examined his cell carefully, using the cantrip that turned his hand into a flickering cold torch. The walls of the circular pit were smooth, almost glassy, as if a giant heated poker had been thrust into the rock and then withdrawn. There was no way to climb them; he was well and truly trapped until Trisandela returned.

He knew that Amber would be concerned; would know immediately, with the powerful intuition that her magic granted, that something had happened to him. As powerful as the pain of knowing that the world's fragments were spiralling toward destruction was the torment of contemplating her worry and fear.

He wished he had had the chance to see her again before this had happened. Staring into the darkness now, Pandrogas realized that he was having trouble visualizing Amber's face. Though their cathexis had been powerful initially, the year spent apart had made the link tenuous. A tragedy that he would now never know whether or not it had survived their time away from each other.

Pandrogas shook his head irritably. He felt he had no right to dwell on the relatively petty matter of his love for Amber—not when so much more was at stake. The world was slowly but inexorably coming to an end. Though it would be centuries, perhaps even millennia, before all the fragments had collided and ground each other into floating dust, eventually that was what would happen. And all life would be destroyed long before that. Only Necromancy might prevent it; and only he had sufficient knowledge of that shunned art to work toward that goal.

The sorcerer coughed and choked as another cloud of sulphur suddenly swirled about him. Turning, he spoke the spell of light and once again beheld the Lady of Bats, eyes glowing and teeth gleaming in the darkness of her enfolding wings.

"All is in readiness," she told him. "Your skill at revivification will now be put to the test, sorcerer."

Before Pandrogas could question her ambiguous statement, Trisandela raised her hand, fingers bent in a gesture of power. She spoke no spell, but an orange light glowed nevertheless with dazzling intensity about her hand—and a section of the wall before them wavered and melted like black smoke.

The sorcerer followed the Chthon into the passageway that was revealed. Trisandela walked with wings half-spread, and, in the uneasy light that he wore, Pandrogas could see the dark sheen of fur on her buttocks ripple as her hips shifted. The sexuality implicit in the sight was surprisingly powerful—he looked away uncomfortably.

There were no stairs, but the corridor descended as it twisted and turned, as though an enormous worm had eaten a tunnel through the rocky core of Zarheena. Pandrogas could feel pressure building in his ears. His burning hand illuminated pre-human carvings on the walls—glyphs and runes that seemed to writhe with dreadful power. He averted his gaze as he passed them; he did not trust his sanity to hold if their meaning should suddenly come clear to him.

Trisandela did not speak, and, though his mind burned with questions, the sorcerer knew the futility of asking them before she was ready. And so he followed her in silence, feeling as though he walked the corridors of a nightmare.

After an indeterminate time the corridor opened into a chamber whose walls and ceiling were far beyond the limited range of light from Pandrogas's hand. The flat sound of his boots against the rock told him that its size must be gigantic.

Trisandela led him to a dais surrounded by a dolmen of glistening obsidian. At the head of the steps rested a huge sarcophagus, which seemed to have been cut from a single multi-faceted crystal. It glittered milkily in the uncertain light. Trisandela mounted the steps, then turned and faced Pandrogas.

"This is your task, sorcerer," she said; "to breathe life once more into the remains of the first ruler of the Chthons—he who was Demogorgon before Sestihaculas, in that ancient time prior to humanity's mastery of fire: Yasothoth, the Lord of Scorpions!"

Pandrogas stared at Trisandela in shocked disbelief. "Return to life a Chthon? This is not possible! Your kind do not have souls that can be netted from the nether dimensions!"

"True enough—but we *do* have a tenacity of the life force that you cannot even begin to comprehend. Recall how you blocked the sun's rays from Sestihaculas, and how swift his reconstitution was."

Pandrogas remembered quite well—in his mind's eye he could vividly see the desiccated, charred husk that had been the Demogorgon, crisped by the deadly light when they had faced each other at the Cliffs of the Sun. He had used Kan Konar's cloak to shade Sestihaculas's body, and had watched in amazement as the Chthon had returned to life, tissues rebuilding and rehydrating themselves in a matter of moments. Chthons lived for thousands of years—indeed, he had never heard or read of one of them dying a natural death, and they could only be killed with weapons of silver or iron. He suspected that they were otherwise virtually immortal.

He looked again at the vault. It was nearly twelve feet long, and he shuddered at the thought of what it contained. Yasothoth had been one of the primal horrors of the world—though his time of ruling the Chthons and the cacodemons had been that of the prehistoric past, when mankind had cowered in caves and rightly feared the night, still had the fear of him survived, his name whispered in trepidation by even the most powerful of sorcerers.

Sestihaculas, so the legend went, had defeated and destroyed Yasothoth in a battle ages before. Was the legend true, then? Had Yasothoth existed once—and was it possible that he could exist again?

"Why?" he asked, in a voice barely above a whisper. "Why would you have me do this?"

"Because," Trisandela replied, "only Yasothoth can stand against Sestihaculas. And I have learned, in my studies of the ancient runes carved in the walls of these corridors, ways to bend him to my will. While you are reforming his dust, before his mind and will are strong again, I will lay my geas upon him. Yasothoth shall be under my command—he will cast down Sestihaculas, and through him, I shall rule the Chthons!

"Should you refuse," the Lady of Bats continued, "be assured that I will enspell you as I plan to do to Yasothoth, and force you to perform the task. I am willing to take the chance that your resurrectional skills might be impaired by the geas."

She was, Pandrogas could see, in quite deadly earnest. The choice, then, was either to attempt the spell in full possession of his abilities, or under her domination. Either avenue seemed to lead directly away from sanity. He could only play for time and hope to find a way to foil her plan.

"I am still not entirely skilled in the necromantic arts," he said. "For an undertaking such as this I will need to do research, preparation . . ."

Trisandela looked at him suspiciously. "Tell me what you need, and it will be provided."

"To return to Darkhaven, where I might—"

"No!" She snapped her wings open with an echoing crack that caused Pandrogas to retreat a step. Her eyes were embers of feral fury. "This is a ploy, an attempt to escape! You know that no Chthon dares enter Darkhaven!"

"I give you leave to trespass," Pandrogas replied desperately. "You must understand—what you ask is beyond anything even the Necromancer ever attempted. To raise a Chthon—it would be the supreme test of necromancy—the greatest accomplishment of any magician since the dawn of time! I must have every opportunity to prepare!"

Trisandela eyed him narrowly. His one chance, he knew, lay in convincing her that he was captivated by the concept of what she proposed—swept away against any better judgment by the possibility of pitting his new-found expertise against such a challenge.

"Very well, Pandrogas," she said slowly. "But no shadow ever dogged your steps closer than I shall in Darkhaven. I grant you one commonweek in which to make ready. Then we shall return here and see the task completed."

"Agreed," Pandrogas said. He held his face carefully expressionless. Once within the interminable hallways of Darkhaven, where his power was at its strongest, he could challenge Trisandela with some hope of winning. It would not be easy—but he had cast out Endrigoth, the Lord of Rats, and even the Demogorgon himself from Darkhaven in the past.

However, the Lady of Bats was devious—that he knew well. It would not be an easy battle. *Is it simply age that saps my confidence,* he wondered; *or some intuitive knowledge of the future?*

His speculation was cut short as Trisandela raised her arms, and the sorcerer felt himself engulfed once more in a stinking whirlwind of darkness.

Kyra walked with Thrisus, master of the Guild With No Hall. There was disapproval in his lean, scarred face, and disappointment in the harsh whisper that was his voice—the result of a knife slash across his throat many years ago.

"You have not acted professionally. I sent you to kill Jagar the High Counselor. Not only does he still live, but now, thanks to your bungled attempt, he is aware that a plot exists against his life."

Kyra felt shame burning her face. She remembered the scene from yesterday vividly—crouching on the balcony outside the Counselor's chambers, watching him relax in luxurious ease on a brocaded couch, slave girls rubbing oils into his pasty, fat limbs. She had brushed her hand against the black marble balustrade as she had aimed, and he had reacted to it, turning his head. The tiny quarrel of the arbalest had struck a platelet of hammered silver on the torque about his neck, instead of burying its poisoned tip in his artery. She had barely escaped.

"Have you any explanation to offer?"

"None, Guildmaster." She did not see how she could tell him that she had not been sleeping well lately; that her keen edge had been dulled by the constant nightmares of dark, fiery-eyed shapes stirring restlessly beneath the ground like maggots writhing in dead meat. Her irrational childhood fear of cacodemons had taken on new intensity since her discovery of the underground corridor and the pit. But she could not tell Thrisus that she had bungled an assignment because of this.

"Our profession is very unforgiving of failure." They continued their walk down the quiet, curving lane for a time. To those few who passed them, they appeared to be merely a man and a woman out for a stroll in the early afternoon sun. "Were you in my position, what action would you take?"

Her voice was quiet. "Dismissal from the Guild."

He smiled slightly. "You would make a harsh Guildmaster." He was silent once more for another few steps; when he spoke again, it was on a subject apparently unrelated.

"There has come to me a woman who has made application to join our ranks. While she is somewhat old to begin the training, she has an interesting talent, one which may or may not prove useful. She is a shapechanger—a werewolf, to be exact.

"See to her discipline and instruction, Kyra. I will be guided by your opinion of her. Tell me if you think this wolf woman would make a good assassin."

Kyra nodded; she did not trust her voice to remain steady. She had, in effect, been removed from the active roster and relegated to a teaching role. Though she felt that Thrisus was being more than fair, still the humiliation of it was galling.

There was no appealing his decision, however. She would have to make the best of it. She raised her head and looked at him levelly. Perhaps, if she did an exemplary job of training this new assassin, she would be reinstated. It was all she could hope for, at the moment.

It took the better part of a day and most of Amber's meager savings to have a chartmaster consult his orreries and tables and determine for her the quickest route to Darkhaven. With the last of her currency she bought a small and obviously very well travelled dragonship, and provisions for the voyage. According to the chart, it would take her nearly three commonweeks to reach the fragment of Oljaer, about which Darkhaven orbited. It was evening by the time she set sail; however, the eternal day of the Abyss quickly returned as Tamboriyon fell away from her. Her sense of urgency had not lessened during all of this; if anything, it had increased. She felt convinced that Pandrogas was in grave peril.

As to whether or not she could help him—that she could not guess. Her power—the gift that she possessed, according to such masters of mantology as Pandrogas and Ratorn, in greater degree than either of them—was all but useless to her without the training to use it properly. True, she had been able to call upon it in life-threatening moments, but she had not been in control of it. She still had much to learn; her newly-attained rank of conjuress was only the second piton driven into the side of a very tall and very steep cliff.

Nevertheless, she could not continue her studies

now. She did not know whether or not she still loved Pandrogas, but she knew that she owed him whatever help she could render, up to and including the risk of her life and soul. He had done no less for her, many times.

She kept the sun over her left shoulder as the charts instructed. Though the winds could be capricious, there were relatively steady currents of air that could be relied upon. A simple spell would awaken her if the craft veered too far from its course. Thus prepared, the conjuress settled in for what she hoped would be a quiet and uneventful voyage.

She continued on her way for two commondays, according to the small sandglass that was a part of the boat's stock. The worst part about travel through the Abyss was that progress was impossible to measure. The sun neither rose nor set, and the ship's runestone, by providing weightfulness, also negated any sensation of movement. Amber could not hear or feel the wind that filled the sails, for the ship moved with it. And the fragments were scattered too far apart for her to see more than one or two of them during the course of her journey, and those would be only the smallest specks in the sky.

On even the most prosaic of voyages this would be frustrating; for Amber, concerned as she was about Pandrogas's fate, it was maddening. But there was nothing that could be done about it, and so she used the opportunity to practice spellcasting and the rigorous physical disciplines that were a part of sorcery. She also played her alicorn flute, letting her music bring her forgetfulness, for a time, of her concerns.

These periods of exercise and meditation helped, but could not distract her completely from her worry. A pervading sense of doom was building within her; during one meditative trance, when she had gone deep into the realm of no-mind, a vision appeared before her with startling abruptness—a vast conflagration, a forest being consumed by blinding flames that seemed to fall from the sky, sending billows of black, greasy smoke skyward. The scene was so vivid that Amber was jolted from her calm state with a gasp of horror.

From that point on, fear was a physical presence that travelled with her. Something terrible was going to happen—it was only a matter of time. But would it happen to Pandrogas, or to her?

She soon found out. At the close of the third "day" Amber prepared for slumber. The small cabin, which consisted of dragon hide stretched taut over curved ribs, was scarcely big enough for the hard mattress. It took her some time to fall asleep. She tried to think of her impending reunion with Pandrogas, but that fantasy, instead of comforting her as it had so many nights before, now merely increased her anxiety. Though the air within was the usual pleasant temperature of the Abyss, she felt unusually hot and stifled. She was able to achieve some measure of comfort by disrobing completely, and at last drifted into an uneasy slumber.

Almost immediately she began to dream. In the dream, she was walking through a huge chamber, past crystal columns as thick as she was tall. She was not naked in her dream, but wore a robe or cloak of some shifting dark fabric. A light burned ahead of her; she approached it, feeling cold hatred and hostility emanating from it in almost tangible waves.

At last she was close enough to see what the source of the light was. It came from a gigantic coffin carved of faceted crystal, which stood upon a dais of black stone. As the conjuress watched, the light, which pulsed faintly and regularly, began to deepen from icy white, taking on a reddish tint.

Impelled by some unquestioned inner urge common to dreams, Amber mounted the steps of the dais. Though the sense of malign intent surrounding the sarcophagus seemed nearly palpable to her, she nevertheless put both hands on the cold lid and began to push.

It slid back easily, and, though the entire vault was ablaze with its light, within it was darkness. She could see something stirring . . . afraid at last, she stepped back hastily.

Pandrogas sat up from within the sarcophagus. Amber stared at him in amazement, her surprise too great to let her speak. He smiled at her—but there was something hideously alien about the way he looked at her.

"My love," he said. "You have freed me."

And then, as she watched, the flesh began to slough away from his face, crumbling to yellowing, parchment-like shreds, revealing the white, grinning skull beneath. The eyes still stared unblinkingly from the naked sockets . . .

She could not breathe. She awoke, choking on a fetid stench that burned her lungs—and opened her eyes to see the gargoyle face of a cacodemon bending over her.

She had no time to recover from her surprise and shock, to speak a cantrip which might have banished him. The crouching monstrosity, its bulk filling the tiny cabin, laid a black palm across her face. Its temperature was painfully hot. Another hand seized her around the waist and lifted her roughly. Then it straightened—its shoulders and wings burst apart the hide of the cabin, and the sun's glare dazzled her—she heard its screech of momentary pain, which almost drowned out the tumultuous beating of its wings—and then the brimstone fumes overcame her.

CHAPTER IX

The Assassination

Pandrogas had left several students behind, mostly members of the Cabal and some gifted younger mages, in the vast castle when he had left Darkhaven. The unlocking of the secrets of Necromancy could not stop because he was not there to supervise it—all those who labored within Darkhaven's walls were grimly aware of the deadline imposed upon them by the steadily-decaying orbits of the world's pieces.

But any hopes he might have nurtured of enlisting his colleagues' aid against Trisandela were quickly expunged. The Lady of Bats had materialized them in one of the many secret corridors that lay between the walls and floors of the castle's chambers, and immediately enshrouded them in a spell of indetectability with which Pandrogas was not familiar. It was marvelously effective, however—not only were they able to venture into the scriptorium, where young conjurers and conjuresses bent industriously over their inkhorns and codices, but when Pandrogas, at the Chthon's urging, lifted volumes necessary for his research from shelves and even from the lecterns next to the copyists' desks, their only reaction was that of bafflement and annoyance that they had so thoughtlessly misplaced their work.

At any other time, Pandrogas would have been eager to learn more about this cloaking spell, but now he was only frustrated. "A sorcerer of your rank or near it would sense us," Trisandela said, "which is why you will make no attempt to alert your guests here of our presence. To insure this, I have made arrangements."

At her demand he led her to a small darkened chamber whose sole object of furniture was a huge ornately-framed speculum. It cast no reflection, but rather glowed with an inner light in which shifting colors moved like oil on water. At a gesture from Trisandela the clouds cleared beneath the glass, to reveal—

Pandrogas staggered; the image in the mirror seemed to recede suddenly from him as if falling down a dark well. He gasped. He was looking at the dank cist in which he had been imprisoned only a short while before, and there, crouched on the cold stone, was Amber!

She was naked, and obviously cold; she hugged her legs to her chest, shivering. She snapped her head up, looking about as though somehow aware that she was being watched—and given her power, he knew that was entirely possible. Then, with another gesture, the Lady of Bats caused the image to dissipate into luminous mist once more.

"She will not be harmed," the Chthon said, "if—"

Pandrogas raised one hand wearily, suddenly feeling as old as the ancient walls surounding him. "If I perform the task you have set me," he finished.

"Just so."

Pandrogas said no more. He turned and picked up

the armful of heavy books he had chosen for his research, and made his way slowly toward a reading room that perennially faced the sun.

Trisandela had posed him quite a conundrum—if he did what she asked and aided in the revival of Yasothoth, the resulting struggle for dominance among the Chthons could well destroy what was left of the world. But if he tried to find a way to trick or defeat her, Amber would pay the price.

He was quite effectively trapped. He could not betray the remnants of humanity that clung to life on the thousands of fragments, but he also could not face the thought of condemning Amber to death.

Moving as stiffly as might one of the many corpses in the catacombs far below him, he sat and opened one of the volumes arrayed before him. The yellowed, brittle pages were covered with writing almost too faded to decipher—knowledge that could help save the world, or destroy it. How it would be used was his choice.

Though he heard nothing, Pandrogas abruptly sensed that he was not alone. Trisandela stood behind him, looking over his shoulder.

"How long do you estimate your research taking you?" she asked.

He moistened dry lips and tried to sound unconcerned. "A commonweek—perhaps less, if all goes well."

She moved into his field of vision, taking care to avoid the dusty beams of sunlight. "Remember—the quicker you learn what you must learn, the less your beloved will have to languish in the bowels of Zarheena." And with that, she vanished.

The thick smoke of her departure made his eyes water—or was that in fact the reason? He stared at the wavering lines on the page, uncaring of the falling tears that caused the ancient Rannish text to blue and run. There had to be some way to rescue Amber

without loosing the Lord of Scorpions. There *had* to
be.

But, in all the vast stores of knowledge that
Darkhaven held, could he find it in time?

Kan Konar sat on a mossy log near one of the huts
of the Deathlings. Though nearly close enough to
reach out and touch, the rough mud and sticks of the
hut's wall were still almost obscured occasionally by
the drifting mist.

Across from him, on another log, sat Telice. She
was the woman who had first spoken to him, however many hours or days before—the perpetual
twilight of the fragment, combined with the mist,
destroyed all sense of time for him. He had been
here long enough to grow hungry and eat, and to
sleep once. And to learn much about these pitiful
people called the Deathlings.

It was a plague, Telice had told him. A plague that
had struck the fragment of Aldean, several commonyears ago. Unlike most scourges, this one had not
reduced its victims to hideous pockmarked traves-
ties of humanity; its curse was more insidious and
terrible than that. Those afflicted had grown pale, as
though their blood had thinned within them. The
skin had taken on the appearance of snow or alabaster, seeming almost to glow like the fabled Moon.

Their strength and endurance declined rapidly,
along with other effects that were more subtle but
equally as devastating. As much as their muscular
capabilities declined, their senses grew more acute—so
much so that the light of even a cloudy day seared
their eyes and their skin. Their body temperatures
had dropped to such an extreme that the touch of a
normal man or woman was like the application of a
brand. And the sensitivity of their hearing was such
that the striation of a nearby cricket could be
deafening.

He had heard stories of them on occasion, in his journeys from fragment to fragment, but had not given credence to the tales. Now he was face to face with their reality. He whispered, "This is why the youth collapsed in pain when I seized him."

"Yes." He had to strain to hear Telice's reply—for her to speak any louder would be to cause herself pain. "And why we dress like the dead—the loose-fitting rags are all we can bear to have touch us, though they are still better than risking being cut or scratched by branches or rocks."

After a moment, she continued. "The only blessing was that the plague was not terribly contagious. Only those who knew each other in a carnal way, or who had sustained physical contact for long periods of time, contracted it.

"We fled to this nameless, uninhabited worldlet. It was our decision—only in the depths of this cloud valley, where silence and darkness rule, can we exist without unendurable pain—at least, for a time."

"What do you mean?" Despite himself, despite his conditioning never to show emotion, he shivered. Perhaps it was only the dampness.

Telice smiled. All of her reactions and gestures were performed slowly, to minimize the pain of movement, but the ironic result was that of a dreamlike, languorous attitude on her part. "You have heard the sound of the dirge and seen the light of the pyre?"

He nodded.

"Though it causes us pain, nevertheless we sound the death knell whenever one of us dies, that its notes might help speed the departing soul from this sad place. In the final stages of the disease, you see, even the pressure of an ant's tread upon the skin is agony; the sound of dripping water is unendurable; the faintest glimmer of light torturous. The victim endures it until his or her will can no longer control

his reactions; then the convulsions that result quickly
magnify the pain to such an extent that death swiftly
follows."

Kan Konar was silent, contemplating the horrible
end that Telice and all the others within this valley
faced. He admired her courage—the equanimity with
which she spoke of that hideous, inevitable death
was inspiring.

"There is no hope of a cure, then? No chance of
remission, no way to save yourselves?"

"None. Some of us have chosen a quicker and less
painful death by suicide. That is the only alternative."

Kan Konar wished he could enfold himself in the
comforting confines of his cloak—not only would he
feel warmer, but also more protected, insulated from
these depressing surroundings.

The irony of his presence here did not escape
him—a living dead man, he had found his way into a
valley of the living dead. But was he here merely to
complete his dying, or for some other reason?

The cloakfighter looked up from his ponderings.
Telice had not moved; her gaze, luminous as a pane
of milky glass filled with sunlight, rested on him.

A new question had occurred to him. Even as he
formulated it, he realized he was afraid to hear the
answer. Why, he could not have said, save that he
knew, somehow, that it would be a crucial element
in deciding his fate.

"Such a disease must, it would seem, have an
unnatural origin," he said. His mouth was suddenly
dry as he asked the question: "Where did this plague
come from?"

"From Xoth," she replied, as he had known she
would.

Kyra's task of instructing the shapechanger in the
ways of assassination were not as arduous as she had
anticipated. Mirren was quick-witted and learned

easily—she was also, though older than Kyra by almost ten years, in excellent physical conditioning.

The two women quickly developed a mutual, though guarded, respect for each other. They could not be said to be friends—Kyra had never had a friend, had never allowed herself to become close to anyone save Roge. Yet it was sensing this same aloofness in Mirren that caused the assassin to feel a vague kinship to the shapeshifter. Mirren was obviously a woman who, like herself, could ill afford to trust anyone. Kyra knew how it felt to be so isolated. She respected the other woman's reserve—and Mirren responded to this with respect in kind.

Perhaps most impressive, however, was how readily she grasped, in only the first few days of her instruction, the basic principle of the Assassins' Guild—the concept of administering death as a work of art, dispassionately save for pride and care in the performance itself. No sense of compassion or empathy could be allowed to dilute the purity of the task—likewise, the blow could not be struck in anger or sadistic joy. The mark of the true professional was detachment.

Kyra had not expected Mirren to be able to grasp this most basic fact. After all, she was a werewolf, and, in common with most people, Kyra believed that animals, even more so than man, killed for savage sport. Yet Mirren professed, at least, to understand the concept, and the questions she asked indicated that she was not merely lying.

Kyra led her about the city of Zarheena for several days, familiarizing her with the narrow streets and crowded buildings in which most of the guild's assignments were to be found. This was followed by several hours of instruction in various weaponry—the tiny arbalest that was Kyra's favorite weapon, as well as poisons, knives, garrotes and other silent means of murder.

Kyra found also that Mirren had a number of good suggestions as to how to make the best use of her singular abilities. As a wolf, her tracking and stealthiness were as good as the most skilled masters of trucidation. Kyra reported to Thrisus that, with the proper training, Mirren would make an excellent addition to the Guild in perhaps as short a time as a commonyear.

"There is, however, one problem that needs dealing with," Kyra told the Guildmaster as they supped in a dimly-lit tavern.

Thrisus cocked an eyebrow. "And that is?"

"Impatience. She feels that her lycanthropic abilities are all she needs to perform an assassin's duties. She understands the philosophical underpinnings of our work, but cannot accept that she isn't ready yet for the application of them."

"What is your recommendation?"

Kyra nibbled thoughtfully at a fruit. "That she be allowed, under carefully controlled circumstances, to show what she is capable of. Then we can judge her capabilities more fully, and better decide how best to use her."

Thrisus considered this. "This is an unusual suggestion. The normal method of dealing with overenthusiasm is stern discipline. What are your reasons for this proposal?"

"Mirren is no ordinary applicant to the Guild. Think of her as a specialist in a form and style of killing that no other of us has mastered. The wolf within her is quite powerful—and, used properly, could be of great advantage to us. But we have to know what we are working with."

After a moment, Thrisus nodded. "Very well, Kyra," he said. "But mind—you are responsible for this werewolf. Do not let her bring embarrassment to our Guild."

Kyra nodded, showing no sign of the concern she

felt. Thrisus was right—Mirren's performance would reflect on her, for good or ill. If the strike was carried out in a manner pleasing to the Guildmaster and the others who would watch and judge, then she would have gone a long way toward reinstating herself as a full member of the Guild. If not—she might face expulsion, possibly even death.

It was a risk she was willing to take. Her standing in the Guild was all that was important to her—she would risk all to be returned to her former status.

And, she promised herself, woe betide Mirren if the shapechanger failed her.

When Kyra told Mirren the news, the shapechanger was so pleased that she nearly gave in to an impulse to hug the assassin. She knew, however, that to do so would be a grave mistake. Mirren liked the assassin, but she did not trust her. She had never seen anyone, man or woman, who was so tightly contained. Such a spontaneous outburst of gratitude might well precipitate violence, and would certainly hinder the professional relationship they had developed over the last few commondays.

She felt vindicated—she knew it was not necessary for her to endure the long and ritualistic apprenticeship that other aspirants to the Guild With No Hall had to undergo. Her wolf would serve her well, as it had always done in the past. It could pad silently through the dark streets, taking advantage of every cranny and shadow—it could scent the victim unerringly, and take his or her life with a single snap of strong jaws on a soft throat.

This method of death, however, was what Kyra and Thrisus had the most trouble with. The Guild did not perform in a haphazard or crude manner—each death had to be carefully designed and executed with skill and elan. Only thus did they maintain the mystique of terror and fascination that brought them much of their business. To savage a victim with teeth and claws was not a death that Thrisus felt would reflect honorably upon the Guild.

Very well—if they wanted a virtuoso performance, she could see to that. The assassins could grasp intellectually the fact that she retained her human mind while wearing the body of a beast, but emotionally they seemed unable to believe it. No matter; all she needed was a chance to convince them.

And now, it seemed, she would have it.

Her first assassination would be a simple one, closely supervised. A jealous wife had learned that her husband, a cartographer in public employ, had been keeping a mistress in one of Zarheena's poorer sections, and had hired the assassins to dispatch the woman.

It was a job chosen for its complete lack of court connections. Even if she botched it, Kyra, who would be watching her closely, could finish it successfully. Mirren did not intend to botch it, however.

The next evening, after the eight bells had tolled, Mirren strolled down the cobbled narrow length of Hazard Street. It was just past supper time; she could smell the thick scent of lentils and potatoes from various pots. A few children still played with crudely-carved wooden swords, darting in and out of dark alleys to frighten each other; a few potters and basketweavers still sat in doorways with their wares set about them. Mirren passed taverns with names like The One-Eyed Basilisk and The Gibbet; the men and women who moved in and out of these dives were, for the most part, dressed in cheap, ill-fitting cloth and worn leather, their weapons carried within easy reach. Occasionally, however, Mirren would see people frequenting the establishments who wore glossy damask, nankeen or cambric, with ruffled collars and jewel-inlaid belts, their hair and beards trimmed and perfumed, their stride arrogant.

Mirren felt no fear for herself as she made her way along, though she was aware of the appraising and lecherous glances given her by both sexes. Kyra and Thrisus dogged her path, she knew, as inconspicuous as the mist that curled from the warm cellar windows. And even if they did not, the wolf could be summoned in mere moments. Her only concern was carrying out her assignment properly.

She stopped at the base of a flight of wooden steps that led to a garret above an apothecary. The weight of her foot on the first step told her she would not be able to ascend without the creaks and groans of the aged wood warning those above that someone was coming. She looked at the line of rowhouses, crowded together like an old hag's teeth. There were other ways to approach the garret.

Two doors further down the street she found another flight of stairs. A moment later Mirren stood on the top of a dormer.

There was no reason to proceed further in human form. She had accomplished the metamorphosis successfully on more precarious footing than this while performing in Cardolus's troop. She pulled off the simple shift she had worn and crouched, naked and shivering slightly in the cool night air. Her ring and a few other pieces of jewelry she deposited in a small pouch of soft leather that she put about her neck. Then she relaxed the inner tension that she had held for so much of her life that it was as natural to her as breathing.

A moment later the wolf hunkered on the narrow, sloping shingles. She turned and leaped to the crest of the roof, where she paused for a moment, savoring the various night scents which were now so much more intense and suggestive than they had been to her human nostrils. Then she began to make her way toward the garret, from which her keen hearing could already detect the cries and moans of illicit passion.

Her plan was a simple one—to leap into the room and rip the woman's throat out with her jaws. She had not had as much difficulty convincing her overseers that this was a properly artistic killing as she had thought she might. They were not opposed to bloodletting as long as the purpose of the assignment was carried out. In this case, it was to shock and horrify the philandering cartographer and insure that he would never stray from his wife's bed again. Their only concern was that it be accomplished swiftly and smoothly.

She crouched on the landing outside the door, listening to the creaking of the floorboards and the groans and thrashing limbs. There was an open window next to the door—a single spring would carry her through it. She listened carefully, pricking her ears to better catch the couple's cries. The timing had to be precise—she intended to make her appearance at the moment of the man's climax.

It occurred to Mirren that this tactic might succeed too well—it would, in all probability, not only insure that the cartographer never cheat on his wife again, but also that he would never be able to perform with her again. Her black lips drew back over her fangs in a wolfish grin at the thought.

She tensed, preparing to spring. She could tell from the timbre of the moans that it was almost time. She could feel the delicious anticipation of the kill building within her. A moment more—

Now!

She leaped. The wolf's body completely cleared the windowsill and she landed on the bed within. She could see their faces, ecstasy turned to stunned disbelief, then quickly metamorphosizing to superstitious horror, the man's fleshy jowls quivering with fear. Mirren snarled. The woman's throat was within easy reach . . .

The man leaped from the bed, hurling back the coverlet as he did so. It fell over Mirren as she leaped toward the strumpet, and the wolf became entangled in it.

The woman, shrieking, scrambled from the bed as well. Mirren thrashed herself free and her powerful hind legs hurled her from the bed, but too late—both the cartographer and his trull had reached the door and now fled, naked, their flabby white skin startlingly bright in the outside darkness, down the stairs.

Mirren gave chase, feeling fear almost as intense as that of her victims. She had bungled it! If she did not kill the trull now, most likely her own death would be the only reparation that would satisfy the Guildmaster and Kyra.

She bounded down the shuddering steps. The cartographer had reached the bottom and was running toward the street, screaming, his buttocks quivering as he tried to force more speed out of his rotund form. The woman fled the opposite way, into the dark, odorous depths of the alley. Mirren was about to follow her, when suddenly she saw the man stagger and then collapse, rolling with a horrible limpness across the slimy cobblestones. He rolled over into the flickering light of one of the street lamps. One look at his face was enough for even the relatively weak eyes of the wolf to realize that his heart had succumbed to the terror she had inflicted.

Snarling, Mirren turned, to see the woman disappearing into the night.

There was only one hope for her now—she would have to rely on her animal skills and cunning to see her safely out of Zarheena and away from the revenge of the assassins. She loped into the alley.

*   *   *

Kyra had never seen Thrisus so angry. The two assassins had watched the fiasco from the parapet of a nearby building, and Kyra had lost no time in following the wolf. She was angry as well—angry at herself, as well as at Mirren. She had trusted the shapechanger, had let herself believe that Mirren could carry out the assignment. Having produced a star pupil possessed of such a unique ability, it would have been easy to convince Thrisus to reinstate her to full Guild status.

None of that would happen now. She would be lucky indeed to escape with her life now—certainly she would be expelled from the Guild and forced to leave Zarheena. But before that happened to her, Kyra would see that the werewolf suffered for failing her.

She moved swiftly and silently into the alley night. A thin sliver of starcrystal was enough to reveal to her the almost-unnoticeable tracks in the mud. Her arbalest was loaded and cocked, just in case the beast decided to turn and attack. Kyra doubted that would be the case, however. Mirren had seen her abilities demonstrated in the training sessions—she knew that, even as a wolf, she was no match for the assassin.

All the wolf could do was run. And that would not be enough. Kyra would follow her to the edge of Zarheena and beyond, if need be, to expiate the mistake she had made in trusting the werewolf . . .

She stopped abruptly. The tracks led into an open cellar door. The blackness within seemed thick, velvety—almost palpable.

Kyra swallowed, her mouth suddenly dry. She would have followed the werewolf anywhere, it was true—through the densest forest or the most dangerous part of the city.

But the beast had gone underground.

The assassin forced herself to take a closer step, holding the shard of starcrystal up. There was, for an instant, the faintest glimmer from within—twin points of green, feral light. The eyes of the wolf—or the burning gaze of a cacodemon?

Kyra hesitated. She looked back over her shoulder. Though she could see no movement for the length of the deserted, narrow lane, she knew that Thrisus was watching her, perhaps had an arbalest or a blow-gun even now trained upon her. She had no choice. She had created this problem—now she would have to resolve it, somehow.

She turned back to the cellar doors, and, shoulders back and head held high, she entered the unknown darkness.

CHAPTER X

The Pit of the Chthons

Amber had no sense of how long she had spent languishing in the pit. There was no slightest change in temperature or light to give any indication of the passage of time. The air was just cold enough to make her uncomfortable.

Twice, so far, a cacodemon had appeared with food—half-seared, half-raw mushroom steaks whose odor nauseated her. She had shrank back against the wall when he appeared, the stench of brimstone making her cough. The thing took no notice of her, however; it merely dropped the rancid meal and vanished again. Amber had to wait until she was quite hungry before she was able to choke the steaks down. They temporarily assuaged her hunger, but seemed to do little to replenish her strength.

Over and over again she inspected the slick black walls for the slightest sign or hint of an escape route. She found none—not even chisel marks to indicate how the excavation of the pit had been accomplished.

Fortunately, one of the first spells she had learned at Taggyn Saer had been the Flaming Hand, for which she was profoundly grateful—without light, she felt she would surely have gone mad. She had always been marginally claustrophobic, and the stifling darkness had made it almost impossible to breathe.

Paramount in her thoughts was escape, of course—but escape seemed impossible. She had tried what few spells she knew against the adamantine walls, and none had proved even the slightest bit effective. Nor was she at all sure she wanted to somehow pass beyond those walls; when she closed her eyes and tried to reach out with her other senses, Amber could feel a presence of evil lurking somewhere in the depths of the rock—a horrific sense of brooding, alien presence that left her even colder than the chill air of the pit.

She did not remember falling asleep; when she awoke, most of one side of her body was numb from lying on the cold stone. Wearily, she pulled herself to her feet and began to walk about the small circumference of the pit, gradually warming and relaxing her muscles.

Second only to considerations of escape was her constant conjecture as to why she had been captured and incarcerated. Sestihaculas seemed the most likely one responsible—and yet she found it hard to believe that the Demogorgon would have broken his pledge never to interfere with Pandrogas or those close to him. Such oaths were binding—and the Chthon was, by his own lights, a creature of honor.

It was all speculation, however, and the most frightening part of it was that she might very well never know who or what had brought her to this dreary hole.

The light generated by the spell turned back the darkness only a few feet—Amber could not tell how high the ceiling was, or if indeed there was a ceiling. Not that it mattered; she could not climb the glassine walls even if she knew that an escape route existed above her.

Once again she fought down a rising black tide of despair. She wished desperately that she had clothes, of any sort—her nudity exacerbated her sense of helplessness and vulnerability, as well as adding to her discomfort. She felt no hope of rescue; no one on Tamboriyon knew where she was, and as for Pandrogas, she had no idea if he was even still alive.

But at this point, even thoughts of her helplessness was not the worst of the situation.

Once more she murmured the words *"Limnus diam"* and once more her left hand ignited in algid fire. For perhaps the hundredth time she stepped close to the wall, seeing her distorted reflection in the obsidian sheen.

Though this section of wall was no different, so far as Amber could determine, from all the others, nevertheless it was here that the unsettling sensation of evil was at its strongest. Somewhere within or beyond the stone, *something* lurked—something so malefic that, even filtered through solid rock, its emanations still reached and unnerved her. She had never felt such virulence before—not in the catacombs of Darkhaven, not in the cemetary of Dulfar, not even in the unhallowed warrens of the Chthons. It repelled and frightened her, and yet, as in all things abhorrent, there was a strange sense of fascination that kept drawing her back to it, like a lodestone pulling a helpless shaving of iron.

She did not feel that the presence, whatever it was, was a threat—it seemed to be unaware of her existence. In fact, were it anything she felt to be human, Amber might have thought it to be sleeping. And she had the very distinct impression that this somnambulance was the only thing that saved her from instant annihilation.

What was most unsettling, however, was the equally strong feeling that, if a way out of the pit existed at all, it would be found here. She felt a growing certainty that, by using the power that was still largely untapped within her, it might be possible to breach this part of the wall. If she could survive the passage through whatever evil lurked beyond it, she might find her way once more to the clean skies and light that seemed more and more like a fleeting dream to her now.

But, even if she could somehow pass through the unyielding stone, what of the horror that lay beyond it?

Hesitantly, Amber put out the hand she was not using for light and touched the wall. It felt the same as it had felt to her the many times she had touched it before—cold and solid.

The conjuress closed her eyes, remembering those times in the past when, due to fear or stress, she had been able to summon the reservoir of ectenic force that was a part of her. The faint orange glimmer of her other hand against her closed eyelids seemed to change, to take on the blue glow she always associated with her power . . .

The coldness of the stone, which a moment ago had been communicated to her only through her fingertips, was now coating her fingers, her hand . . .

With a gasp, Amber opened her eyes—and saw that she had let her hand sink *into* the stone nearly to her wrist! She could barely make out the outline of it beyond the wall—it was as if her hand was surrounded by thick black smoke.

With a convulsive movement she pulled it out; the force of her reaction caused her to stagger backwards several steps. Amber looked at her hand, half expecting to see it hideously malformed or injured—but it was unharmed. The only lingering sensation was that of coldness.

Amber backed away until she reached the far wall, then slid down it and huddled on the floor, knees pressed to her breasts, arms around her legs. She shivered, more from fear than cold.

It would seem that she did, indeed, have the power to pass through the wall—*if* she could trust her peripatetic abilities not to desert her and leave her trapped within solid rock. But it was not the fear of dying inside the stone wall that left her shaking with dread. She was quite willing to take that chance for the possibility of escape.

But what of the horror that lay beyond?

"This spell," Pandrogas said wearily, resting a finger on the faded Rannish text of *The Book of the Black Skull*, "—and this one." He indicated another page from a second volume of forbidden lore. "Selected passages from the two of them should provide sufficient recussitive power to reconstitute Yasothoth."

Trisandela peered intently at both sets of writing, then raised her yellow eyes to Pandrogas. "You are more conversant with the ways of Necromancy than I, sorcerer," she said. "If you say this will work, I have no choice but to believe you." She paused. "You know the consequences to your beloved if you lie."

Pandrogas nodded. The Lady of Bats stood back from the reading table, spreading her ribbed wings. "Then there is no more reason to remain here. We will return immediately to Zarheena."

"Wait," the sorcerer said, holding up a hand. "I must have one day more to rest—to prepare myself. This will be by far the most powerful spell I have ever attempted—and at the moment, I am exhausted from my research. I must have food and sleep."

The Chthon hesitated—Pandrogas could see suspicion flaring quickly in the nonhuman gaze. Then Trisandela nodded, slowly. "Very well."

"I will return to my chambers, to rest and meditate. I must not be disturbed, Trisandela. Only in solitude can I prepare myself for this task."

Once more the Lady of Bats reluctantly agreed, and Pandrogas turned away. Carrying his weariness like a cloak of lead mail, he left the reading room and made his way through the cold, silent halls of Darkhaven, back to the chambers he had shared so long ago with Amber while her husband Tahrynyar had tossed, sleepless and irresolute, in another part of the vast castle.

He had not lied to Trisandela—he would, in fact, need as much rest and mental preparation as possible were he to attempt to resurrect the Lord of Scorpions. But he had no intention of doing such a thing.

He hated to think that Amber would have to remain in the pit of the Chthons another day, or even another minute. But it was necessary if he was to have the slightest chance of rescuing her and defeating Trisandela.

Within his chambeers, Pandrogas lost no time. With a few words and gestures he created a simulacrum of himself, seated in a meditative pose on the bed. It would not fool Trisandela should the Chthon choose to make an appearance in the room—however, if she merely used a spell of extended awareness to sense whether or not he was still there, the ectoplasmic doppelganger would satisfy her.

Years ago, when he had first come to Darkhaven, he had spent long periods of time exploring the maze of secret passages and tunnels that honeycombed the walls of the castle. Nearly all the living chambers had at least one hidden exit, and it was of this option that the sorcerer now made use.

The pressure of his hand on a certain point of the

frescoed wall caused that part of it to silently open. Carrying a small rod of starcrystal, Pandrogas descended a narrow, curving flight of stone steps.

For the past five commondays he had cudgeled his mind in search of an escape from this dilemma—how to keep from aiding Trisandela in a scheme that would surely have severe repercussions against humanity, while simultaneously somehow avoiding seeing Amber pay for his resistance. In the meantime, with Trisandela watching over his shoulder, Pandrogas had had no choice but to search for the vivimantic spell that might accomplish her unholy intention. Now he had found it, and he still had no plan to avoid using it.

In desperation, he knew there was only one place he could go for advice. He would have to commune once more with the shade of the Necromancer.

The steps ended in a narrow passage that led through many abrupt angles as it bypassed rooms and halls. Pandrogas moved swiftly, hesitating only briefly at intersections, though it had been years since he had traversed this particular route. Another flight of steps took him lower still into the depths of Darkhaven, and the light of the starcrystal was now reflected in the dampness of the walls. A final turn brought him to another secret panel.

There was only one way to reach the Necromancer's tomb, and that was through the Labyrinth that lay at the end of the Warped Stairs. Though Pandrogas had negotiated their confusing length a number of times since he, Amber and Beorn had first attempted to reach the tomb, finding his way to the end of them had never become any easier. Total concentration was needed to traverse them; the slightest lapse could result in the stairs leading one back to their beginning, or into the vast caverns beneath the castle, or even in being lost, doomed to wander an endless series of steps leading nowhere.

Pandrogas was tired, both emotionally and physically—he hoped he had the strength of will necessary to keep the Warped Stairs under control. Now, as he opened the gate and stepped onto the first slick black step, he tried to concentrate, to focus all of his mind on the task of reaching the Labyrinth at the far end of the stairs.

It was an exhausting sojourn. By the time he finally stood before the massive wooden door that led to the Labyrinth, the sorcerer was trembling and bathed in sweat. Despite his efforts, twice he had lost his way and had had to start over again, once from the beginning and once from the caverns where Amber and he had pursued the bear over a year before.

Now he opened the door and stepped into the musty dry air of the Labyrinth's first chamber. He sat down, taking a few moments to recover.

I am beginning to feel my age, he thought with grim humor. It was true; over the last year he had found it harder than ever to maintain the physical conditioning that was a necessary complement to his sorcerous abilities. The temptation to let his regimen drop had been quite strong at times. He had been subject to periods of severe depression since he had left Amber on Tamboriyon; black moods in which his constant battle against entropy, both on a personal level and in his attempt to find a way to save the remnants of the world from extinction, seemed futile. Eventually all would be dust and darkness anyway—the best his efforts could do was stave off the inevitable for a vanishingly short period of time, for himself and for the world.

He shook his head and performed a series of calming hand gestures designed to relax him. Such thoughts led only to despair. Life was its own reason for living, after all. If he went through his days at less than the best of his ability, than he might as well hurl himself into the Abyss and be done with it.

Pandrogas stood and contemplated the three doors that began the maze of death. At least he would not have to fight his way again through the pitfalls and traps set by the builders of Darkhaven so many ages ago. Around his neck he still wore the medallion with the safe route through the Labyrinth etched upon it.

The absolute silence pressed down on him as he made his way through the Labyrinth. He negotiated it fairly quickly despite his exhaustion, and soon was in the catacombs beyond, where the thousands of Darkhaven's dead had been entombed over millennia.

As he had become increasingly skilled in the ways of Necromancy, Pandrogas had come to find the catacombs at first a disturbing place, and then a haven of restful peace. He could sense the omnificent and infinitely patient power of the dead, waiting to be tapped. Over a commonyear ago he had served as a conduit for that power, and its white-hot potency had been enough to recharge the drained Runestone of Darkhaven and to lift the entire fragment from its collision course with Oljaer and restore it to a stable orbit.

He had once believed that the energy inherent in all those souls, still tethered by tenuous means to the dust that once housed them, could be used only for evil. In the moment that he held the Runestone at the Necromancer's bomb and opened himself to the power of the dead, he had thought that it could not be used at all; that the best one could hope to do was to survive the galvanic force. He had since come to understand, through his studies, that it was possible to direct it toward specific ends, as the Necromancer had done when he had attempted to divert the cosmic body that had broken the world. He knew also, now, that the power could be used for evil as well as good—it contained no ethic in and of itself. And so he knew that it would be very easy indeed to use Necromancy to restore Yasothoth to life.

Only the Necromancer, he felt, could tell him how to avoid having to do this. From believing, in common with the rest of the world, that the one who once ruled Darkhaven and who now lay entombed in its heart was the world-breaker, the scion of ultimate evil, the sorcerer had come to realize that the Necromancer had been, in fact, a man much like himself, a man whose quest for knowledge had been all-consuming. Now he felt a certain kinship with the mysterious, long-dead magician. And so it made sense to him to turn to the Necromancer for help.

He looked at the hundreds of tiered receptacles that lined the narrow corridor. Within each was the dried remnants of one who had once inhabited Darkhaven. The sorcerer had estimated once that there were at least fifteen thousand such liches within the catacombs, each representing a source of potential strength. The aggregate had been enough to change the montiform castle's orbit. What else might such a force accomplish?

Pandrogas slowed as he came to the end of the catacombs. Just ahead, beyond the obsidian columns, were the great stone doors to the Necromancer's tomb. He could see the cracks in the floor and walls—results of the temblors that had wracked Darkhaven in the final moments of its fall. He looked back at the loculi and mausolea he had just passed, and suddenly the knowledge of what he had to do was plain to him.

"Of course," he murmured. There was no need to seek aid from the Necromancer. The knowledge of Necromancy he had gained before was all he needed to defeat Trisandela. All that was necessary was to have the courage to use the power at his disposal. For surely the strength inherent in the catacombs of Darkhaven was enough to overcome the Chthon.

It was a frightening prospect, true enough, but it was also his only real choice. His worry over Amber and his reluctance—even after his studies over the past commonyear—to use Necromancy had been responsible for his inability to see the answer until now.

Pandrogas turned his back on the tomb of the Necromancer and re-entered the twisting passages of the dead.

He stopped in a vault which he judged was roughly at the center of the catacombs. He stood next to a sarcophagus carved from white jade and closed his eyes, preparing himself. He could feel the power surrounding him, filling the air like static electricity on a dry day. It would be more than enough to drive Trisandela from Darkhaven—that he knew.

To open himself up to the overwhelming force was a frightening thing—it required that he completely abandon his identity as Pandrogas, become nothing more than a vessel through which the awesome strength coursed. It was the ultimate abdication of control. Still, he had done it before, and he knew that he could do it now. And certainly the stakes warranted it.

He thought of Amber, and found himself, for the first time in long months, able to visualize clearly her face, the highlights of the sun in her hair, the delicacy and strength and love in her gaze. For her, he knew now, he would take any risk.

He felt tired no longer. Instead, it was as if the strength he sought from these tombs about him had already suffused him. He was ready to do what had to be done.

Pandrogas closed his eyes and surrendered himself to the power of the dead.

CHAPTER XI

The Power of the Dead

Kan Konar sat on a carpet of dead leaves, his legs folded in a lotus position, his lower body wreathed in mist. For an hour, as best he could estimate, he had been attempting to clear his mind of all thought, to induce a state of mental relaxation and serenity. He was no stranger to this mental exercise; such meditative disciplines had been part of Shadowmaster's training, and he had practiced them daily since then. Usually he could, with very little effort, enter a state in which his mind was as calm and untroubled as the placid surface of a pond.

But today such tranquility eluded him; there arose constantly before his mental eye the image of Telice, and he kept hearing her statement about the origins of the Deathlings' plague. And then anger would burn within him, such anger as he had seldom felt even in those now dreamlike times before his former life had been ended by Zhormallion's bite.

Telice had told him the reason for the Demogorgon's

curse. On Aldean, a group of small children had stumbled into a nest of adders and been bitten, with several deaths resulting. To prevent this happening again, the people had instigated a purge of all snakes in the immediate area. It had been in response to this purge that the Demogorgon had visited the plague.

In the short time that Kan Konar had spent among the Deathlings, their courage and quiet acceptance of their horrible fate had impressed him greatly. They had neither asked for nor deserved such a curse as the Demogorgon had placed upon them. The cloakfighter closed his eyes, picturing Telice's face—the alabaster perfection of her skin and the sadness in her luminious eyes. He felt an unsettling attraction to her, both physically and emotionally. For years he had sternly suppressed such urges, until he had thought that they had passed and would trouble him no more.

But Telice's image stayed before him. He felt that this fascination was engendered somehow in part by the effects of the disease, though how he could not have said. Perhaps it not only made its victims hauntingly beautiful, but also caused an increase in the production of subtle bodily chemicals that governed sexual attraction.

He sighed and opened his eyes, then stood. For a time beyond counting he wished he had his cloak to enfold himself in—not only to take away the perennial damp chill of the cloud valley, but also for the security and protection he had come to associate with the garment. He wished he had never investigated the sound of the dirge; wished he had stayed above the clouds in the safety of his isolation.

He turned, feeling the need to walk, to rid his muscles of tension—and saw Telice behind him.

His senses were as acute as they had always been, and not since his training with Shadowmaster had anyone ever been able to approach so closely without his hearing them. But it was as though Telice had materialized out of the fog itself, so quietly did she move.

"You are troubled," she said softly. It was not the first time in their conversations that she had shown an uncanny ability to sense his moods.

Kan Konar nodded, momentarily not trusting himself to speak. He felt an urge, dismaying in its intensity, to take her in his arms, crush her to him and kiss her. To do so, he knew, would be more exquisite agony for her than any torturer could devise—it would kill her. He said, "I wish there was something I could do that would mitigate the suffering of you and the others."

Telice smiled slightly, and he felt his heart break at the sadness of which her expression spoke. "If there is any positive aspect to this sickness, it must be that it induces a certain fatalism. Events are as they are—there is nothing we can do to alter them. As well try to reassemble the pieces of the world."

"The impossible *can* be accomplished," Kan Konar replied. "After all, did I not return to life and escape from Zhormallion's web? Perhaps—"

Telice held up a blue-veined hand. "It is futile to indulge yourself in such thoughts. You have your course to follow, and we have ours."

"And what *is* your course?" he asked. "What do the Deathlings plan to do with their lives?"

Telice looked at him, and the cloakfighter would have said that there was compassion in her gaze, had he not known of her circumstances. Surely no one in such desperate straits could have the time or the capacity to feel compassion for others. "We plan to die," she said softly. "There is nothing else. It is to be hoped that the disease will die with us. That was the purpose of this quarantine, and it is a good plan.

When the last of us passes on, the rest of humanity will be saved from this plague."

She took a few steps toward him, wincing at the pain the movement and the weight of her body on the sensitive soles of her feet caused. "There are not many of us left. It will not take long."

"I wish to do what I can, then, to make your passage easier," he said, and was surprised to realize, as he heard himself speak, that it was so. He had no desire to return to his isolated eyrie above the clouds; rather, he realized now that the purpose of his remaining days was to help care for these sufferers.

He had never been motivated by altruistic urges before; his duty and loyalty had always been to his daimyo, and in the course of that duty he would either save lives or take them, as ordered. But he had been waiting for it to be made clear to him how he would expiate the shame of his cowardice in the Spider Lord's web, and now he knew. This was how he would end his days.

He stepped toward Telice. "Come," he said. "Tell me what I can do."

In one of the inmost chambers of the castle Darkhaven the Lady of Bats rested, hanging upside-down with the talons of her feet embedded in one of the room's rafters. Enshrouded in her wings, dreaming utterly non-human dreams, she suddenly snapped awake, made aware by some subtle sense of a building danger. Its cause she was unsure of, but she had no doubt that it originated somewhere within the castle.

She released her grip on the rafter and dropped lithely to the stone floor. "Pandrogas . . ." the word came out in a sibulant hiss. Quickly she extended her awareness until it encompassed the immediate area, including the sorcerer's chambers. He seemed to be there; she sensed his still form on the bed.

Momentarily puzzled, Trisandela applied more of her will to the spell, then bared her fangs in a snarl as the simulacrum Pandrogas had left in his bed dissolved before the expanding wave of her cognoscence.

Simultaneously with the realization that she had been tricked came the attack—a burst of ectenic force so overwhelming in its intensity that she was helpless before it. It felt like the searing rays of the sun, like a deluge of concentrated acid, like a scouring blast of sand driven by hurricane winds. There was no hope of withstanding it, not even for an instant—the Lady of Bats screamed as she was hurled from the material world and down those echoing, lightless corridors of aether by which the Chthons bypassed distance.

In the moment that she felt herself gripped and flung by this irresistible force, Trisandela realized what was being used against her—the awesome power of the dead. Pandrogas had managed to tap the ectenic force pooled in the multiferous corpses of Darkhaven's catacombs, and was now directing it against her. She also knew, in that same instant, where her only faint chance of victory lay.

She had not realized that Pandrogas's mastery of Necromancy had progressed to such a degree. That had been her mistake. But it was obvious from the bludgeoning way in which he had struck that he was still incapable of refining and shaping the power—all he could do was use it as a savage might wield a club.

Therein lay her only advantage. Even as she tumbled helplessly outside the plane of existence, Trisandela knew that she could seize the power that carried her, guide it and use it. She could not turn it back against Pandrogas—not even the Demogorgon himself could overcome the inertia of this mystic tide. But she could channel it, shape it into a narrow, purposeful stream—and ride that to a destination of her choosing.

This she proceeded to do, using the ability common to all Chthons and cacodemons to find and reach a particular place in the material plane. In the flicker of an eye, Trisandela stood once more beside the crystal sarcophagus in the cists of Zarheena. Then, opening herself unresistingly to the devastating force, the Lady of Bats let it flow through her—and into the mummified lich within the sarcophagus.

She had neither the time nor the ability to formulate a geas that would bend Yasothoth's redeveloping brain to her will. It was all that she could do to keep herself from being incinerated as the power coursed through her. Her body arced and jerked as galvanic surges made her muscles spasm; orange fire crackled about her, causing every hair in her pelt to stand erect. The pain was unbelievable, beyond endurance—as though the blood in her veins had been heated to the boiling point. But she held on, directing the power through the conduit of her will and into the dry form that had once been the Scorpion Lord.

She had no idea if it would work—but it was the only receptacle that she could think of which might accept the sheer strength of that which Pandrogas had hurled at her. To try to absorb it all herself would have left her a cloud of ashes drifting in the remote reaches of the Abyss. She could only hope that her will and ability had been strong enough to direct it to the task she wanted performed.

And then, just as suddenly as it had begun, moments or unknown ages before, the screaming onslaught of energy halted. Trisandela collapsed to the floor, which had been heated to a painful degree. She had never, in all the long centuries of her existence, known such pain. She would almost have preferred death—even the black, soulless nothingness which the Chthons called death.

And then, through the pounding of blood in her ears, through her gasps for air, she heard another sound—a grating, creaking sound, as stone makes when sliding over stone. Both hopeful and fearful, Trisandela managed to raise her head and look at the sarcophagus.

It was glowing—the crystal that formed it seemed suffused with lambent light. Trisandela managed to stagger to her feet. Still dizzy, wings partially spread for balance, she cautiously approached the dais.

Though the crystal itself was glowing, the partially-open lid revealed a narrow triangle of blackness. Trisandela peered within. At first, she saw nothing— then, with shocking suddenness, a bronze insectoid arm shot from within the tomb and seized her in its chelated grasp.

Pandrogas lay gasping for breath on the dusty tiled floor of the catacombs. His body felt as if it had been racked, but the physical pain was nothing compared to the anguish in his soul.

He had failed. He had sensed what had happened, had felt the echo of Trisandela's actions reverberate down the fluid shaft of power that had linked her to him. But he had been no more able to stop the flow of ectenic force than a man could dam a coursing sluiceway with his bare hands.

When finally he had managed to summon enough strength to break the connection, it had been too late. The sorcerer knew, as clearly as if he had been a spectator within the far-away tomb, that Trisandela had used the power of the dead to accomplish her revivification of Yasothoth. The Lord of Scorpions lived—whether in complete possession of his mind and power, or a mindless monster instead, Pandrogas did not know, for he had severed the link between himself and Trisandela.

He had underestimated his opponent. He had struck

hard and brutally, hoping to eliminate the Lady of Bats before she could gather her wits. Instead, he had given her the power she had needed for her task.

The sorcerer pulled himself to his feet. There was no time for recriminations now; Yasothoth lived, and he, Pandrogas, was responsible. Somehow he had to find a way to undo this calamity.

To travel by dragonship to Zarheena would be folly; it would take weeks at best. To summon a cacodemon to carry him outside the dimensions to his destination would be just as foolish—Sestihaculas would know of it immediately, and Pandrogas had no wish to alert the Serpent Lord to his plans.

But the sorcerer had seen, had sensed, the way in which Trisandela had ridden the cresting bolt of force he had sent against her. Might he not, with sufficient concentration, use the power of the dead to carry him there as well?

It required a skill, an ability to choose one's destination, which Pandrogas was not sure he possessed. And if he was unable to direct his course, he might find himself lost forever in the black clouds of nowhere, doomed to wander between the moments of worldly reality as one might wander lost in the endless passages that honeycombed the walls of Darkhaven. Still, it was a risk the sorcerer felt he had to take.

He wished he could take the time to rest and replenish himself; his stomach was empty, and he felt dizzy and ill. But he could not afford the long hours it would take to retrace his steps through the Labyrinth and up the Warped Stairs. He would have to go here and now, while his resolve was still firm and his strength still sufficient.

He concentrated his thoughts upon Zarheena, tried to visualize the dark pit in which Trisandela had incarcerated him; the pit in which Amber was now. Then he summoned the power of the dead again.

The ravening force seized him once more; this time, however, instead of making of himself a conduit for it, he offered resistance, spread himself against it as a sail is raised against a wind—and felt it seize him, lift him and hurl him at unimaginable velocity into an abyss far greater and more terrifying than the one in which the world's fragments drifted.

Amber had made her decision. No matter how dangerous whatever lay beyond the wall of her prison might be, she would sooner attempt escape than wait passively for her mysterious captor to decide her fate. Besides, whatever waited on the other side of the black stone was dormant—that much she could sense with certainty. Assuming that her intrusion did not awaken it, it was possible that she might be able to make her way beyond it and find some route to safety.

She had no illusions as to her chances; she realized it was entirely possible that she might be trading her present plight for one far worse. Nevertheless, any action was better than none.

Amber approached the wall once more. She stood before it and closed her eyes, composing herself, striving to commune with the power that lived so strongly within her. She had given herself no illumination this time. Instead, she waited for the blackness to be relieved by the clean blue flame that represented her mystic force.

Nothing—the darkness was complete. The conjuress felt a tiny glimmer of panic, but willed it away; she kept her breathing regular, her heartbeat steady and slow. She concentrated on the unseen wall before her, visualized it melting like ebon smoke. Almost unaware of what she was doing, she raised both hands and extended them. There was a ring of azure fire about the periphery of her vision now; as she stepped forward it became stronger, encroaching on the night.

She hardly felt the cold of the wall envelop her.

Amber walked forward. Again fear threatened, but this time as though from a great distance; again she firmly turned it away. Now was definitely not the time to let her concentration falter; she did not want to find herself incorporated into solid rock.

How far she walked through the cold stone she had no idea. She could not tell if her eyes were open or shut—it made no difference in what she saw, which was flickering blue flames. She knew, with some remote and academic part of her mind, that she had not become a wraith capable of penetrating solid matter; rather it was the stone that she had willed insubstantial by activating an ancient spell of crossing.

And then, in the space of another step, she was free. Amber opened her eyes, at the same time murmuring the Payan words that caused cold fire to flare about her hand.

The light illuminated a high-ceilinged corridor that curved toward the right. Like the cist which she had just left, the walls, ceiling and floor were featureless and glassy smooth.

The conjuress felt a tiny glow of pride amidst the fear. No matter what she might encounter, still she had taken action to free herself—and it had been an action that few magicians, even after years of practice, would be capable of. To successfully activate and negotiate a Chthonic spell—that took power. When she learned to control it fully, none would ever imprison or threaten her again.

But that time was still in the future, and might not come at all if she did not keep her wits about her. Amber proceeded cautiously down the corridor. Unbidden to her thoughts came a sudden memory of the dream she had had—the crystal sarcophagus, and Pandrogas rising from within it . . .

Before she had time to do more than shake her head in distaste at the recollection, chaos broke loose. She felt a sudden surge of ectenic force in the air— and then a thunderclap literally hurled her backward, the concussion rebounding in the enclosed area with enough strength to deafen her and bring blood from her nose. Amber was cast against the far wall and slid to the floor. Dazed, she gaped stupidly at the curve of the corridor, from which now came surges and flashes of intense orange light. Fat sparks and careening spheres of odylic power spattered and rebounded into her field of vision, like fireworks on a dark night.

The pyrotechnic display lasted only a moment— then it was over, and only the sharp tang of ozone was left—that and a pale, somehow ominous light that slowly waxed and waned. The conjuress slowly rose to her feet. There was no place to go but forward, unless she wished to return to the pit. Cautiously, keeping close to the wall, Amber advanced around the curve of the corridor.

She could see that the passageway opened into a large chamber. Before she had moved far enough to see into it fully, she became aware of another sound—a grating, scraping noise. Then there was a strangled gasp, as though the air in the lungs that was its source had been suddenly cut off.

She felt fear then, black, abysmal terror. Whatever had lain asleep for eons in the heart of this fragment was now awake, that she knew beyond question. She tried to turn, to flee back to the relative safety beyond the wall, but it was as if her legs were no longer subject to her will. Heart pounding, unable to stop herself from looking, Amber stepped onto the light.

And saw the glowing crystal sarcophagus of her

nightmare, and, standing within it, a form that no nightmare, no matter how demonic, could have conjured—a Chthon like none she had seen before, standing easily ten feet in height. She had a brief impression of a long, segmented tail like that of a manticore's rising to curve over the head, which was an obscene crossing of human and arachnid features, and two arms that ended in lobster-like claws. One of them held Trisandela as if the Lady of Bats were a child's toy.

Then the head turned, and the eight burning eyes of the monster fixed their gaze upon her.

BOOK III

Zarheena

There is the world of light, and the world of darkness. And some in the world of light prefer the darkness.

—Loren Eiseley,
The Night Country

CHAPTER XII

The Lord of Scorpions

The wolf trotted along a damp and dank underground corridor. The darkness was complete, her ears heard only the dripping of water on rock, and her nose detected nothing save the faint reek of sewage and decay.

She had no idea where she was—some ancient passage built to allow members of the nobility escape from the fickle moods of the populace, perhaps. Sarkeet was a very old city, she had heard; parts of it had existed before the Shattering. It did not matter where she was—all that mattered was that she had a place to run.

She had no doubt but that she was being pursued by Kyra—some feral sense for which she had no name assured her of this. The assassin had taken a risk in recommending Mirren for the job, and her only way to reinstate herself with the Guild With No Hall would be to kill the werewolf. Well, let her try, Mirren thought. She would find that a wolf was not so easy a victim as a helpless human target.

There was a faint blue light up ahead; she rounded a corner and saw a lone rod of starcrystal, left in a sconce who knew how many ages ago. She hurried past it, eager to regain the protective darkness beyond. The pouch about her neck bounced in cadence with her lope.

She stepped suddenly, a baffled snarl rising within her throat. The passage ended in a wall of mortared bricks, no doubt erected there years before to prevent just such an escape as she now attempted.

The werewolf listened—it seemed she could hear, from far down the corridor, the nearly-silent footsteps of her stalker. The wolf quickly returned to the starcrystal rod and, rearing up on her hind legs, seized it in her jaws and pulled it from its sconce. She laid it down on the slimy stones, and then crouched down over it, concealing the light with her belly. It was not a large rod, and her pelt was thick— after some adjusting of position, she found she could make the darkness complete once more.

Thus positioned, she waited. There was nothing else to do. She would have to hope that the element of surprise would give her the edge. One swift lunge for the throat, before the surprised assassin could use her formidable arsenal of weapons . . .

It was regrettable that it had come to this. Mirren actually liked Kyra—the two had a great deal in common. Both were loners, used to making their own way without the help of any man, and both had skills that set them apart from normal humanity. She wished it could have ended differently.

Abruptly she stiffened—she had caught the faintest sound of leather brushing over stone. She snorted once, softly, to moisten the nasal cavity. She would need all her senses at their most acute, for she would only get one chance.

Kyra came around the corner, moving cautiously. The wolf tensed, then sprang. The soft blue light of the starcrystal was blinding to one unaccustomed to it; Kyra stepped back, instinctively putting her hands up to shield her eyes. By the time she realized her mistake, the wolf was upon her.

The heavy body knocked her down; she crossed her arms before her throat to prevent the wolf's jaws from closing on it. They rolled about on the filthy floor of the corridor. Kyra managed to ram one forearm into the wolf's mouth, blocking the teeth momentarily; the other hand groped for the dagger at her belt.

Mirren realized that she had lost her advantage. There was only one way out now; back the way she had come, and hope that no others had followed Kyra.

She rolled free of the assassin and was about to flee back up the corridor, when she saw something. The new position of the starcrystal illuminated an opening in the wall—a black patch where one of the large blocks of stone had been removed.

There was no time to consider the relative merits of the new route. The wolf leaped across the corridor and slid headfirst into the hole, wriggling into the darkness. In a moment she was gone.

It had taken all of Kyra's courage to follow the wolf into the cellar, and from there into the black passageway. The fear of having to face a savage beast in the darkness was nothing compared to her absolute certainty that a cacodemon lurked somewhere in the underground warren of tunnels and passages. And yet, follow she had; her sense of duty and honor had left her no other choice.

When she realized it was the wolf who had attacked her, she had felt almost a sense of relief—the sudden blaze of light and the hurtling form silhouetted before it had momentarily convinced her that she faced her greatest fear. But the relief was only momentary—it died when she saw the wolf wriggle through the hole in the wall, and realized that she would have to pursue her.

There was no other choice. If she did not bring back proof that Mirren was dead, Thrisus would attend to her own death, that she knew. She picked up the starcrystal and thrust it through the opening, peering after it.

There was another corridor, running at right angles to the one she was in. This one was much narrower, and sloped downward at a perceptible degree. Mouth dry with fear, Kyra eased herself through the opening.

There was no way of knowing which way the wolf had run, but it seemed logical to assume that she would have gone up, back toward the surface. Kyra certainly had no desire to descend deeper into the fragment, and so she turned her steps toward the ascending grade.

She was doomed to disappointment there, however; after only a few feet, the rising passage ended in a flight of stone stairs that led downward. Kyra knelt at the top step and examined it, holding the starcrystal close. Barely visible were several gray hairs on the top step.

There was no hope for it, then. She would have to go down.

So far, she had seen no signs of the cryptic wall carvings or other prehuman architecture like that in the corridor beneath Visantes's house. Evidently these tunnels were of human origin, having been built literally on top of each other during the long ages of the city's existence. But the further down into the bowels of the fragment she ventured, the more certain seemed her chances of encountering a cacodemon . . .

But even greater than the fear of the unknown depths was the fear of not performing her duty. She was an assassin, and she would carry through with her assignment. That was all she had—it was the only definition of her life. There was no greater terror than the thought of failure.

Holding the starcrystal rod high, Kyra started down the steps.

The clawlike grasp squeezed Trisandela painfully; she gasped for breath. Initially she struggled, but that only caused the pressure to increase, and so she stopped.

It was obvious that, whether or not the Lord of Scorpions was in full possession of his faculties, he was by no means in thrall to her. Though she was accustomed to reading emotions in the varied non-human countenances of her fellow Chthons, she found Yasothoth's expression inscrutable. She could not tell if he intended to kill her or release her.

Then a noise from the entrance caused her to turn her head. What she saw was so astonishing that she nearly forgot her danger momentarily; there, illuminated by the pulsing light of the crypt, stood the sorcerer's woman. She had somehow escaped from the cist; Trisandela felt a brief surge of admiration and respect. The woman's powers were obviously far greater than she had suspected.

Yasothoth turned his head as well, and stared at her. The Lady of Bats could see the stark terror on Amber's face as she ran quickly past the entranceway and down the corridor. For a long moment Yasothoth made no further move; he seemed almost puzzled. Of course, Trisandela thought; he is mazed and confused by his sudden return to life. No wonder he acts indecisively.

Then the Lord of Scorpions turned his spider-like gaze to her again. In a voice that was deep, yet somehow also brittle and chitinous, he said, "Why have you returned me to life?"

Trisandela knew with instinctive certainty that to lie would be to invite annihilation. "To use you in a plan to overthrow Sestihaculas," she replied. It was difficult to speak with the ring of crushing pressure about her ribcage.

The burning eyes became thoughtful. "Sestihaculas," Yasothoth said. "I remember Sestihaculas . . ." He looked toward the corridor again. "The woman," he said. "I sensed great power in her. Who was she?"

"Merely a tool in my effort to revive you."

Yasothoth nodded. "Summon a cacodemon," he ordered. "There seems to be much that is new in this life to which I have reawakened. I must learn my way carefully."

Trisandela said painfully, "I cannot do as you request unless you put me down. Your strength is perhaps greater than you realize."

Again that odd hesitation, as though the Lord of Scorpions were suspiciously weighing everything she said. Then he lowered her to the stone floor of the chamber and released her.

Trisandela inhaled, feeling pain shoot through her as she did so. The chela hovered nearby, ready to seize her again. She noticed that it was not really as much like a scorpion's claw as she had first thought—there was a greater range of motion available to the pincers, and their tips were only slightly larger than the ends of her own fingers.

Judging by his order to her, Yasothoth did not care if Sestihaculas was aware of his return to life or not. She had intended to keep his existence a secret, but it was all too apparent now that she had no say in the matter. Quickly she made the summoning gesture, and a burst of carbonaceous smoke heralded the arrival of Daimar the cacodemon.

The creature reacted in shock and servile awe at the sight of Yasothoth. "My lord," it stammered. "It has been long ages since you—"

The Scorpion Lord silenced him with a peremptory gesture. "There is a woman in the outer corridors. Find her and bring her to me."

"At once." Daimar spared a glance at Trisandela, in which she read volumes. Then the cacodemon turned and loped out of the chamber.

Yasothoth turned back to the Lady of Bats. She could see the glistening menace of his tail rising over his cephalothorax. "Now," the Lord of Scorpions said, "we will speak of your plan."

When she saw the nameless Chthon turn toward her, Amber was filled with utter terror. The creature's gaze was so non-human that merely to look into its blazing eyes was to risk complete madness. Her reaction was totally atavistic and instinctive—she ran, past the entrance of the tomb's chamber and down the corridor into the blackness.

She expected the Chthon to pursue her, or to at least use its magic to somehow retrieve her. But nothing of the sort occured. She ran, feeling her bare soles strike painfully against the rock, rebounding once with numbing force from the wall of the curving passage.

After an unknown time of terror her legs would no longer carry her, and she collapsed to the cold stone floor. She gasped for breath, momentarily unable even to rise to her knees. Slowly the thunder of the blood in her ears subsided, and the blackness that surrounded her was no longer tinged with red.

She began to think clearly again. The most important thing was escape, of course—she had to find a way out of this underground maze. Amber tried to compose herself, breathing slowly and evenly to calm the beating of her heart and still her frantic thoughts. By using her intrinsic powers, she had in the past been able to find her way out of worse traps. She had successfully negotiated the Warped Stairs and the

Labyrinth of Darkhaven—surely she could now make her way out of these tunnels.

She let her awareness extend from her, probing with it, trying to intuit the proper course. But then her lungs filled with a quick intake of breath that was almost a scream, and her eyes opened wide in the darkness.

There could be no mistake—her expanding awareness told her of this new danger as surely as if it had been standing before her.

A caeodemon was following her.

Pandrogas's return to consciousness was slow and painful. He became aware first of an overpowering stench, and opened his eyes to find himself lying next to the reeking splatter where someone had emptied a chamber pot. He pushed himself to his knees, gasping for breath as he tried to crawl away from the offal. Something was holding him in place, however; the hem of his tunic seemed somehow caught on one of the cobblestones of the narrow street he was in.

A moment's investigation showed that it was not caught—it had somehow *melded* with the rock, as if it had been impossibly woven into it.

The sorcerer tore the fabric, freeing himself, and rose to his feet. He had been extraordinarily lucky, he knew—his all-but-ungoverned flight through the aether might have left him embedded within the street or a nearby wall. It required far more skill than he possessed to successfully navigate the corridors that lay outside space and time.

As far as he could tell, however, he was in Sarkeet—he had succeeded to that extent, at least. The journey had lasted little more than an instant, but the pain of it had been excruciating—he had not known how much the enfolding grasp of a caeodemon shielded one from the twisting, searing experience. Every muscle ached, and he felt dizzy and nauseated. Reluctantly, Pandrogas realized that he could proceed little further in his quest without at least some nourishment, and possibly some sleep as well.

He followed the narrow street until it intersected with a larger thoroughfare. It was well into the Zarheenan night, and the few pedestrians still about at that hour gave him only incurious glances. Pandrogas looked about him. He was in one of the poorer sections of town, that much was obvious; the tumbledown houses, crowded close together, the strong scents of ripe sewage and rancid vegetables, and the casual weaponry worn by both sexes made that apparent.

He knew only one person in Sarkeet: the enchanter Visantes, who lived at the edge of the city and the fragment. Pandrogas had written to him some commonmonths ago, asking him to consider adding his talents to those already at Darkhaven—Visantes had been trained in the Black Sun system, a style of sorcery well respected for its knowledge of the Chthons—but there had been no reply. He hoped the silence did not indicate an unwillingness to help, for he would now have to find Visantes's house and ask him for shelter and aid—his precipitous departure from Darkhaven had brought him here with only a few copper coins in his purse.

He began walking, looking for a friendly face—or at least one not openly threatening—of whom he could ask directions. By one of those familiar and maddening quirks of fate, however, now that he had made his decision, all the other travellers on the street seemed to vanish as though by a preordained signal. Pandrogas kept walking. There was little else he could do. Sarkeet, he knew, was not a large city—even in his exhausted condition he could traverse its length before sunrise.

He was almost wrong—dawn was beginning to

brighten the sky when, after finally receiving directions, he turned at last onto the wide avenue known as the Verge, which paralleled the Abyss. In the distance, catching the first light of the sun, was the enchanter's mansion, perched on the edge of the fragment.

Pandrogas felt lightheaded as he lifted the heavy knocker and let it fall. There was no response at first; then slow, hesitant footsteps approached the door from within. It opened a crack, and the face of an older woman peered out.

"Your pardon," Pandrogas said. "I am a collegue of the enchanter Visantes . . . if I could speak with him . . ."

The woman closed her eyes momentarily in an expression of pain. By the intuition that manifested itself in Pandrogas far less often than he liked, the sorcerer suddenly knew that Visantes was dead. The realization must have shown on his face, for the woman—the enchanter's widow, surely—said, "He died a commonweek ago. They say it was natural causes, but I think it was the assassins. Visantes had enemies in Sarkeet . . ."

"I'm sorry," Pandrogas said. He could think of nothing else to say. He would have to find someplace else to rest, to rebuild his strength for the coming battle. But as he turned to descend the steps his vision darkened, as if night had somehow pushed back the dawn. He felt himself falling, but did not feel himself strike the hard stone of the street.

CHAPTER XIII

Into the Abyss

Amber moved quickly but quietly down the curving, nighted corridors of the chthonic maze, her route illuminated by the cold fire that enwrapped one hand. She had to resist the panicky urge to run wildly down random side passages in an attempt to lose the creature that was stalking her. Such attempts would be futile, she knew; the tracking abilities of the cacodemons were supernally acute. Her one hope lay in finding a route to the surface and the daylight before the thing overtook her.

She rounded a corner and saw before her a flight of stone steps rough-hewn into the black rock. Quickly she began to ascend. She fancied that she could hear the cacodemon's shuffling footsteps in the darkness beyond her pitiful radius of light, but when she stopped and listened, the silence was absolute. These feelings were only nerves; she knew that if it were that close upon her, it would spring forward and seize her.

Amber wondered as she made her way up the stairs why it did not simply appear beside her and so cut short the pursuit. Perhaps there were rules, unknown to her, governing the ways in which the Chthons and their servants apported themselves. Or perhaps it merely enjoyed prolonging the hunt.

The conjuress knew it had not given up; she could sense it, somewhere back there in the darkness. Her skill was not sufficient to tell her conclusively if it was gaining or not, but she suspected that it was.

For a time beyond counting, Amber wished that Pandrogas was at her side. Though the sorcerer had proved himself less than the all-powerful and all-wise mentor she had first thought him, still there was no denying his power and, more importantly, his knowledge of how to use it. She would have given much to have any human being, versed in magic or not, with her now—almost as great as the fear of the cacodemon pursuing her was the terror of being alone in such a situation. But her first choice was Pandrogas, of course, though she had no desire to see him exposed to the danger she was in. Still, the selfish and human desire to be with the one she loved once more before this horrible fate overtook her was so strong that it seemed almost as if she could see his face before her in the darkness, hear his voice counselling her as it had so often before.

"Fear is the greatest enemy of the magician," he had told her many times. "When a threat is faced, you must be calm—you must learn to master the instinctive reaction that prepares your muscles for flight or battle. You must channel the surge of your blood into your power, use it to make your spellcasting swift and sure."

She took hold of this thought as she would a rope thrown to her in an angry sea. Fear could destroy her—could spread her power thin like oil on water.

She had to keep focused. *Concentrate on what lies ahead,* she told herself fiercely, *not on what follows from behind.* Ahead might be salvation; behind was only capture and possibly death.

Once again she let her power quest into the darkness before her, hoping to sense a way to the surface. Then, as she reached the top of the stairs, she felt something—a locus of magical power that impeded the waves of her awareness as a submerged rock might disrupt expanding ripples in a pond.

Ahead of her in the tunnels was someone or something which had been imbued with a certain amount of ectenic force, Amber realized as she made her way past unintelligible carvings in the rock wall. Quickly she made her way toward it. She had no idea what it might be, but it did not repel her with the choking sensation of evil as had the thing she had sensed in the pit. If she found it, she might find help as well, or at least a way to the sunlight. It was a slim chance, but her only one, and so Amber hurried forward, letting her sensibilities guide her to the locus.

She came to an intersection of two tunnels. The sense of power was stronger now, much stronger—then, with a flash of unease, Amber realized that it was moving as well, moving toward her.

She had no time to speculate on what this might mean. She rounded a corner, heard a soft growl and saw two points of green lambent light reflected in the flickering light from her hand. Heart hammering, Amber raised her mystic brand, the better to see.

A wolf stood in the corridor before her.

Mirren recognized the woman immediately, though it had been over a commonyear since last she had seen her. Then they had been on the sinking caravel called the *Elgrane,* and she had watched in terror and fury as Beorn the thief, astride the gryphon that

had been Cardolus's prize exhibit, chose this woman
to rescue instead of Mirren and the dryad. Despite
the time passed, despite the completely different
circumstances, she knew this woman who now stood
naked before her, one hand blazing with magical
light.

Two things prevented the werewolf from leaping
forward and ripping her throat out. One was the
imminent threat of the assassin, who was still following somewhere behind her. The other was the obvious fact that she faced a conjuress—Mirren could see
the ring on the blazing hand. She realized that the
conjuress might strike her down, believing her a
dangerous wild animal, and so she quickly cringed,
hunkering down and whimpering, as well as looking
back over her shoulder to indicate danger approaching.

She could see the fear in the conjuress's eyes
replaced by puzzlement. The woman had also noticed the pouch containing the talisman she had taken
from the sorcerer's spire. There seemed to be no
immediate danger of being struck down by magic
now, but there was still the approaching peril of
Kyra. The wolf rose and trotted forward. She licked
the conjuress's other hand, then seized it gently in
her jaws, tugging her toward a side corridor.

She felt the woman hesitate, then follow. From
the affrighted look she cast back over her shoulder,
Mirren surmised that she was being pursued as well.
Very well, then—she now had an ally, for the moment at least. Time enough for revenge later.

The two hurried through the darkness. The wolf's
keen nose detected a slight, almost imperceptible
change in the air—its dry and musty flavor was subtly becoming moister, fresher.

There was a way out somewhere ahead.

The realization gave her new strength; she hurried

forward, and the conjuress ran with her. But now there was another scent, this one coming from behind them—the burning smell of brimstone. In addition Mirren could hear running footfalls, heavy ones indicating the stride of some large creature.

They rounded a final corner and gray light illuminated an exit ahead. The conjuress cried out in relief—and then the cry turned to terror. Mirren looked back over her shoulder and saw a cacodemon come around the tunnel's curve, its expression wrinkled and snarling in reaction to the pain even the indirect rays of the sun caused it.

It lunged forward, one splayed and taloned hand groping for the conjuress. Mirren put on a burst of speed, as did her companion. There was only one alternative to the monster's searing grasp, and nothing less than the primal fear of being torn limb from limb could have driven them to it.

Side by side, the conjuress and the werewolf leaped through the exit and into the sunlight that filled the infinite Abyss.

Pandrogas awoke in some pain—he had hit his head when he had fallen, and now a sizable swelling on his temple told him that he was lucky he had not broken his skull.

Before he could open his eyes, he felt a poultice being applied to the wound. He looked up and saw the wrinkled and concerned face of Visantes's widow as she ministered to his injury.

The sorcerer tried to rise to his feet, only to sink back as she put a hand gently but firmly against his chest. "You appear to be at the end of your strength," she said. "Rest—I have made some dinner for you when you feel like eating." She indicated a tray near the bed, from which smells of incredible flavor were wafting.

"Thank you," Pandrogas said. "You have shown much kindness to a stranger at your door."

She looked at him with an unreadable expression. "You named yourself a colleague of my late husband," she replied. "I can see by the ring on your hand that you are a sorcerer. Had you wished me harm, you would not have used so elaborate a subterfuge to gain entrance to my house." She stood, gathering her robes about her. "Visantes is dead now, but I still honor his friends." She turned and left the room.

Pandrogas carefully raised himself to a sitting position and addressed himself to the food. It was simple fare—onion soup and black bread, with gryphon's milk cheese—but it tasted as delectable as any feast that might be served in a king's hall. The sorcerer felt substantially stronger after he sopped up the last drop of soup with a crust. He then fell to considering his situation.

He still felt weak as a result of the transition from Darkhaven to Zarheena, and he was injured as well, but that could not be helped. There were spells that would increase his vitality temporarily, though he would pay for it later. The important thing was not to waste any more time.

He looked about him. He was in a small room; the sloped ceiling told him it was a garret under the eaves of the house. The air was chilly, though growing warmer because the morning sun was pouring through the only open window. There was little in the room besides the bed, a table with a cracked washbasin and pitcher, and a chamber pot and an old wooden armory.

From where he sat he could see the cloud-strewn welkin of the Abyss. The house extended out over the fragment's edge—yet, due no doubt to some magical connection Visantes had made with Zarheena's runestone, everything within it retained weight-fulness. Pandrogas stared into the infinite blue depths. There were those who found such contemplation restful, but it had no such soothing effect on him.

He blinked and squinted his eyes against the sun's glare. For a moment he thought he had seen two figures floating out there—a man or a woman, and a large dog. A more intense look, however, revealed nothing. Either a drifting wisp of cloud had obscured his vision, or, more likely, it had been some remnant of hallucination caused by his head injury.

He leaned back against the headboard. The vision had been oddly disturbing—for an instant he was tempted to reach out with his mind beyond the boundaries of the house to learn if the two figures had been real or just momentary phantasms. He decided against it, however—he needed to conserve his strength.

He reviewed his situation. Somewhere within the tunnels that honeycombed Zarheena, the Lord of Scorpions lived again. According to the legends, Yasothoth, who had ruled the Chthons as Demogorgon when the world was whole before Sestihaculas had arisen to supplant him, had nearly wiped out the primitive human race on several occasions, seeing them as potential threats to the Chthons as the dominant race of the world. Only the fact that primitive mankind had also possessed, albeit sporadically and in embryonic form, the ability to command the ectenic force, had saved them—that and the Chthons' inability to withstand the sunlight.

After Sestihaculas overthrew Yasothoth, the Lord of Snakes instituted a policy of isolationism—the Chthons and their demonic servants remained in the underworld of caverns, letting mankind multiply and build cities on the surface. And so matters had remained until the cosmic disaster that had shattered the world and caused the Chthons to flee to the shadowy fragment of Xoth.

Now Yasothoth was back, and Pandrogas had no doubt that the Chthon meant to institute a new reign of terror with terrible consequences for humanity. Trisandela had meant to use him to overthrow Sestihaculas, and no doubt such a plan was now uppermost in Yasothoth's mind. Pandrogas had to find him and stop him somehow before he departed for Xoth.

As great, if not greater, a concern to him than the defeat of the Lord of Scorpions was rescuing Amber. The thought of her fate in the hands of Yasothoth was almost enough to drive him mad with worry.

He pushed himself unsteadily to his feet, preparing to perform a most dangerous spell—a cantrip which would mitigate the effects of his weakness and injury by drawing from his own life force. He had had to use this on rare occasions in the past, and always he had paid dearly for it later in extended periods of recuperation. But there was no other choice now; he had to be at his strongest when he faced Yasothoth.

He intoned the phrases and made the proper gestures, and felt new strength surge through him as a result. Revitalized—he only hoped it would last long enough for him to find and somehow banish the Lord of Scorpions back to eternal night—Pandrogas left the room.

He met Visantes's widow on the stairs. The woman, who was carrying a pot of herb tea up to him, reacted in astonishment. "You'll make that wound start to bleed again—" she began, but he raised a hand to quiet her.

"It was not as severe an injury as it seemed," he replied. "I thank you for your care and concern. Please accept my condolences for your loss—if there is anything I can do to make your lot easier . . . ?"

She gave him a slight and wistful smile. "Thank you—but fortunately Visantes has left me not only this house, but the means to live comfortably. My only concern is the loneliness—and that only time will deal with."

Pandrogas nodded. "Still, if you are in need of anything at any time, do not hesitate to write to me—Pandrogas of Darkhaven."

Her eyes went wide at the sound of his name. "Pandrogas! You are the one who was searching for a way to restore the power of the runestones! Visantes was planning to travel to Darkhaven; he wanted to help you in this endeavor!"

"I regret he was unable to," the sorcerer replied.

The woman turned and started down the stairs, saying over her shoulder, "Come with me, Pandrogas—there is something he wanted you to have—something which he felt might aid your efforts."

Though anxious to begin his search for a way into Zarheena's underworld, Pandrogas nevertheless felt he owed it to Visantes's widow to see what she wanted to show him. He followed her into the enchanter's laboratory, which occupied the lowest level of the house. It was well stocked and equipped, Pandrogas noted as they entered—shelves filled with copper- and leather-bound volumes of research and lore lined the walls, and rows of glassware containers full of herbs, salts and elixirs stood in cabinets. A huge bay window afforded a magnificent view of the Abyss.

The woman bent and lifted a corner of the rug that covered most of the floor, revealing a trap door perhaps a foot square. She pulled on the ring set into it, lifting it free of the surrounding wood. Pandrogas leaned forward, peering into the cavity thus revealed. A leathern pouch had been secured to the underside of the house, providing a hideaway no thief would think to look for. And in it . . .

Pandrogas gave a gasp of surprise and reached into the pouch. He lifted from it a wristlet forged of black metal with a simple clasp, from which extended an oddly-curved mount in which was set a large cabochon crystal. The stone itself appeared transpicuous at first glance, but closer inspection showed subtle, shifting hues deep within it.

Hesitantly, almost reverently, Pandrogas fastened the wristlet onto his right hand, that being the one which the curve of the mount fitted. The metal was malleable, and some slight adjustment resulted in its fitting his hand as closely as might a glove. He felt the stone quickly grow warm against his palm.

"What is it?" Visantes's widow asked.

"A heliolite," the sorcerer replied. "One of the few talismans to survive the Shattering. There are only three known to exist. With them, one may channel and focus ectenic force. Your husband was right—this will be of great use. How did he come across it?"

"He was one of the few who dared to explore the warrens of the Chthons and come back," she said. "This was the only thing he ever brought out of those dreadful tunnels. He said it was too powerful for one with as little knowledge as he to attempt to use, but that you might be able to control it."

"As to that," Pandrogas said, "I fear that I shall soon be forced to find out."

Pandrogas left the mansion in the light of the early morning sun, the wristlet now safely ensconced in his pouch. Fate, indeed, he thought—with such a potential weapon at his disposal, he might very well be capable of defeating the Lord of Scorpions in combat and rescuing Amber.

First, however, he had to find the Chthon. This would not be difficult—his ability to sense so powerful a source of magic as Yasothoth would lead him unerringly, once he found his way into the ancient warrens that the Chthons inhabited when the world was whole.

He knew that most of Sarkeet had been built after the Shattering, long past the time that the Chthons had abandoned their underground cities. He knew as well that a number of mansions and palaces had made use of the tunnels for dungeons and escape routes. Exploration of the passages to any great degree had been proscribed, however, largely due to the fact that many who ventured too deeply into them tended not to come back.

He had heard that the tunnels served another purpose as well—they were sanctuary for the city's homeless and criminal elements. Many who had been marked for assassination by the Guild With No Hall had fled into the underground, preferring life in the eternal darkness, feeding on pale rodents and reptiles, to death. But how was this knowledge to help him find an egress? He had no money with which to pay for information.

It seemed, however, that the fates were still with him; even as he wondered, Pandrogas saw a door open in one of the houses, and a man emerge carrying a chamber pot. He raised the lid on an aperture in the pavement between two buildings and poured the contents of the pot in.

Pandrogas approached as the man left. One of the city's points of pride, he recalled now, was that no sewage ran in the open gutters—this was another use to which they had put the tunnels. By diverting streams and rivers from the hills outside the town through the tunnels nearest the surface, they had achieved a system of underground sluiceways that washed the offal under the streets and eventually out of an opening in the underside of the fragment.

Pandrogas lifted the lid. The stench from it was

enough to make him gag, but he knew that this
might be his only avenue into the underworld. The
unpleasantness would be a small price to pay if by
enduring it he could find Amber and, possibly, stop
Yasothoth. With that thought in mind, the sorcerer
gingerly lowered himself into the reeking darkness of
the hole.

CHAPTER XIV

Resolution and Rebirth

Time was a vague and elusive thing on the fog-enshrouded fragment of the Deathlings. There was no day or night, and the mist added to the sense of dreamlike unreality. Kan Konar ate when he was hungry and slept when he was tired, with no knowledge or care of the passing of hours or days. His sole absorption was toward improving the miserable lot of the Deathlings.

To cut down on the length of their journey to a nearby stream for water, he dug a stream that brought the rivulet through the center of the small collection of huts. He carpeted the ground with soft leaves, packed mud around sharp rocks and pruned branches that might scratch their delicate flesh.

He felt an incredible peace and serenity as he attended to these and other details. The mausolean silence of the village was not oppressive; rather, he found it soothing. This was, after all, the perfect way

187

for one whose life was over to end his days—caring for others of the living dead.

Telice spent much of her time with him. They huddled together, discussing other ways to help her people. During these talks the physical desire the cloakfighter felt for her did not diminish, but never by word or gesture did he give any indication of it. If Telice suspected it, she gave no sign of it either.

He felt privileged to have been given such a task to carry out, and he gave himself to it with a devotion that was wholehearted. The Deathlings quickly accepted him as one of them—it did not matter that he did not share their affliction. That he shared their burden was enough.

There were occasions, however—particularly when he was alone and in a contemplative mood—when the magnitude of the Demogorgon's injustice and cruelty troubled his new-found peace, like subterranean rumblings that can ripple the placid surface of a pond. Though Kan Konar was content with his decision to remain among the Deathlings, the similarities between Zhormallion's plague of spiders on Typor's Fist and Sestihaculas's visitation of this disease did not escape him. But when such thoughts did trouble him he set them aside, secure in the knowledge that his duty was to mitigate that evil as much as he could be remaining here.

He had not been there long before he witnessed his first death by the sickness. The disease's course had culminated in one of the older men. The practice was to allow those in the final stages to die alone, since their shrieks and thrashing brought pain to the amplified senses of others. But Kan Konar, repulsed and yet fascinated by the process, remained in the hut, hoping to learn by observation some way in which to ease the passing of others. He forced himself to watch as the man writhed in unendurable

agony on his bed of leaves and grass. Blood burst
from desiccated skin, which was glowing as if by
some weird bioluminescence. He saw the cachetic
form wracked with spastic shudders. Then, to his
horror, the man literally *disintegrated*—the skin began to slough away in flocculent pieces. The hut
filled with the stench of blood and bowels as dissolu-
tion proceeded at an incredibly rapid pace. When he
glimpsed bones protruding through the rotting flesh,
the cloakfighter could stomach no more—he turned
and fled the hut.

Thoughts of revenge on the Chthons returned again,
stronger than ever, after this experience. Gone was
the new-found serenity; it was as though he had
arisen from the dreaming languor of a long delirium.
The hatred he now felt once more for the Chthons
was the first real emotion that had stirred him since
he had awakened in the Spider Lord's web. For that
reason, if for no other, it was to be relished.

But at the same time that hatred gnawed at Kan
Konar, triggering within him fantasies of revenge
and destruction. He was no longer content with the
life of servitude he had chosen. The more he talked
with the soft-spoken Deathlings, the more he observed their pain and noble suffering, the more he
wanted to seek out Xoth again, this time to attempt
to somehow cleanse what was left of the world of its
corruption.

But such fantasies were just that, the cloakfighter
knew. He had failed to kill the Spider Lord—what
possible chance would he have of destroying the race
of Chthons as a whole?

He struggled with this new demon for some time
before confiding in Telice.

"These feelings will pass," she told him. "All of us
have felt the same way on many occasions. But to
attempt to pursue them does no good. Everything
passes—even Chthons. We will all die eventually."

"You may die," Kan Konar said, his new resolve firming within him as he spoke, "but not without purpose, and not without revenge. I'll see to that."

Telice smiled sadly. "I'm afraid that is not possible. You have been exposed to the plague—we cannot take the chance, small though it may be, that you might have been infected and might carry it to another fragment. I am sorry, cloakfighter, but we must keep you here."

Kan Konar stared at her. He suppressed an urge to laugh, which sprang both from astonishment and disbelief. "Setting aside for a moment the fact that you might find such a task—difficult—what makes you think that I may have contracted your contagion? You told me that only by sexual congress or prolonged exposure—months of exposure—could one be infected. I have neither been here long enough nor been intimate enough to be in danger."

"We don't know that much about it; there is always the possibility that you are especially susceptible. The risk cannot be taken."

Kan Konar was suddenly aware that other Deathlings had silently approached, materializing out of the mist like revenants. "This is absurd," he said. "The only way to keep me here is to kill me. As long as I'm alive, I can leave if I wish to—you cannot watch me constantly."

"We do not intend to," Telice replied. "We have already insured that you will stay."

She was going to say more, but the cloakfighter suddenly realized what she must mean. With a muttered curse he ran past her. The others parted to let him by, and in a moment were lost in the soft grayness behind him as he charged up the hill, dodging trees that appeared suddenly out of the fog.

The fragment was small, and the portion of it wreathed in clouds smaller still. Kan Konar's heart had not even begun to beat rapidly by the time he burst out of the fog. He continued on up the hill through the thinning trees. The slope steepened, became dotted with banks of snow—and then he was before the cave in which he had spent most of a commonyear. He entered it and moved quickly to the back, where he had placed the tiny pyx. He had not bothered to conceal it initially; what does a dead man care, after all, if he is robbed?

The pyx was empty. The cloakfighter dropped it and slowly emerged from the cave.

All about him were the disassembled pieces of the dragonship—the ivory planks that now floored the cave; the sails of leather and peritoneum that draped the entrance and made a hard pallet within; the ropes, the rudder—everything. It would have been possible, though tedious, to reassemble it. But to do so now would be useless, for the runestone that gave the little craft weightfulness and the ability to navigate the Abyss was gone.

He was indeed trapped on this fragment now, unless there was another dragoncraft to be found, and the cloakfighter doubted that this was the case. His lips twitched in a grim smile—how ironic that now, when he had begun to consider the possibility of living once more, he should be condemned again, and this time without reprieve.

He looked down at the enigmatic mist wreathing the treetops. "This is not the end," he murmured. "I have found a reason to live again, a reason to fight again. And I will *not* see it taken from me."

In the Abyss, surrounded by the limitless blue of the sky, Amber and Mirren floated. The impetus of their leap from the tunnel of the Chthons had carried their weightless forms far enough from Zarheena for them to be seized and blown away by the endless

winds of the void. Now Zarheena was no longer
visible, and Amber knew that, barring a miracle,
their deaths were assured.

Both she and the wolf woman were naked—Amber
had found nothing to clothe her in the dark barren
tunnels, and Mirren's transformation from beast to
human had not, of course, included garments. Already the endless rays of the sun were beginning to
burn them. Death by exposure and starvation in the
Abyss was not a pleasant way to die, Amber had
heard. She remembered the story Beorn had told
her of being adrift after the storm had blown him
away from Darkhaven. He had forced a vampire to
carry him to land, but Amber knew full well what
their chances were of encountering any form of life
in the trackless sky, much less anything or anyone
that would help them.

She had thought of Beorn much in the past few
hours—her memories of him had been spurred by
her discovery of who Mirren was. After she had
watched in astonishment as the wolf had changed
into a dark-haired woman perhaps ten years her
senior, she had remembered the lurid advertisements
painted on the side of Cardolus's wagon, which she
had seen more than a commonyear before. This was
the lycanthrope with whom Beorn had lain, the woman
who had attempted to take Amber's place on the
gryphon that Beorn had liberated during the sinking
of the *Elgrane*.

Mirren now floated next to her. They held hands
to avoid separation—the thought of being alone in
the Abyss was more than either could bear, even
though the resentment the wolf woman had felt for
Amber for leaving her and the dryad behind in the
maelstrom had not diminished.

"Were you not a conjuress, I would have tried to
rip your throat out," she told Amber. "Because of

you, Ia is drowned at the bottom of the Ythan. And I have endured such hardships as you would not begin to comprehend—"

Amber said, "Don't blame me because Beorn chose me instead of you. As I recall, I did what I could to save you and the dryad—I pushed her log into the water that you might have something to cling to. It was all I could do."

"It was not enough," Mirren said sullenly.

"Be as that may, we have more pressing matters to attend to. There is a bare chance that my power might save us. Do you want to come with me, or would you rather perish slowly here in the sky?"

Obviously, Mirren had had but one answer to that. Amber now focused her concentration, attempting to use her knowledge and her intrinsic magical strength to do something she had done before, though never at a great distance—to sense the location of something and to orient herself in regards to it. In the past, the object of her search had usually been Pandrogas; now it was a fragment, some source of land. Whether it was Zarheena or another did not matter; even Calamchor, the jungle fragment, swarming with manticores, basilisks and other dangerous creatures, would be welcome haven now.

She closed her eyes and filled her thoughts with visions of land, of a green and blue island hanging jewel-like in the sky. At first, nothing—then, gradually, she felt a subtle but unmistakable pull, as if from the faraway attraction of a fragment's runestone. Keeping her eyes closed, the conjuress extended her free hand. She heard Mirren gasp, and knew that the hand was glowing with a sapphire refulgence noticeable even against the bright blue backdrop of the Abyss. Amber felt a breeze begin to caress her skin and pluck at her hair and she knew that they were moving, being drawn in the direction of whatever fragment she had sensed.

"Hold on," she told Mirren, and then spoke no more, keeping all of her mental focus on that clear vision of land, maintaining the ethereal attachment that pulled them with ever-increasing speed.

How long would it take? She remembered Beorn's tale of how his arms had been cramped and numb from clinging to the vampire for what had seemed like an eternity before they reached land. She was not in so uncomfortable a position, fortunately— dragging the wolf woman along with her was not a difficult task, given their weightless states. Still, it could be days, even weeks, before they reached the fragment . . .

Amber shook her head. She must not allow herself to be distracted by such worries. As in meditation, the thrust of her consciousness had to be sharp and clear, arrowed in on only one thing.

She cleared her head of all thoughts save the vision of land. The breeze against her face had quickened to a wind now, and she could feel the power within her burning coldly on her free hand.

She had no idea how long it was before Mirren gasped "Look!"

Amber opened her eyes. She was momentarily dazzled by the glare of the sun "beneath" her; then her vision cleared and she saw, directly ahead, a floating mass of stones and dirt, tapering to an irregular root of rock at one end and capped at the other with a mountainous and verdant surface. Mirren must have been sleeping, or she would have noticed it before now, she thought.

It was impossible to tell how large the fragment was, floating as it did against the featureless sky. It had to be of fair size, however, for Amber could make out considerable variety in its terrain. At one end were several snow-dusted peaks which sloped into a cloud-filled valley. They were approaching the mountainous end.

Amber closed her eyes quickly, unwilling to lose the focus of her power. While it was true that their inertia would tend to carry them on their course toward the fragment, she was well aware of how capricious the abyssal winds could be. She remembered all too well seeing her husband Tahrynyar hurled into the void by such a wind, even though he was literally only inches away from the mystic field that inspired weightfulness on the fragment.

There was no faltering of their progress, however, and soon she felt secure enough in it to open her eyes again. The fragment grew in size before them, too gradually to be seen at first, but then more rapidly. It had evidently been broken off of a larger mountain range during the Shattering—one of the taller peaks seemed riven in half.

It did not appear to be moving, but Amber knew that appearances could be deceiving; she had to make sure that her velocity matched that of the fragment's, otherwise they could easily be crushed by the million-ton mass as it hurtled by. To make landfall was much more complicated than it looked. Given their mutual nudity, she had no particular desire to set Mirren and herself down in the snow. It appeared, however, that she was not to be given that choice. Though she had some measure of control over their flight, as they drew closer to the fragment the play of wind around the escarpments and declivities made it impossible for her to judge their landing site. In the last few moments of flight it was all she could do to make sure they were not seized by an updraft and hurled high above the land, which would insure a bone-breaking fall.

As it was, their landing was none too gentle. A blast of wind hurled them over the cliffs. Though she

still felt weightless, it was frighteningly obvious to
Amber that she was now falling—the ground rushed
up at her, and she could vaguely hear Mirren's screams
as she too fell. They both landed in a deep snowbank—
Amber felt her shoulder graze a rock painfully. The
plunge into icy coldness took her breath away. She
pulled herself out of the snow and stumbled to a dry
patch of land where she stood shivering, her breath
fogging the air before her. It was amazing how the
temperature could be comfortable in the Abyss and
so much colder on land.

Mirren scrambled free of the snow as well, and
joined Amber. She said, "I suppose freezing to death
is better than starving to death."

"If our luck continues, we'll do neither," Amber
replied. "And it appears it might." She pointed up
the gentle slope they had landed on. Near the crest,
nearly obscured by foliage, was a cave.

Within it they found more than just shelter—there
was a meager supply of fruit and dried rabbit meat,
the remains of a fire by the entrance, and, best of all,
soft dragonskin blankets that they wrapped themselves in. The cave was outfitted and furnished with
the disassembled parts of a small dragonboat. They
also helped themselves to the food. Amber was not
especially hungry, but she was thirsty to the point of
pain, and the small keg of cold water just within the
entrance was most refreshing.

"We must be careful," Mirren said, chewing on a
tough piece of rabbit jerky. "Whoever lives here
might return, and they might not be friendly."

Amber cupped one last swallow of water to her
mouth, then turned and smiled at the other woman.
"I am a conjuress, and you a werewolf. From the
looks of things, no more than one person lives here.
I doubt we have that much to fear."

Mirren stopped chewing suddenly, looking past

Amber to the entrance. Amber turned quickly and
saw the silhouette of a man backlit against the glare
of sunlight on snow. Quickly she rose, pulling the
blanket close about her. The man, somewhat short
and compactly built, stepped inside. He was wearing
torn leggings and a shirred tunic of dark cloth. His
hair was also dark, as were his eyes, which held
surprise and wariness but no sign of pleasure. Good,
Amber thought. At least he is looking at us as intrud-
ers first and women second, if at all.

"How did you come here?" he asked.

"We floated," Amber replied, "out of the Abyss."
She saw the man's gaze widen slightly at this, but
otherwise he showed no sign of surprise, or of any
other emotion.

"I met someone once before to whom that happened," he said. "A long time ago." He crossed to a
chest in a dark corner of the cave and opened it,
pulling out garments and boots of supple dragon
leather. "See if these fit you," he said. He then
stepped outside to allow them privacy for dressing.

"Our lucky day, it looks like," Mirren said as she
quickly donned the clothes. They were somewhat
large, but not inconveniently so. Amber's fit more
closely—the one for whom they were made must
have been a small man, or perhaps a woman.

Everything from the clothes to the planks that
covered the cold rock floor seemed to have come
from the hide, sinews or bones of dragons. A chaseboat
from a dragonship, most likely, Amber thought. The
man was probably a dragoneer who had been cast
away on this forlorn fragment. She remembered the
time she and Beorn had spent on board the *Dark
Horizon*, and the mad pursuit of one of the huge
skyworms ordered by Captain Asran—a chase that
had resulted ultimately in the thief and her drifting
to Xoth in a chaseboat much like this one once was . . .

She sat down to pull on the boots. As she did so,

she caught sight of a word carved in the chest and illuminated by a stray reflection of light—a word that caused her, for a moment, to doubt her very sanity. There before her, in flowery Perese text, was the name *Dark Horizon.*

CHAPTER XV
Converging Paths

Deep within the flexuous passageways beneath Zarheena, Kyra the assassin searched for the wolf woman. Her heart was a constant hammer of fear in her chest, and her mouth was dry with anticipation every time she turned a corner. But she kept searching. It was her duty to find Mirren. She did not fear the wrath of the Guild With No Hall more than she feared the possibility of encountering a cacodemon— quite the contrary, in fact. But her sense of duty kept her going, even though her terror was a palpable thing that seemed to ride on her shoulders and dig talons into her neck muscles.

She was sure that she could find her way back once she had dealt with Mirren—her sense of direction remained unconfused even by the twists and turns of the tunnels. The search seemed futile, however; there were so many different routes, and the wolf could have taken any one of them.

She heard a noise ahead—a scraping sound as might be made by claws on stone. Kyra hurried forward, hoping to corner Mirren before she could get away again. She had loaded a poisoned quill into her arbalest—one shot was all it would take—

And then she rounded the corner, and there in the unforgiving light of the starcrystal, hunched with bowed back and legs but nonetheless filling the corridor, skin glistening like rough black stone and eyes blazing, stood her worst nightmare embodied.

In the chamber of the sarcophagus, Trisandela watched as the Lord of Scorpions sat brooding. Her plans were now completely out of control, she thought—there was no possibility of her controlling Yasothoth and forcing him to do her will. She could only do her best to survive the impending war—for it would be nothing less than that when the previous Demogorgon challenged Sestihaculas. Chthon would be set against Chthon, and battle would rage across the nighted fragment of Xoth. And if it became known that she was the instigation of all of it . . . the Lady of Bats felt a shudder ripple her pilose skin.

A sound in the corridor outside the chamber caused her to look up. She saw Daimar enter, clutching the limp figure of a woman in one hand. The cacodemon laid the unconscious human, who was dressed in pale loose-fitting robes, before Yasothoth. At first the Chthon showed no sign of interest; then, as the woman stirred and groaned, he turned his head to watch her.

Trisandela watched also. The woman's eyes flickered, then opened. Incomprehension, swiftly followed by horror, filled her face as she looked from Yasothoth's countenance to Trisandela's. The woman made a strangled, glottal sound, and then Trisandela could see clearly all comprehension and sanity leave her eyes, as though the light of reason had been extinguished by a wind from some dark pit. The woman began to laugh— a low chuckle that built swiftly to piercing shrieks.

The cries of her madness were annoying. Evidently Yasothoth did not find them so, however—he watched the grinning creature as she jerked and trembled with the force of her insanity. Then he lifted one of his chelae. The pinchers glowed with a white light, and the woman was abruptly silent and still. Trisandela realized that Yasothoth had put her in a trance.

The Lord of Scorpions turned to Daimar. "This is not the woman I sent you to find," he murmured.

The cacodemon cowered back nervously. "Your pardon, my lord—there was another, but she hurled herself into the sunlit Abyss before I could reach her—"

Trisandela fully expected to see Daimar disintegrated on the spot for this. Yasothoth, however, merely nodded, as though he found the explanation satisfactory. He made a gesture of dismissal and the cacodemon, relief apparent in its rugose features, backed hastily from the chamber.

Yasothoth turned to Trisandela. "I have determined my course. It will be necessary to lure Sestihaculas to a place of battle where I may face him alone. It is also necessary that an ally of some sort be ready to intervene if necessary. Sestihaculas defeated me once—I do not intend to let it happen again."

"Understood, my lord."

"This woman whose power I sensed would have been ideal—her mind would be easily controlled, and her ectenic strength might have been used to tip the scales of battle." Yasothoth thought for another moment. "We must find another human of comparable power."

Trisandela nodded. Yasothoth's plan was simple and direct—and, if implemented properly, virtually foolproof. Should he become Demogorgon once again, however—than what of her? Would she be better or worse off under his rule than under that of Sestihaculas?

Whatever the outcome, it was obvious that her plan of becoming the dominant force on Xoth was no longer viable. She hoped now merely to insure her survival.

Pandrogas had made his way through the sewers and into the Chthonic passages that honeycombed the fragment with relative ease. There had been much power expended during the quickening of the Lord of Scorpions, and its residue guided him unerringly.

The heliolite nestled securely in his right palm. It was a source of comfort to him—though of no intrinsic power itself, it could focus and magnify ectenic force to an astounding degree. With all three of the talismans used together, it was said, even a sorcerer of no particular power would be invincible.

He hoped that this one would be enough to aid him against Yasothoth. He did not have much time, he knew, before he would have to pay the penalty for the revivifying spell he had used on himself. He had to find and deal with Yasothoth before then.

The tunnels were complex, but his sense of the recently-expended magic in the revitalization of Yasothoth led the sorcerer unerringly. He had given much thought to his priorities: should he seek Amber first and attempt to move her to a place of safety before dealing with the Chthon? Reluctantly he had come to the conclusion that such was not the wisest course. Great as his love for Amber was, it had to come second to the task of defeating Yasothoth—quite literally, the fate of what was left of the world depended on the latter. He had to strike hard and fast, while there was still strength in him to do so.

From around a corner, albescent light spilled from the rough-hewn entrance of a chamber into the passageway—light that slowly waxed and waned as though alive and waiting. Pandrogas paused, breathing deeply and slowly, concentrating. The heliolite on his palm seemed to pulse warmly in time with the light. He looked at it and could see golden motes stirring deep within it.

Now was the time, for good or ill. His mind formed an image of Amber for what he was well-aware might be the final time—then he stepped around the corner to face his adversary.

Trisandela's first realization of the attack was very nearly her last—a beam of aureate power, seemingly as solid as a battering ram, passed close enough to her that she could feel the fur of her pelt stand and crackle in the static it generated. As she leaped to one side she saw the lance of light strike Yasothoth squarely, lifting the huge Chthon from his feet and slamming him back against the irregular surface of the crystal sarcophagus. Turning, she beheld the source of the incredible burst of force—Pandrogas, standing in the entrance to the burial chamber, one hand extended, palm out. The cupped hand glowed brighter than the hated sun.

She realized almost immediately what the source of the beam had to be—a heliolite, one of the most powerful and ancient of human talismans. Yasothoth would not be familiar with it, for it had been crafted after his defeat and entombment.

There was no time to seek cover behind the sarcophagus—in any event, a sorcerer of Pandrogas's power using the heliolite could burn a hole through it like passing a heated poker through ice. There was only one alternative to incineration, and that was to flee. But even as she prepared to vanish she saw Yasothoth, smoke curling from the wound he had sustained, push himself to his feet with a roar of pain and anger that reverberated from the chamber's walls. The Lord of Scorpions thrust forward one arm, chitinous skin gleaming, and from the chela came a

dazzling explosion of odylic fire that warred with the
beam from Pandrogas's hand, pushing it back. The
two opposing forces crackled and sparked for an instant; then, slowly, Pandrogas's power began to overcome that of Yasothoth's.

Perhaps the sorcerer would have won—but, even
as Trisandela watched, he suddenly faltered, stagger-
ing as though overcome by a sudden weakness. At
that instant the Lady of Bats made her decision.
Pandrogas was going to lose this battle, that she
could see. Better to aid Yasothoth however she could
rather than be thought disloyal. Accordingly, she made
a gesture of her own which produced a band of
orange fire that wrapped suddenly about Pandrogas's
hand, searing the skin. He cried out, distracted—
and Yasothoth struck. The blast of searing white light
enveloped Pandrogas, seemed for an instant to consume him—then it faded, and when Trisandela's vision cleared she beheld the motionless form of the
sorcerer upon the cold stone floor.

As Amber stared in shock and realization at the
name upon the chest, the castaway once more entered the cave. She rose and turned to face him.
"This dragonboat," she said intensely; "where did
you find it?"

He looked at her for a moment without replying;
she could see him weighing the advisability of telling
the truth. Then he shrugged slightly, evidently deciding that there was no harm in it. "On Xoth. Why
do you ask?"

Amber shook her head, stunned with the magnitude of this coincidence. "This was the craft that
carried me to Xoth, over a commonyear ago—Beorn
and I were set adrift—"

"Beorn!" The castaway's tone held astonishment.
"Beorn the shapechanger—Beorn the thief?"

"You knew him?"

The castaway nodded. Amber was aware of Mirren watching them. It is almost too much to be believed, she thought—that three people gathered together by chance from all the myriad fragments should share a common history.

The castaway was looking at her with some form of realization dawning in his gaze. "You and Beorn, then, were on Xoth?"

"I was a prisoner of the Demogorgon, until I was rescued by Pandrogas the sorcerer—"

"And your name," the castaway interrupted, "is Amber."

The conjuress looked at him searchingly. "How is it that you know me, but I do not know you?"

"Since you say Pandrogas survived his encounter with Sestihaculas, doubtless he has spoken of me to you. I am Kan Konar, late of Typor's Fist, once employed by Ardatha Demonhand."

Amber nodded in comprehension. "Of course—the cloakfighter. But how came you here?"

Kan Konar seemed not to hear the question—he was momentarily lost in thought. Then he looked at Amber again. "The sorcerer said you were possessed of great intrinsic power—greater than any he had ever seen." He glanced at the ring of rank on her finger. "Have you learned, then, to control it?"

"To a degree," Amber replied. "To a small degree."

"Perhaps it will be enough," the cloakfighter murmured. Then, his air that of one who has come to a decision, he said, "The runestone for this dragonboat has been hidden somewhere on the fragment. If we can find it, we can reassemble the craft. I assume your power can sense its location?"

"I should be able to do that, yes."

"Then perhaps something can be done," he said, again more to himself than to her. "Perhaps a way can be found." He looked back at Amber. "In return

for my aid in your escape from this fragment, will
you agree to help me in a cause of my own?"

Amber hesitated. Her first impulse was to say
no—there was something about the cloakfighter's intensity that she did not like. But she had seen no
cities, or indeed any sign of human habitation, on
this fragment when she and Mirren had approached
it. The dragonboat from the *Dark Horizon* might
well be the only way to leave it—and she could not
remain marooned here while Pandrogas might be in
danger.

She did not wish to be deceitful, but the stakes,
she felt, warranted it. She could always refuse to aid
him if what he wanted was impossible or reprehensi-
ble, and trust to her skills at conjury to protect
herself.

All this took only a fraction of a moment to consider. Amber nodded and said, "I will. Let my companion and I rest and recover from our ordeal, and
then we will aid you however we can."

Kan Konar gestured at the stores of food and said,
"Whatever is here is yours." Then he turned and left
the cave again.

Mirren came to stand beside Amber. "I don't know,"
she said dubiously. "He strikes me as a nightfellow."

"I don't understand the term."

"A Rhynnish saying—one who prefers the darkness." Mirren stared through the entrance at the
cloakfighter's retreating figure for a moment. "Why
did you tell him we would aid him?"

Amber explained her reasoning. Mirren nodded
thoughtfully. "I'm beginning to have more respect
for you, conjuress. Of course, that still doesn't mean
I like you."

Amber suppressed a smile. "Of course." She
stretched out on a pile of leathern sails in one corner
of the cave. "You may have the hammock," she said
to Mirren. Her last act before falling asleep almost

immediately was to mutter the Charm of Aware Air, which would warn her if anyone or anything approached within a certain radius. There was no sense, after all, in taking chances.

Pandrogas felt as though he were swimming in a cold dark sea, fighting an undertow that threatened to drag him back into the depths. After what seemed an eternity of struggling toward wakefulness, he noticed the barest glimmerings of light against his closed eyes. Opening them was like attempting to lift the stone lid of his own sepulchre.

He was lying on the cold floor of Yasothoth's burial chamber. The Lord of Scorpions loomed over him, regarding him with his alien gaze.

"You are mine now, sorcerer," he said. "Your attempt to destroy me has failed, and you will have no second chance. Instead, your power will aid me against Sestihaculas." He paused. "Rise."

Pandrogas felt his limbs moving as though under the command of another mind—he stood, arms hanging limply at his side, eyes staring straight ahead. Waves of exhaustion caused his muscles to tremble.

He had gambled and lost—the revitalizing spell had taken its toll too soon, and his power had failed him just when he needed it most. And now Yasothoth had placed him under a geas—his will was no longer his own, and he knew he would obey unquestioningly every command the Lord of Scorpions issued him.

Amber was irretrievably lost to him now, if indeed she was still alive. Even if he were to come face to face with her, he could not attempt to rescue her or help her escape without being commanded to do so by Yasothoth. According to the strictures of the geas laid upon him, he could not even feed himself unless so ordered; if the Chthon willed it, he would die a slow death by starvation.

"I think this is unwise, my lord," Triasandela said abruptly. "I have had dealings with this sorcerer before—he is cannier by far than most mortals. Even the spell within which you have enwrapped him may not prevent him from somehow contriving mischief."

"You credit him with too much ability," the Lord of Scorpions replied. "He cannot break the geas. He will be my unsuspected weapon against Sestihaculas—and once the Lord of Snakes is destroyed, he shall aid me and the rest of the Chthons in wiping out this pestiferous race which, so you tell me, is the cause of our world's destruction."

Trisandela hesitated. "At least remove the heliolite. Should he find a way to use it—"

"Enough, Trisandela! Do not presume to give me advice!"

Pandrogas fought against despair during this exchange. He had no doubt but that the Chthon fully intended to wage all-out war on humanity—and that he would have to stand by Yasothoth's side during the holocaust unless he could find some way to break the spell that held him.

But, though he was free to think as he pleased, he could not speak the words and make the gestures that would free him from the geas. There seemed to be no hope.

"Come," Yasothoth said to Trisandela. "We have preparations to make. There is much you must tell me about the state of the world since last I ruled it."

The two Chthons left the sorcerer to the silence of the burial chamber and the desperation locked within his skull.

CHAPTER XVI

The Madwoman

Within the darksome caverns of Xoth, Sestihaculas, Lord of Snakes, summoned into his presence the cacodemon Taloroth.

"It has been more than a commonyear since Trisandela left Xoth to seek out Pandrogas," the ophidian ruler of the Chthons said. "She may have fallen before the sorcerer's magic or, knowing the Lady of Bats, she may be attempting to implement some devious scheme of her own. Seek her out and learn what you can."

Taloroth nodded and, unfolding his ribbed wings, vanished in a pillar of smoke.

Following the fading ectenic residue perceptible to senses most humans could not begin to comprehend, the cacodemon materialized in the shadow of a barbican on the sprawling gray roofscape of Darkhaven. Extending his awareness, he realized immediately that Trisandela was no longer within the vast structure, and neither was Pandrogas. When he attempted

to trace her subsequent route outside the boundaries
of reality, however, he found it closed to him—the
Lady of Bats had used a spell to prevent just such an
occurance. This in itself was suspicious.

It appeared, however, that the sorcerer Pandrogas
had also travelled by apportation in the recent past—a
feat of which the cacodemon had not known humans
were capable. Acting on intuition, Taloroth followed
Pandrogas's course.

This he had immediate cause to regret, because it
led him to a street in the city of Sarkeet on Zarheena,
in midday. Several passersby screamed and ran in
panic as the cacodemon appeared, roaring in pain
from the searing rays of the sun. He quickly sought
the shade of a nearby building and pondered what to
do next.

Like others of his kind, he was not particularly
adept at devising contingency plans. He had been
ordered by Sestihaculas to find Trisandela and had,
so far, been unable to do so. It seemed that the next
step was to return to the Demogorgon and explain
the situation. But Taloroth did not like to fail in his
master's eyes—the penalties could be severe. He
recalled the ancient warrens beneath the streets of
this city. There, at least, would be shelter from the
shrill screams of mortals and the deadly sunlight—a
much more congenial place in which to consider his
next move.

Accordingly, Taloroth moved himself at near-
instantaneous speed to a dark passageway far beneath the surface of Zarheena. Once he had done so,
he sensed a strong influx of power—stronger than
any of which he had previously been aware, save in
the presence of the Demogorgon. Intrigued, the cacodemon began to shamble along the nighted corridors, seeking the source of this sensation. It appeared
that he might have much, after all, to tell Sestihaculas.

*   *   *

Pandrogas had no idea how long he stood there in the absolute darkness of the chthonic pits. He could not move unless ordered to do so by Yasothoth, and so he stood, though his exhausted muscles begged for an opportunity to relax. Eventually, he knew, they would simply give out, and he would collapse to the stone floor.

He reviewed the circumstances that had brought him to this pass, feeling self-contempt like the sting of a lash. He had been instrumental in reviving Yasothoth, and unable to rectify that by destroying him—instead he had provided the Lord of Scorpions with himself as a weapon, and as a result of this, all who lived might eventually suffer. As bad as Sestiha-culas was, he at least took no action against humanity unless provoked. But Yasothoth, Pandrogas was convinced, intended to scourge the fragments, not stopping until every man, woman and child was dead.

In addition to all this, he had failed to rescue Amber. He had no idea what Trisandela or Yasothoth had done with her. Did she still live? If so, might she not be better off dead?

He could not move, but he could weep, and that he did, feeling hot and bitter tears on his cheeks, his chest wracking with the harsh sobs of a man who knows others will suffer because of his foolishness and ineptitude.

At that moment his painful introspection was interrupted—by something as overt as a noise, or merely by a subtle shift in air currents, he could not have said, but suddenly the sorcerer knew that he was no longer alone. Something had entered the burial chamber behind him—he could sense it moving, large but withal silent and agile, coming closer and closer to him.

Pandrogas was not a cowardly man, but to be trapped within one's own flesh, far underground and surrounded by enemies of a horrific and nonhuman nature, was enough to unnerve even the most courageous. Then his nostrils caught the faint scent of brimstone, and he realized that it was either one of the Chthons or a cacodemon who now stood behind him. He did not consider himself out of danger, however—Yasothoth would not harm him, but Trisandela, he knew, was not in favor of letting him live. Had she decided to risk the Scorpion Lord's wrath by having him killed surreptitiously?

The thing, whatever it was, moved slowly around in front of him—he heard claws scraping on basalt. Then, abruptly, a burst of yellow flame appeared, wrapped about the misshapen hand of a cacodemon. The flickering light illuminated the creature's tuberous features.

"Ah, Pandrogas," it said. "Do you not remember me—Taloroth, whom you bent to your will and forced to ferry you and your woman from Nigromancien to Darkhaven? I have not forgotten that insult."

Pandrogas was silent—the conditions of the geas did not give him leave to speak. The cacodemon smiled, revealing crooked fangs.

"I sense that someone has placed a spell of restraint upon you. This makes my task easier. My lord Sestihaculas had pledged to take no action against you, but he can hardly be faulted if I decide to bring you into his presence. I am sure he will have many questions for you . . ."

At that moment a lance of orange energy, dazzlingly bright in the darkness, struck the cacodemon squarely in the chest, knocking the creature backwards and eliciting a howl of rage and pain. Trisandela stepped within range of Pandrogas's vision, one hand upraised and still glowing with the force of her power. Taloroth cowered before her. "Mercy, Lady of Bats! I meant no disrespect—"

Trisandela's next gesture enveloped the cacodemon in a whirlwind of candent fire, cutting of his plea. The cacodemon screamed and, within a matter of moments, was reduced to a pile of charred bones on the stone floor.

The Lady of Bats then turned to face Pandrogas. He could see the gleam in her eyes from the light of her smouldering claw. After a moment, Trisandela said, "I can negate, to some degree, the effects of Yasothoth's geas, insofar as granting you autonomy of motion." She made a sign of power, and Pandrogas realized that his body was once more under his own control.

"You are still bound to obey the Scorpion Lord's direct commands," the Chthon cautioned. "But perhaps it will not come to that, if we act swiftly and decisively."

Pandrogas flexed his arms and legs and shrugged his shoulders to warm the stiff muscles. "Is this some new and devious form of psychological torture, milady?"

Trisandela stepped before him. "I am no longer in control of this situation," the Lady of Bats said. "Due to your interference Yasothoth is fully in command of himself, and there is no possibility of subjugating him to my will. It therefore seems appropriate that you aid me in destroying him."

"You do not wish to aid Yasothoth in his battle against Sestihaculas?"

"I have no great love for Sestihaculas, but better to see matters continue as they have been rather than to take the chance of their growing worse. I know where I stand with Sestihaculas. Yasothoth is now an unknown quantity."

Pandrogas nodded. It was an unlikely alliance, and yet, working together they had a better chance than working separately to destroy the Lord of Scorpions.

Trisandela feared Yasothoth—that much was plain. He could not see any way that she might be planning to betray him in order to curry favor with the other Chthon, since the latter already had the sorcerer completely within his power. He nodded.

"Very well. Where is Yasothoth now?"

"He sleeps. We must find a way to destroy him before he awakes."

Pandrogas said, "This will not be easy. Any preparation to kill him by magical means he would detect before we could strike. But there are ways to destroy a Chthon without using magic . . ."

Trisandela nodded. "The simplest way, of course, is by exposure to the sun's rays. This is not practical, considering our location. A blow through the heart with a weapon of iron or silver will also suffice. However, there is a complication: Yasothoth will sense our auras if we approach close enough to attempt such an action."

The sorcerer bowed his head for a moment in thought. "True enough—we cannot take the risk. If only there were someone with no training in magic whom we could trust to—"

"The assassin," Trisandela interrupted.

Pandrogas looked at her noncomprehendingly.

"Another human found us before you," the Chthon continued; "a paid assassin, from what little I have been able to learn from her. Evidently she came here by accident, and the sight of Yasothoth and myself was evidently more than her weak will could withstand—she seems to be quite insane now."

Pandrogas felt a chill of repugnance at the matter-of-fact tone with which the Chthon spoke of the breakdown of a human mind. If Trisandela noticed this, she made no mention of it. "Perhaps we can use her," she mused. "Her instability seems to have removed any resistance she might have to a geas . . ."

Pandrogas was aghast. "What a horrible concept! You are advocating sending a helpless madwoman to what will most likely be her doom!"

Trisandela looked at Pandrogas with glittering eyes. "There is little alternative, sorcerer. Consider what is in store for the rest of humankind should Yasothoth ascend to the throne of Xoth, and tell me whether or not the possible loss of one life is a worthwhile sacrifice.

"Further," she continued, "we are speaking not of some pitiful asylum inmate, but of a highly-trained and skilled murderess. Her reason may have been blasted, but her reflexes and instincts are still there. With her fear and irrationality controlled, she may well be the perfect foil for us."

Pandrogas started to speak again, and then was silent. Trisandela was right, loathe though he was to admit it. The stakes were such that virtually any means used to assassinate the Scorpion Lord would be justifiable. Trisandela regarded him with sardonic humor, then shifted her wings in what seemed to be a gesture indicating that the discussion was over.

"Come," she said. "We will prepare our weapon to strike," and she stalked from the burial chamber. After only a second's hesitation, Pandrogas followed her.

The Chthon led him to another, smaller chamber hewn from the ancient rock. As they entered the dark chamber, the sorcerer could hear a low, muffled moaning that set his teeth on edge. *"Limnus diam,"* he said quickly, and the resultant light showed him a woman, small and compactly built, with short black hair. She was wearing loose-fitting robes of white, and she huddled in one corner of the room, which was little more than a cell, rocking back and forth and crooning softly to herself.

Trisandela eyed the shivering form dispassionately.

"No time to waste," she said. "I will administer the spell, and—"

"No!" Pandrogas said sharply, stepping past her and kneeling before the madwoman. He lifted her head; her eyes, dark and flat as two pieces of coal, stared at him uncomprehendingly. "I will do it," he continued, not sure why it was important to him to do so. He rose and performed the proper gesticulations, speaking the necessary words in Payan, and felt gratified to see the rocking slowly stop, as the enforced calmness of the geas took over.

He looked at Trisandela. "You realize that the spell may not sit firmly upon her madness—we cannot program her as surely as if she were sane."

"There is no other candidate," the Lady of Bats replied. "It is a simple action she must perform, and one for which she is eminently suited. All will go well."

Pandrogas hoped that such would be the case. Any other outcome was too horrible to contemplate. He looked at the assassin. "Rise," he said gently. She did so.

"What is your name?" he asked her.

"Kyra." The word was as flat and emotionless as a drop of water striking a rock.

"There is a task you must complete, Kyra," Pandrogas said. He carefully and meticulously outlined the parameters of the assassination as he and Trisandela had discussed it. The plan was for her to stab the Scorpion Lord through the heart with a spike of iron, which they had obtained by means of a quick apportation to Zarheena. Pandrogas gave the weapon to the assassin—a short, dagger-like torsade broken from a gate. "Do you understand your mission?"

"I do."

Pandrogas nodded. He felt sorry for her—the possibility of her surviving the encounter with Yasothoth was infinitesimal. Even in his death throes the Chthon would be more than capable of annihilating a mortal, particularly one with no spells of protection at her disposal. But Trisandela, unfortunately, was right—better by far that this one person should die than that hundreds of thousands should be exterminated.

Trisandela gave the assassin detailed directions to the chamber in which Yasothoth slept. Kyra, the torsade gripped in her hand, exited, and the Lady of Bats glanced at Pandrogas. "Now we wait," she said.

"Now," said Pandrogas, "you will tell me what has happened to Amber—and woe betide you if she has come to harm."

Trisandela bared fangs in a smile. "You are bold, sorcerer, to threaten me here—or anywhere, for that matter. Nevertheless, I will tell you. The conjuress is evidently possessed of more power than I had suspected—she was able to circumvent my spell of containment and breach the pit in which I had incarcerated her. Yasothoth ordered a cacodemon sent in pursuit, but the brute brought back this woman instead. I do not know the fate of your paramour."

Pandrogas nodded, feeling an odd mixture of relief and concern. He was grateful to hear that Amber was no longer a prisoner, as he was, of the Chthons. But what possible new horrors did she face in the tangled network of this underground city?

There was no way that he could know—he could only hope that she had found her way to safety. For his own part, the next hour would, in all probability, tell his fate.

Trisandela squatted in a corner of the room, wings enfolding her, eyes lambent in the darkness. Pandrogas watched her. "If Kyra succeeds, and Yasothoth is returned to death," he said, "what, then, shall be my fate?"

Trisandela regarded him calmly. "We are partners of necessity and for the moment, sorcerer, no more than that. Do not lose sight of the fact that you were responsible for Yasothoth's premature quickening. By doing so, you ruined my plans—and I do not brook such interference lightly."

She closed her eyes and said nothing more. Pandrogas sat down; there was nothing to do but wait. He could not attack her or take her by surprise— the geas was still with him enough to prevent that. It seemed apparent that, no matter if Kyra succeeded or failed, his own doom was inevitable.

The spell Kyra was under insured that her feet would carry her stealthily along the corridor, which was dimly lit by starcrystal rods of such great antiquity that even their radiance had dimmed to a faint haze. She was aware of the nature of her task—to attempt to kill the Chthon Yasothoth. That she would fail she had not doubt—the monster, whose horrible eightfold gaze burned into her consciousness day and night, was indestructible, immortal—a primal force of evil. Before such a horror one could do naught but flee or prostrate oneself and pray for a speedy death, which she had not been granted.

Kyra wanted to scream, or to laugh—if she laughed loud enough and long enough, the terror that was such a part of her no longer seemed quite so frightening. But she had been commanded to perform her task as the consummate professional she had once been, and her training as an assassin had taken over to insure this.

She entered the chamber. There, on a raised slab of black stone, the enormous, armor-plated creature slept. Though its eyes were arranged on its head as a scorpion's, it had chosen—for reasons known only to itself—to cloak them with human-like lids while asleep.

It breathed by virtue of lungs—she could see the massive chest rise and fall. Trisandela had told her to strike the iron blade as though a human breast lay beneath her—evidently the location of the Scorpion Lord's internal organs was sufficiently similar to her own for that to be effective.

She stopped beside the rude bed, which was half as tall as she. Yasothoth was prone before her, a ridiculously easy target. Before, in a life governed by sane and normal universal laws, it would have been an easy matter to strike and be gone. But things were not so simply decided now. How could she hope to destroy such a powerful creature with a simple blade? How dare she even consider such a task? But there was no real choice left to her—the compulsion to strike overrode all uncertainty, all fear within her. The assassin watched her hand holding the iron blade raise and hover above the Lord of Scorpions as though it belonged to someone else.

The dim light reflecting off the plates of the exoskeleton was hypnotizing . . . hypnotizing and somehow strangely beautiful . . . Kyra realized, suddenly and with awful certainly, that she could not, *must* not, attempt this deed . . . she had been wrong, she saw that clearly now, as if blindness had been lifted from her . . . to strike would be blasphemous, for Yasothoth was in fact a god, a horrific and vengeful deity . . . but not to her eyes, for she was now finding it possible to view him as he really was, her mind unclouded by the petty prejudices of anthropomorphism . . . in fact, in his own way he was beautiful, an awesome engine of power and destruction . . . and her duty was not to kill him, but to serve him . . .

But she could not stop the downward plunge of the knife—the geas overrode her brain's frantic commands to her muscles—in an agony of frustration she did the only thing she could to attempt to prevent this sacreligious act—she opened her mouth and screamed.

She did not feel the pain as the chela closed about her wrist. She watched as the blade fall from her nerveless grasp, to shatter on the stone floor. It seemed to take an improbably long time for it to fall.

Then blackness enveloped her, save for the eight burning eyes of Yasothoth, which had always been before her and always would be.

CHAPTER XVII

Amber's Decision

"He is awake!"

Pandrogas started upright at Trisandela's words. The Lady of Bats' face was filled with inhuman fear—the only time Pandrogas had ever seen such an expression on a Chthon. Then, before he could say or do anything, she vanished.

Pandrogas staggered backward, coughing and feeling his eyes tear from the concentration of sulfurous smoke. He had not fully recovered when a shadow suddenly blocked the dim light from the corridor outside the chamber. The sorcerer turned and gasped in horror.

Standing in the arching entrance was Yasothoth, and beside him was Kyra. The assassin's eyes were vacant, her expression slack.

His inhuman gaze fixed on Pandrogas, Yasothoth stepped forward. "Trisandela has fled," he said. It was not a question.

Pandrogas nodded.

"It does not matter. There is no fragment remote enough to hide her from me. I will deal with her attempted betrayal in good time.

"As for you—" the Scorpion Lord picked up Pandrogas, his claw closing about the sorcerer's waist and lifting him from the floor, applying painful pressure on his ribs. "If I did not have need of you, your death agonies would last longer than your lifetime. But the geas I laid upon you still applies, and now Trisandela will not be around to subvert it.

"Sestihaculas must die immediately, before anything else can go awry." With these words, searing mist once more filled the sorcerer's eyes and nostrils, and he felt himself falling at unbelievable speed between the fragments . . .

When he opened his eyes again, the first thing he saw was what had once evidently been a town mansion. But only the stone chimney and foundations still stood, along with the lower brick walls; everything of wood and glass had been burned away by a fire that had evidently been so fearsome that only the rock and masonry remained.

Yasothoth dropped Pandrogas, and the sorcerer sprawled to his hands and knees next to Kyra. He stood slowly, looking about him in awe and disbelief.

All about them were the blasted and scorched remnants of what had once been a city. All traces of wood, along with any vegetation, had been reduced to ashes. Pandrogas had never seen a vision of such absolute and total devastation.

Yet this scene paled in comparison with what he saw when he lifted his head—for there, positioned "above" them and apparently near enough to reach out and touch, was the hellish surface of Xoth, its elsinorian jungles and morasses spread over the vault of the sky like some mad painting. Pandrogas could clearly see the black monolithic dwellings of the

Chthons and their servants and, to one side of the fragment, the brilliant stretch of arid land called the Cliffs of the Sun, where he had had his confrontation with Sestihaculas.

There was no doubt as to their location. Yasothoth had brought him and the assassin to the nameless fragment, the unknown land that shielded Xoth from the sun. The fragment pursued an orbit close enough to the burning orb to scorch the very rocks upon which he stood.

"Here we shall face Sestihaculas," Yasothoth said. "And before dawn strikes on this worldlet, we shall destroy him—or he us."

While Kan Konar and Mirren worked together to reconstruct the disassembled dragonboat, Amber searched for its runestone, which, according to the cloakfighter, had been hidden by the fragment's inhabitants—those called the Deathlings.

Letting herself sense the talisman's ectenic force and be drawn to it was easily accomplished. The pull of it led her down the gently-sloping declivity and into the perennially mist-shrouded forest. She had heard of the unfortunate inhabitants of this land; Pandrogas had spoken of them once. According to Kan Konar's descriptions of them, they were incapable of hiding the stone anywhere too inaccessible— the rigors of their affliction would prevent them from climbing trees or even lifting rocks to form a hiding place. Kan Konar seemed amazed that there were those among them who had been able to leave the fog and make what was to them an immense journey to his cave in order to steal the stone. It bespoke an awesome nobility and dedication to the task.

Farther thought was interrupted when a woman materialized suddenly out of the fog, swathed in

funereal garb and glowing like a revenant. Amber was
considerably taken aback.

The woman was surprised as well. "Who are you?"
she asked, her voice so soft as to be almost inaudible.
"How came you here?"

Amber spoke her name, recalling the cloakfighter's
caution against loud speech. She added, "You have
stolen a certain talisman from Kan Konar. I am here
to retrieve it."

The woman—from Kan Konar's description, she
had to be the one called Telice—made an almost
imperceptible gesture of negation. "We cannot allow
this," she said regretfully. Amber was aware periph-
erally of other figures now visible, surrounding her.
She lifted her hand, showing the ring of rank. "I'm
afraid you cannot stop me," she replied. "Do not try,
if you value your safety." She had no intention of
hurting any of them, of course, but she felt reasonably sure that Alozar's Cantrip of Confusion would
distract them long enough for her to take the runestone and go. She hoped it would not come to that,
however.

She was quite close to it, she knew. A vagrant
breeze shifted the mist, revealing the rough wall of a
clay and reed hut nearby, and Amber suddenly realized that the locus of power was within that hut.
Quickly she spoke an attrahent, and the runestone
burst through the wall and leaped across the intervening space to her outstretched hand.

She fully expected to have to defend herself against
the Deathlings after this action but, to her surprise,
none of them made a move. As though realizing that
they would have no chance of taking the stone away
from her, the plague victims simply stood there. At
length, Telice spoke again. Amber had to strain her
ears to hear the soft tones.

"It is evidently the will of the powers that be that
the cloakfighter leave this fragment. But be aware,

conjuress, that by helping him to do so, you may be helping also to spread this disease throughout what is left of the world."

Amber felt a chill run the length of her spine. "What do you mean?"

"He has been exposed at length to our contagion. We are not entirely certain how it is communicated. If he *is* a carrier . . ."

"I understand," Amber said slowly. It was, without a doubt, a moral quandary—the cloakfighter's dragonboat represented her only opportunity of resuming her search for Pandrogas, but by helping him escape from this fragment she might be unleashing a virulent epidemic.

Another, much more frightening thought occurred to her. How could she be sure that she herself had not contracted the disease simply by being on the fragment? The possibility caused Amber's breath to catch.

As though she had read the conjuress's thoughts, Telice said calmly, "We are not sure of how the disease is communicated—there is a possibility that even this slight exposure might be dangerous. That is why we sought to prevent the cloakfighter from leaving."

"Then every moment I remain here puts me in greater jeopardy," Amber replied. She turned then, and with no more words, started back uphill. The Deathlings parted their ranks to let her through.

"Tell him," she heard Telice say after her, "that I am sure he will find the final peace he seeks. Tell him he will be remembered here as long as one of us lives to light the pyre."

Amber did not reply to this; she kept walking, feeling more and more nervous, until at last she emerged from the cloud bank into the cold, clear air of the mountain slope.

Leaving behind the forest and the mist, which had

exacerbated her incipient claustrophobia, calmed her somewhat. She sat down, staring at the runestone in her hand, weighing the situation.

She reluctantly admitted to herself that, cowardly though it might be, she could not face the thought of self-exile here based on the remote possibility of her having been exposed to the Deathlings' plague. Thinking about it, she seemed to recall Pandrogas stating that the disease was incommunicable save by prolonged intimate contact. If this were true, then she, at least, need not be concerned about her safety.

The cloakfighter, however, was another matter. Only one solution occurred to her—she and Mirren could take the dragonboat and leave Kan Konar behind. The thought of such a betrayal sickened her. If he had not already taken the disease, to leave him here would almost insure that he would die from it eventually.

The question, then, was: was she willing to sacrifice the cloakfighter's life?

If it were a matter of trading his life for that of Pandrogas, then the issue would not be so difficult. But what she was considering—and it was hard to face the situation honestly—was abandoning Kan Konar so that she could have a remote chance of finding a man she had not seen for over a commonyear, who might not even still be alive.

And, if Pandrogas were still alive, was he indeed in need of rescue? Could she even be certain that he still loved her? No—she was sure of none of these things. She would simply be marooning Kan Konar in order that she and Mirren could escape.

But the alternative was to risk contacting the disease from him herself, as long as she remained even in casual contact with him—and possibly spreading it to others.

Amber stared at the runestone in her hand. She felt incapable of making a decision on this matter;

either choice seemed equally damning. Complicating the matter still further was the fact that she did not have the right to make a choice for Mirren. It was not up to her to condemn the wolf woman to a life of exile. With a sigh of confusion, she began walking slowly back toward the cloakfighter's cave, unsure what she would do when she got there.

In the back of the cave, Kan Konar lifted the lid of the chest and pulled out a cloak of dragon leather. He stood for a long moment in the darkness, hesitating—then, almost reluctantly, he draped the cinnamon-colored garment about his shoulders.

It was not made for fighting, of course—there were no measured stones weighting the ends, no deadly slivers of bone concealed in the hems. But his later training had been concerned with learning to fight and move while wearing different styles of cloaks, as well as none. He spun about once, feeling the distribution of its weight about him, sensing the play of its fold. The leather was heavy and yet supple—it would not be the worst of weapons.

It had been a year and more since he had worn any sort of mantle, save to sleep in during cold weather. He had fully intended never to wear a cloak again, since his own had been lost; to make do with some other garment was shameful to a warrior. But he would need every advantage where he was going. Honor mattered no longer—only expediency did.

He intended to use the power within the conjuress—the power he had heard about repeatedly from Beorn, and from Tahrynyar, and from Pandrogas—against Xoth. He had no plan as of yet—but he knew he could not turn away from the possibility of revenge for both himself and the Deathlings.

He thought of Telice, and wondered briefly if he should return for a farewell. He decided, reluctantly, against it. The Deathlings might try to restrain him, and he did not want to be put in a position of having to prevent them from such an attempt. It was better this way—though they might never know whether or not he accomplished his goal of revenge, that would not matter. He would know. He had a cause worth dying for once again, and that was all that mattered.

The cloakfighter turned and left the cave.

All too soon Amber came within sight of the cave. The reassembling of the chaseboat from the *Dark Horizon* was progressing well; standing in the shadow of a rocky overhang, Amber watched them working on it. He was wearing a cloak of dragon leather—this surprised her somewhat, since the weather was not particularly chill. Mirren, meanwhile, was stretching the leathern surfaces of the ship's wings taut over the supporting network of bone and sinew.

Now was the moment of decision—she could put it off no longer. Neither of them had seen her; from this vantage point she could strike, paralyzing the cloakfighter with a few well-chosen words, if such was her choice.

The conjuress raised her hand, then hesitated. There *had* to be another answer! But, cudgel her mind as she might, she could not think of what it might be. She closed her eyes, attempting to see Pandrogas's features before her, but his face remained resolutely unformed in her mind's vision.

Oddly enough, it was this inability to imagine the features of the man she loved that caused resolve to abruptly harden within her. It was as though all that she had been through since leaving Tamboriyon— indeed, in a sense, all that she had endured since that long-ago day when her dragonship had crashed into the roofscape of Darkhaven and Pandrogas had rescued her from the storm—seemed to well up from the depths of memory, bringing with it all the fear, hatred and resentment concomitant with those experiences. What did it matter if she found Pandrogas or not—or even if he still loved her or not? She had survived and triumphed over too much to let it end here, in such a meaningless fashion.

She would not inflict the possibility of the Deathlings' disease upon an unsuspecting population. But neither would she be bound to a life of exile on this remote fragment. Amber owed the cloakfighter nothing—in fact, he had been indirectly responsible for some of the misery and hardship that she had endured. It had been his decision to associate with the Deathlings and to expose himself to their illness— let him remain here, then, and carry on his self-appointed task.

She did not know what task Kan Konar wished her aid in accomplishing, and she did not care. While telling her and Mirren of his exile, he had spoken much of destiny and preordination. Amber was not sure what her destiny might be, but she was certain that it did not include remaining trapped here. And she would not allow the cloakfighter, or anyone, to be the cause of that.

She raised her hand again, this time with determination—and at that moment something struck her between the shoulder blades, hard enough to make her cry out with surprise and pain. She was driven forward a few steps, into the open. Before she could recover she was struck again—this time in the arm. She caught a glimpse of a furred and winged body streaking across the sky above her, followed by another, and another . . .

Bats.

A barrage of blows drove Amber to her knees. She looked up and saw the cloakfighter and the wolf woman under attack as well. The cloakfighter spun and wheeled, striking bats from the sky with the edge of the dragon cloak. But for every one he killed, ten more seemed to appear—the air about them was thick with the fluttering forms. Their shrill cries seemed to stab into her head. One bit her on the leg, and another on the arm. The pain and confusion made it impossible to concentrate long enough to speak a spell of dispersement.

The bats herded her forward until she stood with Kan Konar and Mirren. The three huddled together, trying in vain to avoid the myriad creatures. And then, suddenly, the attacks lessened. Looking up, Amber saw that the majority of the bats had gathered together in a vast, hovering swarm above the ground, circling, their shadows blocking the sun like a cloud. And then there was a sound like a crack of thunder, or the unfurling of enormous wings.

Within the shadow cast by the living cloud above, the stench of brimstone and a column of ebony mist announced the appearance of the Lady of Bats. She struck swiftly; Amber scarcely had time to recover from her astonishment before she felt herself engulfed in the foul-smelling smoke, just as had happened to her before when the cacodemon in Trisandela's service had appeared on the dragon-boat bearing her toward Darkhaven. Only this time, as she was spun away down a vertiginous tunnel of darkness, the last thing she heard was Trisandela's laughter.

After a journey that seemed to crowd the discomforts of a lifetime into the space of a few moments, the mists cleared. Amber found herself, along with Kan Konar and Mirren, standing on the crest of a hill that was bare scorched dirt. There was not so much as a single blade of grass to be seen—only the cinder-strewn ground.

"Wh-where are we?" Amber heard Mirren say, in a small voice quite unlike the lycanthrope's normal tone. It was Kan Konar who replied. "Back in hell," he said flatly, and pointed above them. Amber looked up and beheld the fragment of Xoth.

The cloakfighter looked at Trisandela with a grim smile. "I thank you, milady," he said. "I was unsure as to how to reach Xoth again. You have provided me with both the route to and the means for my revenge."

"You babble, mortal," Trisandela said. "I had no time to be selective in whom I brought here—otherwise, be assured you and the werewolf would not be here now. It is her I want," and the Chthon pointed to Amber. "Only she," the Lady of Bats continued, "has the power to aid me in the struggle that is to come. Look," and she pointed to an area near the close horizon of the nameless fragment, where Amber, squinting in the dim light, could just make out the remnants of what had once been a city.

"There Yasothoth has come, and there he will face Sestihaculas in battle—a battle that will determine, among other things, whether your race lives or dies."

BOOK IV

The Nameless Fragment

The cape is his tool, and it seems a thin protection from death; yet in the hands of a master the cape is more than cloth, it is a thing of great power."

—Carlos Perito,
Suit of Light

burst into flame. Pandrogas saw several cacodemons flitting across the fragment like ungainly insects, sev-

CHAPTER XVIII

Heliopolis

In the eternal twilight atop the black cliffs on the fragment of Xoth, Sestihaculas brooded. Taloroth the cacodemon had not returned from his mission—this, in itself, seemed to constitute proof that some sort of chicanery was taking place on the part of Trisandela. Perhaps, the Demogorgon mused, the time had come for him to investigate personally.

He had made a pledge long ago not to enter Darkhaven, but he was confident that he could discover Trisandela's trail from another point. Accordingly he let his awareness extend into the interstices between the physical points of location in the world, seeking the ectenic spoor that she had left. Only the most recent of her journeys were still appreciable to him, and these indicated that the Lady of Bats had travelled from Darkhaven to the fragment of Zarheena, and from thence . . .

Sestihaculas frowned. The trail, though recent, was not clear; it was as though someone or something

had obfuscated it by sorcerous means. Further, he
had the impression that Trisandela was not alone in
her journeys, though who had accompanied her was
likewise unclear. He retained the distinct sense, however, that a locus of great magical power was involved.

It was then that a thought occurred to him that
chilled the Serpent Lord's blood. Zarheena—it was
there, deep within the Chthon's ancient warrens,
that Yasothoth had been entombed.

Even as the Demogorgon prepared to apport to
the location to discover if his greatest fear was true,
there appeared before him Daimar the cacodemon.
In stammering, fearful tones, the creature told him
that Yasothoth lived, and issued the challenge of the
Lord of Scorpions.

Sestihaculas nodded slowly in grim realization.
This, then, had been Trisandela's plan—to ressurect
the Chthon whom he had overthrown eons before
and set the Demogorgons against each other in battle. There was no choice—the other Chthons would
quickly learn of the thrown gauntlet and demand
that he pick it up. To not do so would demonstrate
weakness, and such an action would severely under-
mine his authority.

He looked somberly at Daimar, who cringed, expecting to receive a destroying burst of scarlet flame
for being the unfortunate chosen to convey the mes-
sage. Instead, the Demogorgon merely said, "Tell
Yasothoth that I will come."

Daimar nodded, relieved, and vanished. Sestihaculas looked up at the silhouette of the nameless
fragment that shielded Xoth from the deadly sun. He
knew that Yasothoth had planned some form of
trickery—he also knew that he had no time to form
contingency plans of his own. To do so would be
construed as being fearful.

He regretted that there had not been the opportu-

nity to see Pandrogas grovel before him in defeat.
Such a desire seemed almost petulant now.

With that thought, the Lord of Snakes allowed
himself to vanish in a column of smoke and fire.

The cloakfighter wrapped himself within the supple leather of the dragoneer's mantle. It was strange
to be wearing such a garment again after all this
time; particularly since its balance and weave felt
wrong to him. It would serve as a weapon, however,
if one was needed. Of that he was sure.

Even so, he was tempted to doff it, at least temporarily, for even though the thickness of the fragment
shielded them from the sun, it was still astoundingly
hot. He felt perspiration trickling down his back and
beading on his forehead. The temperature was a
grim harbinger of what it would be like when the sun
rose over the close horizon.

He and Mirren followed at a discreet distance the
Lady of Bats and the conjuress. They made their way
through a landscape that was, in its own way, even
more hellish than Xoth. At this point in its orbit the
nameless fragment was close enough to the sun to
ignite wood. Kan Konar's imagination needed no
prompting to visualize what the light would do to
frail human flesh.

He glanced at the wolf woman who paced beside
him. She had seemed brash and obnoxious when he
had first encountered her on the fragment of the
Deathlings; now she was subdued, fearful for her
life. No matter who won in this upcoming battle of
titans, it was obvious that she would lose. The
cloakfighter felt sorry for her, in an abstract way; she
was one of the few innocents who had become involved in this complicated struggle through no fault
of her own.

As for himself, he felt a fierce desire to see, finally,
an end to the quest he had set himself upon so long

ago. He had struggled back from death to life, and one way or another, the battle would soon be over. He had no idea as yet what means he would utilize to gain revenge for both himself and the Deathlings, but that a way would be presented he had no doubt. The gods were cruel, but they could not be so cruel as to deny him consummation at long last.

They had reached, finally, the outskirts of the buildings. Trisandela stopped, as did Amber. The Lady of Bats then turned to face Mirren and Kan Konar.

"I can take no chances of any outside interference at this point," she said, "even from those with no magical abilities. Yasothoth *must* be defeated—that is all that matters." She levelled her burning gaze upon the wolf woman and the cloakfighter and continued, "Therefore, you must die."

She raised a hand glowing with power. Mirren shrank back with a cry against the cloakfighter, who raised the folds of his garment in an instinctive and futile gesture of defense—and then Amber stepped between the Chthon and her victims. "No!" she said sharply to Trisandela. "If you want my help, you will cause them no harm."

The Lady of Bats eyed Amber narrowly. "I could ensorcell you and thus insure your cooperation—"

"You know it is better if you do not," the conjuress replied calmly. "I will aid you freely, and with full possession of my powers and my abilities, if you will leave them alone. They are no part of this."

Trisandela hesitated, then lowered her hand. The talons that tipped the fingers clicked against one another with an impatient sound. "Very well."

Amber turned to the cloakfighter and Mirren. "Go now," she said softly. "If I survive this, I will do my best to see you safely off this fragment."

Kan Konar bowed slightly. "Your intervention is appreciated, Conjuress." He stepped back and watched as Mirren and Amber looked at each other somewhat hesitantly. He had sensed a tension between the two of them since first they arrived at his cave. But now Mirren abruptly and impulsively stepped forward and hugged Amber. "I never truly realized how brave you are," she said. "Be careful—for your sake as well as ours."

The conjuress nodded—she seemed, for a moment, near tears. Then she turned back to the Chthon. "I am ready," she told Trisandela.

Kan Konar took the wolf woman's arm and pulled her away. They stepped behind the length of a wall that had once marked the boundary of a manor's grounds. Lying on the ground near their feet, baked brittle by the sun, was the brown skull and part of a ribcage of some long-dead inhabitant of the forgotten city. The heel of Kan Konar's boot brushed against the skull, which promptly collapsed to powder.

"What do we do now?" Mirren was trembling, glancing apprehensively this way and that as though expecting to see an army of cacodemons materialize from the scorched and skeletal remnants of the buildings around her. "There's no way we can escape— soon it will be dawn and then we'll burn, we'll burn like paper dolls in a furnace—"

"Calm yourself." He spoke quietly, but she reacted to something in his tone as she might have a blow across the face. She looked at him warily, as though realizing suddenly just how dangerous he could be.

"I have no desire to leave this fragment," he continued. "My one purpose is to find a way, somehow, to destroy Xoth and all its inhabitants. My hope is that, should Amber survive this upcoming conflict, that I can somehow use the power within her to accomplish this."

"This is insanity," the werewolf said slowly, staring at him. "What you want is impossible—"

"I have spent the last few commonyears accomplishing the impossible," Kan Konar interrupted. "I see no reason to stop now. Somehow I will find a way to do this. I owe it, not only to myself, but to the Deathlings."

Mirren raised a hand in an agitated gesture, brushing back her hair. "Madness. From what you've told me of the Deathlings, they want only to live out their days in peace. They've put aside their thoughts of revenge—as had you, for a time. You were better off then."

Kan Konar only half-heard her words, however—he was staring at the ring on her hand. Embedded within a base of resin was a sliver of stone, and it glowed with a blue-white light, faint but still quite visible in the gloaming. He took her hand, staring curiously at the ring. "Why is it glowing?" he asked. "What does it signify?"

She pulled her hand from his. "Amber told me that the ring is made from a fragment of a runestone," she said. "It evidently reacts this way whenever one is nearby. The sorcerer Thasos used it to seek out runestones for his—"

She stopped in shock as he grabbed her hand again, twisting the ring from her finger and wresting a cry of pain from her as well. Holding it up, he turned this way and that, studying the way the glow waxed and waned. "The runestone," he murmured, when he had determined the direction in which the glow was brightest. Then he glanced overhead at Xoth, noticing in particular the thin line of blinding sunlight at one edge that marked the Cliffs of the Sun. "Yes, of course!"

He turned and started down what was left of the lane, following the glow of the ring. He heard Mirren running after him. "Wait! What are you doing?"

Kan Konar looked at her over his shoulder, his teeth bared in a grin no less feral than the snarl of her wolfish alter ego. "You have granted me the means to accomplish my revenge, wolf woman," he said.

"I don't understand! What do you mean?"

"The runestone," he replied. The ring's light had led him to the fissile walls of what had once, evidently, been a temple. He moved up the steps. "The lynchpin of this nameless fragment. It will be the tool of my revenge!"

He turned and plunged into the darkness and relative coolness of the temple's interior, with Mirren close behind him. Inside was as barren as the rest of the city; only a few piles of ashes remained to mark where wooden benches and tables had once stood. Kan Konar moved quickly past these, following the increasing luminescence of the ring, which lead him to the nave of the structure.

A stone altar stood on a raised platform. He braced himself, pushing against it with all his strength, and it slowly rocked backward, revealing a dark aperture beneath its base. The glare of the ring was blinding now; it cast eerie highlights as he reached into the hole and felt the tingle of power as his fingers closed around the small, smooth stone.

He held it up triumphantly, showing the black rock to Mirren. "If I can find a way to destroy this," he said, "then this fragment will shift in its orbit and the sun will scour the surface of Xoth, burning away those loathsome forests and destroying the Chthons and their cacodemons." He laughed, feeling a wine-like rush of triumph fill his soul. For the first time since escaping from Zhormallion's web, he was truly alive.

It was then that the attack came from the shadows about him.

Her master had spoken, and so she must obey. There was no question of that; even had she not been ensorcelled with a geas, she would have offered no resistance to his orders. For he was Yasothoth, Lord of Scorpions, soon to be ruler of what remained of the world, and she was fortunate enough to be his servitor. He had not killed her when he might have, when he had been most certainly justified in so doing. Now her life was his, utterly and completely.

Kyra felt the sense of fulfillment that comes with total abdication of one's self. Faintly, in the dim far reaches of the chaos that had once been her mind, the echoes of the terror she had felt still reverberated. But by the time it reached the forefront of her consciousness it had been transmuted by her madness into servile awe and adulation. She would die happily for Yasothoth—could, in fact, think of no more sublime or fulfilling way to meet her end.

The Lord of Scorpions had ordered her to make sure that no surprise attack came from any unsuspected quarter while he prepared for his final confrontation with Sestihaculas. She had prowled the immediate area of the city, using all the ingrained talents of her profession to move like a shadow among shadows down the nighted streets, searching for signs of danger to her lord. She had seen the flash of light from the ring that the cloakfighter carried and had followed him and the wolf woman, whom she recognized vaguely through the mists of her madness. And had waited for the opportune moment to attack . . .

Kan Konar caught the barest flicker of moment from the depths of one of the shadowy corners. Long years of practice and conditioning took over, and he whipped his cloak up and across his body just in time to feel the impact of what seemed to be a small throwing knife as it caught in the folds of the garment. Then he was moving, spinning in the direction of the attack, the dragoneer's cloak fanning out from him in a manner calculated to be confusing and distracting to his enemies.

The light of the ring illuminated the dark corner, but, to his astonishment, there was no one there. Whoever had attacked him had faded into the shadows as quickly as he had moved to meet him. Kan Konar dropped into a defensive crouch, looking quickly in various directions. The posture would only be marginally effective, since the dragon leather, though tough, did not have the same ability to turn a knife's blow as his own cloak had.

He looked down at its folds and saw the weapon he had been attacked with; not a throwing knife, as he had suspected, but a tiny quarrel no longer than the width of his hand. He looked about again. He was alone in the large, empty chamber; Mirren had evidently fled when the attack came. A sensible reaction, one small part of his mind commented. He would be wise to do the same. His reflexes were swift enough to block the flight of a knife, but there was no way save by luck that he could continue to protect himself from these small arrows.

Accordingly, he began to move, making his way toward the entrance in a complicated and hypnotic dance, weaving the folds of his cloak around him to present a difficult target. He was almost to the door when another arrow struck—this one he felt pierce his tunic, grazing the skin just above a rib. Then he was outside, where at least there was room to maneuver and cover to be had.

The cloakfighter still clutched the runestone in one hand; now he quickly transferred it to an inner pouch in his clothing. His fingers gathered the edges of the cape even as he wished he had weighted the ends of the garment with rocks inserted in the hems. As a weapon, this cloak was pitifully inadequate—still, it was all he had.

There was no sign of an enemy—the avenue was

utterly quiet and still. Whoever had attacked him preferred skulking about in shadows to a direct confrontation. Kan Konar felt a surge of contempt—a warrior's reaction to such cowardly tactics. If he could just catch a glimpse of his adversary, force him into a face-to-face confrontation, he had no doubt of the outcome.

The merest breath of movement alerted him; only in the silence of this dead city would be have heard the whisper of fabric on flesh. He spun about, hands raised in a defensive posture—

Mirren crouched in the shell of what had once been a recessed doorway across the street, staring at him fearfully.

With a muttered curse he turned again, but it was too late—the momentary lapse in vigilance had been the opportunity that his adversary needed. Even as he noted a blur of movement from the other side of the street, he felt a blaze of pain erupt along the side of his head, and darkness subsumed the world.

CHAPTER XIX

Confrontation

In another part of the forgotten metropolis, Yaso-thoth and Pandrogas stood together in the ruins of what had once been a vast coliseum. The sorcerer waited passively, arms at his side, unable to resist whatever order the Chthon might give him.

Kyra had already received her instructions; Yaso-thoth had told her to patrol the city and deal with any danger that might conceivably threaten. Pandrogas could not conceive of any reason for such danger to exist, but Yasothoth was evidently as inhumanly cautious and suspicious as the vermin he espoused. The sorcerer had no doubt that, if the Scorpion Lord had not thought Kyra's presence necessary, the assassin would now be a dry dead husk in the tunnels of Zarheena.

Only a moment before, Pandrogas had watched Yasothoth dispatch Daimar to issue an ultimatum to the Demogorgon. Given the Chthonic means of travel, Sestihaculas would in all probability arrive momen-

245

tarily to do battle for the rulership of Xoth. Yasothoth
was obviously aware of this also, for now he turned
and looked down at Pandrogas. "Secrete yourself in
some advantageous part of this structure," he instructed the sorcerer. "From there you will observe
the battle and, at the appropriate moment, do whatever must be done to turn it in my favor, if such is
needed. Sestihaculas defeated me once—I will not
see it happen again."

Obediently, Pandrogas turned and started toward
what had once been the walls of the arena. The air
was hot, a dry, baking heat that ominously presaged
the day that would soon arrive. Pandrogas remembered how hot it had been on the Cliffs of the Sun,
that tiny area of Xoth unprotected by shadow. Given
the angle at which the fragment of hell lay, the sun's
rays fell obliquely across it; even so, they had still
been powerful enough to turn the cliffs into a barren
wasteland.

Whatever the outcome of the clash between the
two Demogorgons, the sorcerer knew that his fate
was sealed. Whether he was destroyed by one of the
two Chthons or left to be reduced to cinders at the
dawn mattered little. He could envision no scenario
that did not lead to his death.

Oddly enough, the prospect no longer frightened
or depressed him—whether it was an effect of the
geas, or simply because he had faced death for so
long in so many ways, Pandrogas's capacity to care
seemed to have been eradicated. He no longer had
any control over his destiny; in effect he had already
died, although his death was, so far, incomplete.
However, the sorcerer knew that that would be rec-
tified very soon.

His one regret was that he had not been granted
the opportunity to see Amber again, to tell her that
he still loved her. He hoped that she had not been

too disappointed when he had failed to make their rendezvous on Tamboriyon. He had no doubt that she had pursued her studies on mantology to good effect—she might even have reached the rank of conjuress by now. It was good to imagine her happy and content in her new life; Pandrogas hoped it would be a long one, and that the rapidly increasing disintegration of the fragments' orbits would not adversely affect it. A pity that their story could not have had a happy ending, as so many childrens' fables did.

Pandrogas made his way up a flight of steps leading to the tiered seats. It was hard to imagine this blasted husk of a city as being once filled with people. Various sports and events had thrilled thousands within this coliseum once—now, not even shadows disturbed the ruddy twilight.

He saw where he could best hide and fulfill Yasothoth's orders—an arched entrance near the top. From here he could view the entirety of the arena and strike when and if necessary.

The heliolite was warm in the palm of his right hand—the perspiration beneath it made his skin itch. He recalled the moment of awe, almost fear, that he had felt when he had willed the ectenic force within him through the focusing properties of the gemstone. It had been a rush of strength, a sense of invincibility second only to what he had felt when he had allowed the power of the dead to fill him. And this focusing element was only one of three; he felt almost dizzy as he contemplated the devastating force that could be released through all of the heliolites used in conjunction, particularly if the energy being channeled was that of the dead. Could any mortal flesh survive such searing power?

It seemed fairly obvious that he would never find out. Pandrogas reached the secluded spot he had picked and and, as he did so, caught a glimpse of a crimson flash from the corner of his eye. He turned in time to behold the dissipating column of smoke that announced the arrival of Sestihaculas on the nameless fragment.

There was no time spent in preamble. The sorcerer shielded his eyes as red fire warred with white. Almost immediately the smell of ozone was sharp in the atmosphere around him, and he felt the reverberations of the conflict between Yasothoth and Sestihaculas transmitted through the tons of stone that separated him from them. The sound was like the thunder of a summer storm; the amount of odylic energy being expended by the two Chthons was almost beyond his comprehension.

Squinting against the dazzling light, Pandrogas tried to determine which of the two Demogorgons was getting the better of the battle. At first it was difficult to determine—the glare of their magic and the distance to which he had removed himself reduced both Chthons to little more than dimly-glimpsed silhouettes in the coruscating brilliance. Gradually, however, as his eyes became accustomed to the glare, he was able to follow the course of the struggle.

Sestihaculas appeared to have the upper hand already—the advantage of strength, both brute and mystical, had been his when they fought eons before, and it did not appear to have changed now. The Serpent Lord was quicker than the Scorpion Lord as well—Pandrogas saw Sestihaculas dodge a blow from Yasothoth's curving tail which struck the shiny floor of the arena with a force sufficient to leave cracks that radiated for ells in all directions. Sestihaculas then countered with a blazing sphere of ectenic force that knocked the Scorpion Lord sprawling; the concussion sent the sorcerer reeling backward several steps.

Against his will, or rather without it, Pandrogas stepped forward, raising his right hand, his fingers crabbed in a sigil of significance. He could feel his power gathering, compressing to a single lance of deadly intensity, as he murmured the words of a cantrip. Such a blast, striking the Lord of Snakes from behind, would easily distract and weaken him long enough for Yasothoth to destroy him.

Another moment, and Yasothoth would be the new ruler of Xoth—and however many years were left to the remnants of humanity clinging to the world's fragments would be spent hiding in abject terror from the demonic ferocity of the Scorpion Lord. His would be the hand that made all of this possible—and there was nothing he could do to stop it.

He extended his arm, feeling the heliolite pulsing with barely restrained energy—and then, from behind, he heard a voice cry out his name.

Amber's ability to sense magical loci had led her unerringly to the coliseum. Trisandela, she knew, was somewhere close behind her, but the Lady of Bats did not intend to show herself unless absolutely necessary. Amber was to be the first line of offense—her power, strategically used, could tip the scales in favor of the Serpent Lord.

She paused a moment before climbing what had once been stairs that led to the top of the edifice. It had been only slightly over an hour since she had decided to maroon Kan Konar on the fragment of the Deathlings in order to save herself and Mirren. The appearance and subsequent actions of Trisandela had left her no time to reflect on her decision—but now the realization of what she had intended to do suddenly welled up within her, bringing her to a stop. Has she really been capable of such a choice? Would

she have carried it out? Deep within, Amber had no
doubt that she would have. It was her first realization, or perhaps admittance, of the changes, the
hardening, that the adventures and privations she
had gone through had wrought within her. She could
no longer think of herself as a person basically altruistic in nature; she may have been that person once,
but apparently she was no longer.

When had this hardening begun? When had this
inner cold core which she had only now recognized
within herself begun to grow? Had it been the first
time Amber had realized that Pandrogas was not the
perfect love, the perfect man that she had idolized
and fantasized about? Or had it happened sometime
during her studies on Tamboriyon? She had taken a
lover there, after all—she had not remained true to
Pandrogas's memory. At the time it had seemed an
innocent enough diversion—looking back on her affair with Zerrad now, however, Amber felt ashamed,
as though she had somehow been unfaithful to the
sorcerer.

She felt momentarily paralyzed by the overwhelming nature of her self doubts. Had her decision to
abandon the cloakfighter to the Deathlings' disease
been made because she was determined to find
Pandrogas at all costs, or simply because she was
afraid of contracting the affliction herself? Did she
really love Pandrogas—had she ever really loved him?
Had she set sail in the Abyss in order to seek him, or
merely to escape from what had become an uncomfortable situation with Zerrad? She had no answer for
these and for other questions.

She had agreed to aid Trisandela freely if the Lady
of Bats would spare the lives of Kan Konar and
Mirren. But was this evidence of true concern on her
part, or merely an attempt to make reparation for
her earlier intentions? Amber felt suddenly weary.

This was not the time for such self examination. She could see the horizon beginning to brighten; all too soon the destroying dawn would sweep over the city. There would be time for such scrutiny later—if she survived.

At that moment, she sensed the first blow in the struggle between the two Chthons; she could feel it vibrate within her mind as well as faintly hear the crackling conflict of forces from inside the coliseum. The conjuress hurried up the stairs. Just past the archway at the top she could see the figure of a man limned against the flickering red and white light. She had no time to be surprised at the unexpected presence of another human within this dead city, for as she reached the final step he turned, raising his right hand, which glowed with auric fire.

Amber stopped, her astonishment and shock nearly sufficient to cause her to faint.

"Pandrogas!"

Pandrogas spun about. For an instant it seemed that he had surely lost his mind, even as Kyra had; for before him, no more than ten yards distant, stood Amber. So astonished was he to find her in this remote and blasted locale that for a moment he did not recognize her, and for a moment after that he felt caught in the throes of some strange, waking dream. Amber could not be here; therefore, he must be either hallucinating or insane.

They both stood frozen, gaping at each other; Pandrogas could tell by the expression on her face that she was just as stunned as he was, and it was this, oddly enough, that convinced him of her reality. A phantasm of his mind would, it seemed to him, be more in control of the situation.

Before he could move or say anything, however, another spell cast by one of the Chthons below caused the entire structure beneath them to shudder slightly. Amber's expression changed to one of concern. "We have to stop Yasothoth!" she cried, and, stepping forward, raised both hands in the beginning gesture of Malrai's Lance of Light.

It was then that Pandrogas knew despair; a sensation of helpless horror that surpassed any he had ever felt before, even during the time he had faced Sestihaculas on the Cliffs of the Sun, or when he had waited for Darkhaven to strike the fragment of Oljaer. "Amber!" he cried. *"No!"* But even as he warned her, he could feel his own power gathering once more, and he was helpless to prevent it. Everything he was experiencing seemed to slow down to a glacial crawl; he watched as though a passive spectator as Amber turned toward him, her expression at first questioning, then disbelieving, and finally horrified, as he pointed the glowing surface of the heliolite at her. In that instant he would have gladly turned it on himself, or hurled himself from the top of the wall to the streets below. But he could do neither of these things; he could only watch helplessly as the geas of Yasothoth forced him to launch a blinding ray of ectenic force at the woman he loved.

Amber's shock was sufficient to slow her reaction; she could only stare in helpless disbelief as the blinding force erupted from the strange jewel that Pandrogas wore on the palm of his right hand and struck her, hurling her backward. She hit the wall of the archway with enough force to drive the breath from her, and even in the extremity of her bewilderment and fear she realized that Pandrogas had used only the merest fraction of his power against her. But *why?* Why had he attacked her?

As though through a darkening tunnel she stared up at him. She could see the sorrow and desperation on his face. His arm was still extended; the jewel, which she recognized now as one of the legendary heliolites, still roiled with golden light.

"A—geas," he managed to gasp with great effort. "Yasothoth . . . I must protect him . . ."

She understood, then. She tried to move, to stand, and cried out—the flash of pain in her side told her that a rib must be broken. That was the least of her worries now, however. It was obvious that Pandrogas was attempting, with every fibre of his being, to resist the influence of the geas—and just as obvious that he was failing. The Scorpion Lord's will was simply too strong. She would have to fight back or be destroyed.

Accordingly, she shouted the words of Yattai's Rings; bands of bright blue force wrapped about the sorcerer, binding his arms to his sides. Only for an instant, however; with the words of an appropriate counterspell, Pandrogas caused them to evaporate into the murky air.

She knew then that she had little chance of survival. Her intrinsic power was stronger than his, but he had much greater experience in how to use it; even though his reaction time was slowed somewhat by the geas, he was still her superior in skill. In addition, he had the focusing and enhancing properties of the heliolite to rely upon. It would only be a matter of time before she was destroyed by the man she loved.

Another, stronger tremor rocked the stadium, causing them both to lose their balance momentarily. Amber stole a glance down at the two Demogorgons, who were still locked in savage combat. They stood braced against each other now, claws and chelae straining against each other's shoulders, while flashes of red and white force crackled about them. Immediately beyond the far wall a single tower rose, high enough to seemingly impale the fragment of Xoth that floated like an inverted bowl above them. The tower was dark against the growing baleful glow of the impending dawn.

The battle between Serpent Lord and Scorpion Lord would have to end, and soon, or the sun would destroy them both. Accordingly, she and Pandrogas could waste no more time in their struggle. Amber looked back at the sorcerer and saw that he had been momentarily distracted by the struggle below as well. Now was the moment in which to strike. The training she had received from Ratorn left no doubts as to the decision she should make. To attempt to immobilize or imprison Pandrogas again would be foolhardy in the extreme—should she fail, she would lose her precious advantage of surprise.

All of this flashed through her mind in the merest of instants; already she could see him beginning to turn back toward her.

Ratorn had once shown her a spell called simply the Devastator; it was one of the most powerful destructive spells known to a sorcerer. He had demonstrated it once as part of a discussion of what she would learn when she attained the tenth ring. It had reduced a stone piling the size of a horse to gravel. He had not intended that she learn it; her remarkably retentive abilities, however, had made it possible for her to memorize the moves and phrases of the spell upon one viewing. Like most very powerful spells, it was quickly and efficiently performed; the opening lines of the cantrip served to effectively paralyze one's opponent for annihilation.

Unbidden now, this spell came to Amber's mind, full and complete. Though she had only practiced it a few times in the privacy of her quarters, never completing it for fear of the destruction it would unleash, she knew now that she could use it on Pandrogas before he could renew his attack.

All this, in the fleeting moment that he glanced down at Sestihaculas and Yasothoth. The decision had to be made in the fraction of a second remaining to her: Would she use this spell against Pandrogas?

If she did not, he would surely kill her. And then he would insure that Yasothoth triumphed over Sestihaculas, and then would begin a reign of horror and destruction unlike any seen since the Shattering.

If she destroyed Pandrogas, she would then be free to strike against Yasothoth and grant Sestihaculas the victory. The status quo would be maintained, and humanity would never realize how near the end had come.

It was that brutally clear. All of mankind on one side of the scales—and on the other, the man she loved.

Amber Jaodana Chuntai Lhil, late the Marquise of Chuntai, now a conjuress in the Taggyn Saer system, made her decision.

Pandrogas had already raised the heliolite to use again. Amber raised her own hands, and then a shroud of glowing orange engulfed him, becoming a solid and impenetrable sheath that began to tighten around him. He would be crushed, Amber knew, before he could bring his own power to bear on it.

Shock immobilized her for an instant that seemed an eternity—then she turned and beheld Trisandela, both hands upraised and glowing with force, standing at the top of the stairs.

"Now!" she cried to Amber. "Use your power against Yasothoth—*now!*"

Without thought, without consideration for the consequences, Amber struck. She willed all of her strength and ability into the words and motions of the Devastator. But her target was not Yasothoth—it was the Lady of Bats.

Caught off-guard, with her own power enwrapped in the destruction of Pandrogas, Trisandela had no

defense. She had time for a single scream as the spell
enveloped her in blue flame. Amber barely had time
to draw a breath before the Chthon was transformed
into a slowly-settling fall of greasy ashes.

The implementation of the destructive spell had
only taken an instant, but it had been long enough—
when she turned back to face Pandrogas, he was
already on his feet. He stared at her, his face stricken,
pale with the realization that he could not stop himself from striking.

That was the last thing she saw before golden light
consumed her vision.

CHAPTER XX

Holocaust

Kan Konar regained consciousness slowly. He was first aware of a throbbing pain along his left temple. He attempted to raise his hand to investigate the injury, and realized then that both his arms were tightly bound behind him. The shock of this knowledge served to clear his head somewhat.

He looked around. He was in a small, barren chamber—evidently some sort of solar room, from the circular shape and large openings that had once been window. Shards of faceted glass laced the edges of some of the windows, and a stairwell ended at a doorway near him. Over the cityscape visible through one of them, he could see the horizon, which was the shade of freshly-spewed lava.

His cloak had been carelessly thrown against a wall nearby. Against the opposite wall stood a small, wiry woman dressed in the pale, loose-fitting garb of one of the Guild With No Hall. He had heard of them: a cult of assassins on the fragment of Zarheena. On the back of her right hand was a tiny arbalest. This, obviously, was the one who had attacked him in the temple of the runestone. The thought of the stone drew the cloakfighter's attention to it; he shifted his weight minutely and was relieved to feel its weight press against him within the inner pocket of his garb.

The assassin looked at him and nodded. There was a strange fixed quality about the stare with which she regarded him. "You are awake," she said. "Good. Here we will wait, you and I, until Lord Yasothoth can spare the time to decide what to do with you."

Kan Konar did not deign to reply. In common with most of his class, he felt a deep and abiding contempt for those who killed by night and shadow instead of facing their opponents as warriors. It seemed that there was no end to the indignities that he was to suffer; now, in addition to failing to avenge his master so long ago, he had been bested by this vermin.

His silence did not seem to impress the assassin, who continued to talk. There was a nervous aspect to her speech; something in it, combined with the way she regarded him, made the cloakfighter abruptly quite sure that the assassin's mind was unsound.

"I could have killed you myself," she continued, "quite easily. Your skill with the cloak means nothing to me. But it remains for the Lord of Scorpions to decide your fate—I am privileged to be only his instrument. When he has disposed of Sestihaculas, then he will determine your fate. And perhaps he will look favorably upon me."

The mingled awe and horror in her tone as she spoke chilled the cloakfighter. He felt quite sure that it had been Yasothoth who had somehow been responsible for the woman's madness. However, mad or no, she was still a formidable opponent.

Further speech was cut short by a strange sound from outside—a continuous crackling, something like the crumpling of parchment or the sound of twigs being consumed by a fire, and yet not exactly that. He heard also rumblings that were similar to thunder; some of these were strong enough to vibrate the stone beneath him. Coterminious with these sounds was an odd flickering light, alternately crimson and pale as milk and occasionally blinding in its intensity, that radiated from the twilight below the level of the room's windows.

The assassin looked down at the city below and smiled. "It has begun," she said.

Kan Konar realized that the lights and sounds came from the battle between the two Demogorgons of which Trisandela had spoken. The fate of humanity would be settled by the outcome of this conflict, but that did not concern him. He had only one goal: to somehow destroy the runestone of the nameless fragment. Once this was accomplished, the orbit of the fragment would shift, and its mass would no longer protect the squalid forests and warrens of Xoth from the cleansing sun. The filthy race of Chthons and their servitors would be burned away, and Kan Konar would have achieved the goal his honor demanded so long ago.

But it would have to be accomplished soon, for the dawn was coming. He was not sure if the proximity of the sun by itself would be enough to release the power of the runestone. He would have to find some other way to do it. He had hoped to enlist Amber's aid, but this was no longer possible. In any event, he could do nothing until he had somehow freed himself from this insane assassin.

He moved surreptitiously, testing the thin rawhide thongs that encircled his wrists and ankles. Though he had made the barest of movements, the assassin turned and smiled at him. "The thongs are treated with chala oil," she said. "They are all but impossible to cut or break. Do not think to escape."

As she stepped back, the cloakfighter noticed something—the edge of one of the shards of glass was glowing very slightly. After a moment's thought, the only possible explanation of this phenomenon came to him—and with it the barest possibility of a way to freedom.

"Yasothoth is doomed to defeat," he said suddenly. "There is no possibility of his winning against Sestihaculas. The Serpent Lord defeated him when the world was whole, and he will do so again."

He saw her expression harden—it was the reaction he had expected. "This is blasphemy, cloakfighter," she said, her tone dangerously soft. "You may be assured that I will tell Lord Yasothoth of your indiscretion. Any mercy he might have considered toward you will surely be forgotten now."

Carefully, now, he told himself. He wanted to taunt her into moving closer, but not enrage her to the point where she would decide to dispatch him herself with her arbalest or one of the throwing weapons like the one she had used to crease his skull earlier. "I have no fear of the Scorpion Lord's wrath," he said. "I do not know how he was able to return from the dead, but his second life will end the same way his first one did, and by the same hand."

"Speak no further," the assassin said. She was trembling with rage now, and Kan Konar wondered if he might have provoked her too far. He could not attempt to pacify her now, however; there was always the chance that she might realize what he wanted her to do.

"You will see," he said. "It is you who will have to face the wrath of Sestihaculas. Perhaps, if you are lucky, he won't kill you—perhaps he will instead take you back to Xoth, to serve him in the crawling darkness—"

"*I said speak no further!*" She raised the arbalest, and he felt a split second of resignation. But then she thought better of it, and took three quick steps toward him, raising her left hand to backhand him across the face. She was fast, faster than he had thought; he barely had time to swing his bound legs across the floor, knocking hers out from under her.

She fell, but even in her rage and madness her reflexes served her well; she spread her arms and slapped the hard stone of the floor, shouting as she hit to diffuse the impact. In an instant she would be on her feet again—the cloakfighter twisted his body around on the floor, balancing on his back and swinging his bound legs, putting all the strength of his contracting stomach muscles into the blow. The side of his left boot impacted with the back of her head as she rose off the floor, sending her sprawling. She shuddered once, and did not move again.

No doubt she had a knife concealed somewhere with her robes, but there was no time to look for it. Since he had woken up, the incardine rim of the sun, grotesquely swollen, had lifted above the horizon. The fragment of glass was glowing more strongly now, focusing the intense light.

Kan Konar knew he had only moments left in which to destroy the runestone. Nimbly he shifted his bound arms from behind him over his head and held the thongs that bound him in the path of the sunbeam. He could not avoid contact of the light with the flesh of his wrists, and he clenched his teeth at the pain—it felt as if a white-hot brand was being applied to them. In a matter of moments, however, the light had burned through his bonds and his hands were free.

Quickly he untied his legs and stood, feeling the prickling of returning circulation. If he could reach the street he would have a few more precious moments before the dawn reached him. Even as he turned toward the stairwell, however, a hand gripped his ankle, causing him to lose his balance and stum-

ble to his knees—and then the assassin was upon
him.

The conflict of titans continued in the ancient coliseum. Red light clashed with white as both Sestihaculas
and Yasothoth hurled energies at each other that
were capable of reducing boulders to dust.

Neither spoke—they mouthed no threats to each
other as human antagonists might have done. Both
knew the stakes for which they struggled—absolute
power versus eternal annihilation. Filled with the
primitive bloodlust of the creatures they had spon-
sored, the two Chthons grappled with each other,
hands and chelae braced against each other's shoulders, while crackling sparks of raw power writhed
along their arms.

Mirren had watched, horrified, as the assassin
dragged the unconscious form of Kan Konar into the
base of the tower and out of sight. Then she was
alone.

She had to find Amber—only she possessed the
power and the possible inclination to rescue her from
the fiery death that would otherwise inevitably consume her. The conjuress had accompanied the Lady of
Bats to find the battleground of the Demogorgons.
But where was that, and how could she find it?

She would simply have to start looking. She could
make better time as the wolf, that she knew, and so
she quickly removed her clothes and willed the transformation to begin.

It seemed to take forever, although she knew that,
in reality, it was no longer than any other time she
had made the transition from woman to wolf in the
past. The wolf trotted quickly down the ruined street,
sniffing the scorched pavement. She picked up the
faint but unmistakable scent of the conjuress almost

immediately, as well as the much stronger scent of Trisandela. The olfactory trail led her to the coliseum.

The cloakfighter managed to grab the assassin's right wrist, thus preventing her from using the arabalest. He was stronger and heavier than she, but her fighting skills were superb. She struck at him with the nails of her left hand; he saw they had been painted with a dark and tarry substance which he had no doubt was poison. He blocked the stiff-fingered blow just before it reached his face, and managed to roll over on top of her. He saw her tongue probe the inside of her cheek; she took a deep breath and he jerked his head to one side just as she spat a needle-sharp projectile at him with enough force for it to shatter on the stone well beside his throat.

She was too dangerous; he had to end the battle immediately. He jerked his head forward, slamming his forehead against her nose. Blood momentarily blinded him as it sprayed from the injured cartilege. The pain distracted her for just an instant, and that was all the cloakfighter needed; he kicked up and out with both feet, hurling her backwards. She struck the wall and rebounded from it to her feet, then leaped toward him again. Kan Konar rolled over once and seized the dragoneer's cloak where it lay on the floor beside him, whipped it up and out. It wrapped about her face, blinding her. Her momentum carried her forward another step; the cloakfighter swung one leg in a long, sweeping arc, knocking her off balance. Still tugging at the cloak, she staggered backwards toward one of the windows that faced away from the dawn. She attempted to recover her balance, failed—and, with a scream of rage, fell toward the street far below.

Kan Konar staggered to his feet, putting out a hand to steady himself. The sun was a finger's breadth above the horizon now. A line of searing light burst

through another of the windows, creeping slowly
down the wall. There was no more time. The
cloakfighter looked down through the window next
to which he stood and saw the flickering emanations
of power that marked the struggle of the Chthons.
He pulled the runestone from the inner pocket, realizing that he had only one infinitesimal chance left to
fulfill the pledge he had made to his dead daimyo
and to the brave woman on the fog-shrouded fragment of the Deathlings.

As the deadly dawn began to spread over the city,
Kan Konar hurled the runestone from the tower. He
watched it fall, and realized that his aim had been
true—and then the sudden cataclysm that was the
result of it hurled him backwards into the tower.

As Mirren reached the base of the steps she saw
and heard the beginning of the pyrotechnical confrontation between Sestihaculas and Yasothoth. Mirren
loped up the stairs quickly. At the top of them she
saw three figures; two human and one decidedly
inhuman. The raised batlike wings gave no doubt as
to Trisandela's identity, and neither did the cocoon
of orange light that she used to enclose one of the
other figures. Even as the werewolf paused, however, she saw the remaining person, whom she now
recognized as Amber, turn and blast the Lady of Bats
with a spell that incinerated the Chthon on the spot.
Mirren had not known that the conjuress was capable of such power.

As Amber turned back toward the other, however,
the latter raised his hands. Mirren saw now that he
was a man, and even caught the sparkle of reflected
light from the arena on the crystal ring that adorned
his tenth finger. He was a sorcerer, and he intended
to attack Amber; indeed, even as the wolf charged
up the remaining steps at full speed, snarling, and
sprang toward the sorcerer, she saw golden lumines-

cence outline his hands just before she seized one of them in her jaws.

The momentum of her attack caused the sorcerer to fall backwards with a cry of pain and surprise. The keen eyes of the wolf caught a glimpse of Amber's astonished face as she flew past her. She also saw something else in the time it took her to knock the sorcerer off his feet. Something small and dark—a ball, was her first thought, or a stone—flew out from a window in the tall tower into which the assassin had dragged the cloakfighter. There was something hypnotizing in the curve of its passage through the air—Mirren watched as it dropped straight down toward the crackling and scintillating display of raw power being given off by the two Chthons. Into that nimbus of energy it fell. A dazzling flash of light erupted from it, and in its wake followed chaos.

Pandrogas had been grateful when Trisandela's spell enveloped him—he had hoped that the Lady of Bats would destroy him and thus free him from the horrible fate of having to kill Amber and insure Yasothoth's survival. When Amber turned and unleashed the power of the Devastator upon the Chthon he would have hurled himself in its path if that had been possible. But it had not, and Trisandela had been destroyed, and there seemed to be no way to prevent him from doing the same to Amber.

Then the wolf had attacked. He had no idea where it had come from; surely no animal life had survived on the nameless fragment. There was no time to ponder the question, however. A moment later brilliant blue-white light filled his eyes, and the stone structure beneath him and the wolf whose jaws were snapping for his throat shook violently, as though in the grip of a massive quake.

The wolf toppled off of him and scrambled to its feet. Pandrogas rolled over and looked down into the arena; he saw a roiling, expanding fireball of odylic energy filling it. For an instant he thought he could see the silhouettes of both Sestihaculas and Yasothoth as they were consumed by the fire. In the same instant he realized that the geas no longer controlled him.

There was no time to feel relief or gratitude, however. He also knew what had caused the eruption of magical force below. Only the destruction of a rune-stone could have released such power. He leaped to his feet and seized Amber's hand, pulling her toward the stairs. "It will consume us!" he shouted. *"Run!"*

Amber hesitated for a moment, then evidently realized that Pandrogas was no longer under the geas. The wolf growled uncertainly, looking from the conjuress to the sorcerer. "It's all right, Mirren," she said to it. "Come with us!"

The three of them hurried down the treacherous steps toward the street below. Their shadows stretched before them, growing darker as the light from the released energy of the runestone continued to expand and intensify.

As they reached the street another quake struck, this one strong enough to cause them all to lose their footing. Amber landed on her back, staring up at the orbiting fragment of Xoth overhead, and Pandrogas saw wonder and horror fill her face. She pointed upward. *"Look!"* she cried.

The sorcerer raised his eyes and beheld a sight sufficiently awe-inspiring as to make him momentarily forget the danger they were in.

Above them, the fragment of Xoth filled the sky. Across it, beginning at the Cliffs of the Sun, the devastating light was spreading slowly across the breadth of the fragment. Everywhere it touched, the enormous mushrooms and rampant vegetation burst into flame. Pandrogas saw several cacodemons flitting across the fragment like ungainly insects, several of them being caught and immolated by the searing light. Even across the intervening miles they could feel the heat. Thick black smoke from the burning forest quickly obscured the apocalypse from view, but not before it seemed obvious that the entire surface of Xoth would soon be exposed to the scourging, cleansing flame.

"The fragment is shifting its path!" Amber shouted.

Pandrogas realized that such was indeed the case. There was still a residual attraction that gave them weightfulness on the surface, although the orbit was changing much more quickly than Darkhaven's had—evidently this fragment had been more dependent of the power of the runestone to maintain its stability.

That would not be the cause of their deaths, however. He could see the light from the rising sun creeping down the walls of the buildings. It would reach the street in mere moments.

The ground shook again; a nearby wall shattered like glass, crashing to the ground. The radiance of the vaporized runestone was rising over the top of the coliseum now, and its pressure was pushing the walls outward. As Pandrogas watched, a crack opened in one of them and blue-white light shone through. The air was beginning to thicken with embers and choking clouds as the winds of the Abyss whipped the smoke across the intervening gulf toward them. It seemed it would be only a matter of chance which factor of the cataclysm claimed their lives first.

The wolf whimpered and crowded close to Amber as a column collapsed across the street. Amber looked at Pandrogas. Her fear was gone now, replaced by a calm that was somehow reassuring to him. "This way, at least," she said, "we die together, rather than at each other's hand."

"Perhaps we will not die," he answered. "Gather close, you and the wolf, and give me the strength of the power within you."

She did not ask why, but did as he bid her. Pandrogas seized her hands and opened his mind and soul, letting the ectenic strength that she possessed mingle with his. There had been a time when she had not had the skill to do this, he remembered. In another second they would know if their power combined would be enough to save them.

"Think of Darkhaven!" he cried out to her. Then he let the power within them both hurl them, together with the wolf, into the lightless atheric corridors that he had traversed once before at such peril.

An instant later one of the walls of the disintegrating coliseum crashed into the street where they had been, and the fierce rays of the sun cut through the swirling dust and smoke.

Kan Konar pulled himself to his knees. The tower shook again; he wondered for a moment if it might fall. He looked out of the window and saw the spreading fireball that had been the runestone, shining like the light from a thousand starcrystals. Then he looked up—and beheld the destruction of Xoth.

The huge mushroom stalks, filled with sticky fluid, exploded as the sunlight reached them. Some cacodemons had the presence of mind to apport themselves elsewhere to safety, but others—many others—panicked and attempted to fly or run from the all-destroying rays. He could see them, through momentary rifts in the smoke, falling like bright sparks toward the ground. He imagined their batrachian and polypous shapes seared into ash as the hated sunlight touched them. He thought of Zhormallion's web becoming a huge, momentary torch, imagined the bulbous Spider Lord scuttling, panic-stricken, into the deepest depths of his den. Sestihaculas and Yasothoth were dead, and the majority of their peers and servants were following them into the oblivion that awaited their kind.

The cloakfighter smiled. At long last he had completed the task he had set himself years before; at long last he had redeemed his honor. His daimyo, and the Deathlings, had been avenged. Now, finally, he could rest.

He sat down crosslegged before the window. The destruction of the runestone had affected the fragment's rotation as well as its path; the window was turning slowly toward the swollen red sun, which was now nearly halfway over the horizon. Kan Konar, erstwhile retainer of Ras Parolyn on the fragment of Typor's First, warrior, ronin, and now destroyer of Xoth, awaited his end.

The fragment turned. The tower turned. And the window came to face the sun.

The cloakfighter greeted the dawn.

CHAPTER XXI

Darkhaven Again

Amber stood in one of the many rooftop gardens of
Darkhaven, looking out at the sun that hovered always at the same low angle over the battlements. It
seemed hard to believe that this was the same ravening furnace that had nearly destroyed them only a few
days before. Over a commonyear ago she had stood
with Pandrogas on the edge of Tamboriyon and noted
how the dust from the impact of the aerolith on
Rhynne had reddened the sunlight. It was tinted
crimson again now, but the cause this time was the
smoke from the burning realm of the Chthons.

Amber took a deep breath and winced—the ban-
dages that supported the broken rib she had suffered
were very tight. It was still hard for her to believe
that they had escaped safely from the holocaust. The
apportation had returned them to the sorcerer's castle, but the expenditure of ectenic energy, and the
pain of the passage itself, had left both her and
Pandrogas almost too exhausted to move.

Mirren had not been in much better shape; the wolf woman had taken to bed and slept the clock around, shielded from nightmares by a sleep-soothing cantrip which Amber had pronounced. Pandrogas had told Mirren that she was welcome to stay in Darkhaven as long as she wished.

Amber turned and entered the castle, moving slowly down one of the corridors without any real destination in mind. She had not seen Pandrogas in several hours, and she had no idea if she wished to seek him out or not. Since their return they had spoken only of the ordeals they had been through, correlating the facts of what had happened. The sorcerer had been astonished to learn that Kan Konar had survived his confrontation with Zhormallion, and had been, according to Mirren, the one who had destroyed the runestone of the nameless fragment.

The sorcerer had hidden the heliolite in his laboratory, guarding it with a spell against any possible depredation—he had not forgotten how Beorn the thief had managed once to breach his sanctum. Since his return he had spent much of his time in the laboratory, poring over charts and armilary models of the fragments. Amber had not asked what he was doing. She assumed she would learn soon enough.

Sooner or later, she knew, she would have to face the fact that she had been ready to kill Pandrogas in order to save what was left of the world. The timely intervention of Trisandela had prevented this; she had struck down the Lady of Bats reactively. But that did not change the fact that she would have annihilated Pandrogas, the man she loved.

For she knew now, oddly enough, without doubt or hesitancy, that she did love him. These past few days of contact and introspection had told her that much. What troubled her was not any uncertainty about that, but rather why she felt no remorse or guilt over what she had intended to do to him.

She had been giving little thought to where she was going, just letting her feet carry her where they would. Now she looked up and was not surprised to see the bronze head mounted over the double doors of the laboratory. They were open; within was Pandrogas, consulting a reference volume of magic. He looked up as she entered. She could read nothing on his face.

"You have been working hard almost since we returned," she said, with a small smile. "Should you not rest for a time?"

He sighed and ran a hand through his hair. "Why not? All of my research here indicates that nothing can be done anyway."

She did not want to hear the answer to the question, but she asked it anyway. "About what?"

Pandrogas stood up wearily and walked around the table. "The force behind the runestones is breaking down much faster than anyone has anticipated. There seems to be some form of synergistic interplay between all the runestones, and moving or damaging any one of them has an effect on all. Thasos caused irrepairable damage in his search for the runestone that would awaken the Necromancer. And now, by destroying the runestone of the nameless fragment, Kan Konar has further exacerbated the problem.

"As the fragments' orbits decay, other aspects of the shielding spells are falling apart as well. The impact that shattered our world also caused the fragments to pursue a very eccentric orbit about the sun—currently we are quite close to it, close enough for it to have the effects we saw on the nameless fragment. The magic established over a thousand years ago protects us from the terrible heat. But as it decays, the outer fragments are affected first." He sighed and rubbed his eyes. "Soon all the various land masses will look like the nameless fragment, and soon after that they will grind together and become, eventually, no more than dust in an airless void."

"How soon?" Amber asked.

"I estimate no more than another commonyear or two before the atmosphere begins to dissipate. After that, without air to nourish us and protect us from the extreme heat and cold of the void, it will not matter."

Again, she wondered why this news left her feeling nothing. Everything that had happened in the past since she had first entered Darkhaven seemed a dream—the only reality was here and now. She looked up at him and said, "You know that I would have killed you in order to stop Yasothoth."

She did not know what she expected his reaction to be. Pandrogas merely nodded, however, and said, "I know." After a moment he added, "It would have been the right decision."

Amber waited, but he did not continue. "Is that all you can say?" she asked. "Do you understand me? I love you, and I would have destroyed you!"

He shrugged. "What does it matter? A few more years and none of it will mean anything."

Amber looked at him, feeling as though she were really seeing him at long last. She understood now that she had been relating to the image of Pandrogas that she had been carrying in her mind for over a commonyear, rather than to the reality. Now she was confronted, not with the image, but the reality. He was not behaving as she had thought and dreamed he would—and, for that matter, neither was she.

They had separated for a year in order to gain some perspective upon their relationship and themselves, agreeing to meet again to see if they still loved each other after enough time had passed to let them recover from the traumatic experiences they had shared. Instead they had been plunged into a new series of adventures that had left them both even more emotionally and physically exhausted. Would they ever, she wondered, be able to see each other truly, unencumbered by such stress?

If what Pandrogas said was true about the disintegrating ectenic force, then they had little time left. They could not afford to waste it.

"Listen to me," Amber said to him. "I no longer know who I am, Pandrogas—the last few weeks have changed me even more than the previous two years. Nor do I know who you are. We have never had a chance to relate to each other as normal people can. Very little is certain in my life right now and, if what you tell me is true, I have very little of life left.

"There is only one certainty I can cling to. I don't know how it came to be, but I have no desire right now to question it. I only know that I love you. I have done things of which I am ashamed and appalled in order to reach your side. All of this should mean something to you."

Pandrogas had not been looking at her while she spoke; now he raised his gaze to meet hers.

"It means a great deal—more than I can say or you can know. But I am not sure who I love—the Amber that I remember, or the one who stands before me now." He looked down again, and shook his head. "We have no time left for love, anyway."

He started to turn away; Amber seized his arm. "Damn you, don't walk away from me!" She was astonished at the vehemence of her words. "If what you say is true about the world ending, then we two are probably the only ones with the knowledge and the power to do something about it! *That* should be important to you, even if love is not!"

He spun around to face her, and the anger in his face surprised her—there was a time when it would have frightened her. "Don't say that love is not important to me! If you know how I longed for you during the year I spent here—how I thought of you and no one else—"

Amber remembered Zerrad and closed her eyes in momentary pain and guilt. "And you think that I have not felt the same?"

"I followed you from fragment to fragment; I faced Sestihaculas and Yasothoth to save you; I—"

"Spare me an account of your privations and hardships—I know them very well! We have both suffered, Pandrogas—the question is, did we suffer *for* each other, or *because* of each other?"

Both of them were silent for a moment. Amber's face was flushed, and her breath came rapidly. She was surprised at the anger she felt. She could see that Pandrogas was similarly exercised, and she suddenly felt overwhelmed with confusion.

"Why are we doing this?" she said softly. "When last we saw one another, we parted with respect and love, vowing to come together as adults and equals. We did not fight then; why are we fighting now?"

Pandrogas was silent for so long that she wondered if he had heard her. Then, slowly, he said, "Yasothoth's geas would have forced me to kill you. The fact that I had no choice, that I was being used as the instrument of his will, means little to me; what matters is that I would have killed you. Had I done that, I could not have lived with the pain, even though it would have been no choice of mine. And now you tell me that, of your own free will, you would have destroyed me. That the circumstances—letting all of humanity suffer Yasothoth's wrath in order that I might survive—really allowed you no more choice than I had should mitigate it, but they do not, at least, not as far as I am concerned." He looked up at her then, and the confusion and hurt in his face stabbed her worse than the occasional sharp pain in her side. "And yet, I love you, and I know that now as surely as you profess to know it about me. I don't know why, but I know that it is true."

Amber smiled wearily, and sat down on a bench. After a moment, Pandrogas sat down beside her.

"When we parted on Tamboriyon, you suggested that we cast the sphere," he said.

Amber nodded, then stood and took the segmented globe from a nearby shelf. She held it at arm's length above the table, then looked at him.

"What question would you ask it?"

"A very simple one: 'What now?' "

She nodded, and released it. The sound of it striking and breaking was very loud.

Pandrogas rose, and together they looked at the oracular configuration of the fragments. After a moment, the sorcerer said, "It is an unfamiliar pattern."

"I do not recognize it either," Amber said. She turned to *The Book of Stones,* which lay nearby, and opened it, searching for a definition to the strewn pieces. After a moment she closed the book.

"It is a new pattern," she said. "Any prophecy it might contain must be extrapolated from the fragments' positions."

"Look at this," Pandrogas said. He pointed to one of the smaller pieces, which lay under the shade of an alembic. The sphere was of hardened gemwood, renowned for its durability; nevertheless, the piece had broken in half.

"What is the fragment?" Amber asked as Pandrogas picked up the pieces.

"I'm surprised you had to ask," he said. "Xoth, of course."

Amber nodded, and sat down again. After a moment she said, "How many of the Chthons do you suppose escaped the conflagration?"

"As many as were able to apport before being struck by the sun, even as we did. Sestihaculas is dead, as are Yasothoth and Trisandela. But I would be surprised if Endrigoth did not survive, and Breelorand, and Shaikor, and Zhormallion. There are plenty of ancient tunnels, such as the ones beneath Zarheena, to which they could have fled."

"And now they will be angry," Amber murmured. "And desirous of revenge."

"One can hardly blame them."

He looked up at him again. "We have to do *something*, Pandrogas. What shall it be?"

She sat down beside her. "About saving what is left of the world—or about saving ourselves?"

"Both, if possible. But whether we can continue is not as important as whether humanity survives. Whether we come ultimately to love or hate one another matters not at the moment—what matters is that we must do something to prevent the disaster you foresee."

Pandrogas nodded. "Yes. But at the moment, I have no conception of what it might be."

Amber looked at the scattered fragments of the globe on the table. It has been a strange and complex journey, she thought, that began so long ago and now has ended in Darkhaven. Along the way she had lost a husband and gained a lover, only to lose him as well. But what she thought she had gained, finally, was a sense of herself, of who she really was. Now, it seemed, even that was ephemeral, like the ever-changing dance of the fragments and the myriad comings and goings of humanity upon them. Nothing was immutable, and all eventually returned to dust.

Nothing was immutable? No, that was not true. One thing was constant, more so even than her belief that she loved Pandrogas, and upon that she would lay her foundation—the desire, the necessity to survive, whether as a person or as a species. She would do what she could to save what was left of the world, just as she would do what she could to save what was left of her life and her ability to love.

To do any less was to not be alive at all.

She looked at Pandrogas, and put her hand on his. "We'll think of something," she said.

Here is an excerpt from Heroing *by Dafydd ab Hugh, coming in October 1987 as part of the new SIGN OF THE DRAGON fantasy line from Baen Books:*

Hesitantly, Jiana crawled into the crack.

"It's okay, guys," she called back, "but it's a bit cramped. Toldo next—wait! —Dida, then Toldo. I want . . . the priest in back." She felt a twinge of guilt. What she really wanted was the boy where she could reach out and touch his hand when needed.

Dida whimpered something. Jiana turned back in surprise.

"What's wrong?"

"Oh, love . . . are we really going—into *there?*"

"Dida, it's the only way. Are you a mouse? Come on, warrior!" He pressed his lips together and crawled toward her hand. When she touched him, she felt him trembling.

"Don't fear. I came through here, remember?"

The tunnel smelled as fresh as flowers after the stench of sewage. Jiana could breathe again without gagging.

The ceiling of the passage sank and sank, until she was almost afraid it would narrow to a wedge and block them off. But she remembered her harrowing crawl from the prison, her heart pounding with fear, feeling the hot, fetid breath of *something* on her neck, and she knew the passage was passable. At last, they were scraping along with their bellies on the floor and their backs against the splintery ceiling. Jiana wondered how Toldo Mondo was managing with his prodigious girth.

Suddenly, she knew something was wrong. She crawled on a few more yards, then stopped. Dida was no longer behind her. She heard a faint cry from behind her.

"Jiana, help me—please help me . . ."

"Lady Jiana," called out Toldo, "I think you had better come back here. The boy . . . seems to have a problem." Jiana felt a chill in her stomach; Toldo sounded much too professionally casual.

"What's wrong?" She turned slowly around on her stomach, and inched her way back to where the two had stopped. She stretched out her hand and took Dida's; it was clammy and shaking. With her fingers she felt his pulse, and it was pounding wildly.

"I can't do it," he whispered miserably. "I can't do it—I just can't do it—all that weight—I can't breathe! —I can't . . ."

"What? Oh, for Tooqa's sake! What next?"

As if in answer to her blasphemy, the ground began to shake and roll. Again she heard the scraping, grinding noise, only this time much closer. Dida continued to whimper.

"Oh gods, oh gods, oh please, let me out, oh please, take it away . . ."

"Too close," she whispered, trying to peer through the pitch blackness.

"Oh my lord," gasped Toldo Mondo, "don't you hear it?"

Again the ground shook, and this time the scraping was closer yet, and accompanied by a slimy sucking sound.

For a moment all were silent; even Dida stopped his whimpering. Then Jiana and Toldo began to babble simultaneously.

"I'm sorry," she cried, "I'm sorry, o Ineffable One, o Nameless Scaly One, o You Who Shall Not Be Named! I never meant—"

Toldo chanted something over and over in another language; it sounded like a penance. The fearful noise suddenly became much louder.

"Toldo! It's coming this way! Oh lordy, what'll we do? Crawl, damn you, crawl, crawl! And push the kid along—I'll grab his front and drag!"

"You fool! It's here! Don't you hear it? Am I the only one who hears it?!"

"Shut up and push, you fat tub of goat cheese!"

In a frenzy, they began to squirm away from the sound, dragging Dida, and Jiana discovered that the tiny crawlway was as wide as a king's hall, though the ceiling was but a foot and a half off the floor. Dida was no help. He was in shock, as if he'd been stabbed in a battle. He could only move his arms and legs in a feeble attempt at locomotion, praying to be "let out."

After a few moments, Jiana realized she was hopelessly lost. Had they kept going straight from the hole by the river, they would have found the next door. But they were moving to the right, and she did not know how far they had gone in the pitch black. In fact, she was not even sure which way they were currently pointing; the horrible noises had seemed to change direction, and they had concentrated on keeping them to their rear.

"Oh gods, I've done it now," she moaned; "we won't ever get out of here!" A sob from Dida caught at her heart, and she cursed herself for speaking aloud.

"We shall make it," retorted Toldo Mondo. "There must be *something* in this direction, if we go far enough!"

Soon, Jiana herself began to feel the oppression of millions of tons of rock pressing down on her. She had terrifying visions of being buried alive in the blackness by a sudden cave-in caused by the movements of whatever was behind them. With every beat of her heart it got closer, and the shaking grew worse. She could clearly hear a sound like a baby sucking on its fist.

"Jiana, go!" cried Toldo in a panic. "Crawl, go—faster, woman! It's here, it's—Jiana, I CAN SMELL IT!"

"How does it squeeze along, when even we barely fit?" she wondered aloud. *You're babbling, Ji . . . stop it!*

She surged and lunged forward, not letting go of Dida, though he was like a wet sack of cornmeal. And then, there was a rocky wall in front of her. There was nowhere left to crawl.

Coming in October 1987 * 65344-X * 352 pp. * $3.50

To order any Baen Book by mail, send the cover price plus 75 cents for first-class postage and handling to: Baen Books, Dept. B, 260 Fifth Avenue, New York, N.Y. 10001. And ask for our free catalog of all Baen Books science fiction and fantasy titles!